Best Wishes to Mel. From Merv

Terror by Candlelight

Mervyn Russen

GW00707446

AVOCADO BOOKS

Avocadobooks.com

First published by Avocado Books in 2016

© Mervyn Russen

ISBN: 978-0-9935658-2-3

Mervyn Russen asserts the moral right to be
identified as the author of this work

A catalogue record of this book is
available from the British Library

Formatting and cover design:
Matt Trollope / JaxEtta.com
© Avocado Books, 2016

To my wife, Susan, who had to live with
the characters in this book as I wrote it.

MERVYN RUSSEN

I know not how it was - but, with the first glimpse of the building, a sense of insufferable gloom pervaded my spirit.

- taken from *The Fall of the House Of Usher* by Edgar Allan Poe (1839)

CONTENTS

Chapter 1

A New Beginning

David Linde returned the spade to the garden shed. The effort of digging had caused him to perspire heavily and his back ached. The garden looked tidier and he was happier it would not look a disgrace, now he was leaving it to someone else. He needed to move on, to change his surroundings – to make a new start. He approached the back door and turned to gaze back at the garden. Nothing remained undone. The magnolia was growing well. The bay tree had been cut back and the lawn looked reasonably manicured.

He closed the door and made his way to the sink to wash the soil from his hands. He watched particles spiral inwards to the waste pipe. Rather in keeping with his life at the moment, a spiral in and down to nowhere. He shook himself from his reverie. These were very negative thoughts. They were unusual for him because he had the remarkable gift of being able to bring a shutter down on the negative aspects of his life and visualise a positive future.

Having showered, he dressed in a pale blue shirt, red silk tie and dark blue suit which was slightly too large for him. Quite tall and slim – a shade over six feet – he had the dark brooding look of a 19th century poet. His luxuriant hair tended to flop forward over one eye and he had a habit of jerking his head back to remove the annoying curl. His dress was not untidy but had the careless air of a man who did not place it at the top of his priority list.

He felt better as he made his way to the front door. He stopped to collect the estate agent's blurb on the hall table. He felt really good about this particular house he was visiting this afternoon. It looked as though it was "just the ticket", as his mother would have said.

*****

The house stood isolated from its companions and had done so for nearly a century and a half. It was a typical Victorian town house that had, when new, been the domicile of a senior professional man...a surgeon probably, with a stiff high collar, mutton–chop side–whiskers and a tall silk top hat.

David Linde mused on these matters as he stood in front of the house and contemplated the brick façade before him. He had arrived early and there was no sign of the estate agent. He preferred to reconnoitre a property before he was bombarded with the fusillade of adjectives which were the stock in trade of such agents.

Sash windows and coloured glass segments were set in the fanlight above a sturdy front door. A front step worn concave by the many feet which had trodden on it and the many servant girls who had scrubbed it. He relished all these as his gaze travelled over the front of the house.

It was a large detached house with a large double gable. The front windows were framed in concrete.

The name of the house, 'The Eaves', was cut into

the concrete by the front door and above the door was the date '1868'. A gravel drive led from the front door to two large wrought iron gates attached to two substantial brick pillars. Linde noted the two rather sad stone lions, which sat dejectedly atop the pillars.

The house would need some work – the window frames were past their best and in places deep–weathered fissures were visible upon their surfaces. Paint peeled back in places on the wooden surfaces but most of the work needed was cosmetic in nature. He would not want to change too much because he felt that the dignity of this old building would be compromised by plastic soffits and frames.

The front garden was overgrown. Suddenly a voice broke into his reverie. He turned to see a fresh-faced youth carrying a Samsonite briefcase striding towards him.

"Morning. You must be Dr Linde. I see you are already enjoying this delightful property blah... blah...blah."

Linde switched on the filter system he had learned to activate when he felt he was listening to padding and irrelevances not just from estate agents but from anybody. It had caused trouble for him in the past and had been one of the problems cited by his wife for the divorce because it had annoyed her to the point of distraction. This and many other problems did not make for an ideal marital relationship and so it had failed and finally ended.

Mr Tayt, the young man, shook Linde's hand and suggested they enter the house. The interior of the building was an even greater delight because it too had not undergone the drastic physical changes which prevailing fashion dictated. It had therefore retained much of its original character. The rooms had high ceilings with attractive pargetted cornices and roses at the centre of the ceilings from which the lights were suspended.

The garden at the rear was much like the front in that neither of them had been tended for a long time and were overgrown. He loved the old perimeter wall. Red brick had been deeply pitted by a century and a half of rainstorms and frosts. It stood seven feet high giving privacy, which he also liked. He loved it all and determined to make it his, provided the price was not extortionate.

So it was that formalities were completed and he took possession of The Eaves, Rill Place, Blackheath the following month.

His friends at work were pleased that he had found a place and that he could now build a new life after the trauma of the disastrous marriage. His work had suffered also during this period. In his field of research one's intellectual cutting edge needed to be honed to a fine sharpness.

Linde was a research chemist with a rising reputation in the field of radiochemistry. His colleagues tended to be young, smart and did not suffer fools gladly. He had at one time been thought of as a future Nobel laureate, but at 35 his age was against him. Nonetheless, he enjoyed his research fellowship at Imperial College and the location of his new house meant that his journeys to and from work were not too arduous.

Linde spent a particularly fogbound Saturday in November moving his possessions into The Eaves, a difficult task at the best of times. By the end of the following week the house was beginning to look like a home and he was down to the detailed tasks such as arguing with a service provider about the installation of a broadband line.

It was at the end of November, a month in which he had spent much of his time at home with a paintbrush in his hand, that he ventured out into the garden. A considerable task awaited him, but, in the early morning sun on one of those rare glorious autumnal days, he was tempted to start hacking at undergrowth. He found a scythe, which he had bought for the purpose, in the old garden shed and started to work from the house outwards towards the old garden wall. Very soon perspiration poured from his brow. He was making some progress, however, and he set to with a strong will. He piled the refuse in the centre of the garden, noting that a trip to the tip would soon be necessary. By this time he was ready for lunch and took a break for a sandwich.

The light had begun to fail as he reached the far left hand corner of the garden relative to the back of the house. He was aware of the intense silence of the garden now and a sharp chill settled over him. Time to pack it in for the day, he thought, and began to clear up his tools. He headed back to the house and washed his hands in the kitchen sink. He felt the satisfaction that follows intense physical labour. He showered, dressed, and went into one of the back bedrooms, which was occupied by his computer and books. He enjoyed his study. It was a haven from the world and the smell and appearance of the books gave him an intense pleasure which nothing else matched.

He checked for new emails and then strolled to the window and looked out into the garden in the gathering gloom.

It was then that he spotted the woman.

Chapter 2

The Woman in Black

She was slowly moving towards the corner of the garden to his far left. He could discern that it was a woman and that she was turned away from him. He could only see her hair and the narrow white crescent of her forehead, cheek and jaw. Her clothes were dark in colour and their outline melted into the gloom beyond her.

His reaction was one of immediate territorial anger. He turned from the window and ran downstairs along the hall, through the kitchen and out into the garden. He paused outside the back door and allowed his eyes to become accustomed to the darkness. He stared into all corners of the garden but there was no-one there. He turned and as he did he heard the faint but distinct rustle of cloth. His eyes strained to make out shapes in the darkness but he could perceive none. In the distance a dog barked but, in the main, silence reigned.

He was determined to search the garden from end-to-end and grabbed a torch from the kitchen. He proceeded to cover every inch of the place in a comprehensive sweep. His search proved fruitless and a puzzled frown crossed his face. She could not have possibly passed him and entered the house. She could not have left by the garden gate, which was hard by the kitchen door. In any case it was bolted with a fairly rusty bolt and its withdrawal would have been accompanied by a considerable rasping noise.

He felt dreadfully cold and realised he had not put a coat on before he had started his search. It was no good – he must have imagined it. He made his way back inside and realised he was very hungry, so much so that a feeling of faintness was stealing over him. He had only had one cheese sandwich since breakfast and had been working very hard. Perhaps he was hallucinating as a result of low blood sugar levels.

That was it, he told himself, as the great Sherlock Holmes had said, "eliminate the impossible and whatever is left, no matter how improbable, must be the truth." It was the only logical explanation and he was a scientist, a dealer in logic. Cause and effect were his watchwords, leave anything outside of that to charlatans and quantum physicists.

Linde changed and phoned a local restaurant, *Le Relais*, and booked a table for dinner.

He was about to open the front door to leave when the telephone rang. It was his friend Jim Flagg, a painter and sculptor, inviting him to a dinner party at his house on the following Thursday. It was to celebrate the sale of one of his paintings to a rich American with more money than sense. David was available and accepted the invitation with a cheery, "see you Thursday. By the way what time?...ok...7.30 it is."

As he stepped out into the night he wondered what woman Jane Flagg would set him up with this time.

*****

Linde woke the next morning at 8.30 am. He reached out and grabbed the alarm clock and cursed audibly. He had wanted to make an early start on taking the mound of garden refuse to the local tip.

By late afternoon, however, the garden was cleared and he was ready for a cup of tea. He made his way downstairs to the kitchen, filled the kettle and turned to plug it in on its stand. Before he could do so he felt a cold draught blow across his face from the direction of the back door. It ruffled his hair and caused him to shiver. He turned; expecting to see the door open, or at least ajar, but was surprised to find it firmly closed. He moved towards the door to identify the cause of the icy blast when behind him there came the distinct sound of a human sigh. It was a sigh like nothing he had ever heard before – it was deep and ended in a groan, the tone of which fell eventually to a sound like a door turning on a rusty hinge. It was a woman's voice but it sounded so full of despair and longing. Although he could only make out a lamenting shamble of sounds but no distinct words. It sounded as if all hope had gone and the owner of the voice was experiencing a world full of care and loss. The hairs rose on the back of his neck as he listened. The sound seemed to emanate from no particular place in the house – it came from first one way and then another. It eventually faded gradually back to a distraught sigh again.

Linde blinked his eyes as the terrible sound died away to the echoes which themselves fell to a silence – frightening in its intensity. He checked the door again and it was still locked. He decided to search the house. His limbs shook as he made his way into each of the rooms downstairs. Completing the search of the ground floor – he made his way upstairs and after looking in his bedroom and finding only what he expected to see; he began to regain control of his nerves. The final place to check was the garden and after yesterday he felt slightly queasy about going out there. Could the lamentations come from that woman?

He curled his hands into fists and hissed through his teeth as he strode towards the back door. "Come on Linde, pull yourself together," he told himself. The sky outside was beginning to darken as the autumn twilight closed in. Linde unlocked and cautiously pushed the door open. He caught his breath as a sudden tumult filled the air. He had disturbed a flock of starlings and for a few moments the air was filled with the sound of flapping wings. He stepped out on to the path at the back of the house and the cold air caused him to shiver again. This time no Victorian phantom met his gaze but he approached the darker areas of the garden with trepidation. Blessed relief flooded over him as he ended his fruitless search and he allowed himself to relax a little. He turned to make his way towards the back door when he saw her again.

Her back was towards him and she was wearing a black dress. He swore he heard the swish of her skirts as she entered the kitchen and disappeared from view. Linde was transfixed for a second time that afternoon. When he was capable of movement he rushed into the house, even though every fibre of his being told him not to do so. He ran through the darkening rooms switching lights on as he went. He was alone. He slumped down at the bottom of the stairs, his head in his hands.

The house was empty – he had searched it twice – so what was going on? He didn't believe in ghosts but he had seen that woman twice now and both times she had disappeared completely. There was the sigh as well; it had come and gone into nowhere and everywhere." He felt frightened...very frightened. He made

17

some tea and sat at the kitchen table with the steaming brew before him. He had begun to doubt his sanity because there were no such things as ghosts. If that was a given then all that he was experiencing was inside his head.

Chapter 3

Dinner At Eight

Julia Davenport stared up at the Flagg house. It had been built in the 1930s by a rich industrialist and was the ultimate in Art Deco design for the times. It was an unusual shape and looked like a combination of a battleship and Broadcasting House. There was a massive studio extension facing north – this was the haven where Jim Flagg, the artist, worked his magic with paint, pastels and clay.

Jane Flagg opened the door to Julia and they greeted each other with kisses on cheeks and a hug. They had been school friends and were devoted to each other. Physically they were very different. Jane was a dark haired, long-legged beauty with the figure of a model. Today she wore a classic short black cocktail dress, clinging provocatively to her body. It was fairly low cut, revealing a tantalising hint of cleavage.

Julia was 27 years of age, of average height and was slightly above average weight for her height. She was dressed immaculately in a navy blue suit with a very pale blue silk blouse beneath it. She made considerable efforts to dress well at all times because she was a career astrologer. It was a profession graced by people who tended to wear beads, enormous earrings and tent-like flowered kaftans. Others in her field also exhibited a combination of wild enthusiasm and oodles of gush. It was no wonder that clients did not take them seriously.

Julia believed in what she sold but was also an acutely aware businesswoman. She spoke with a gentle southern Irish lilt. Her hair was Celtic reddish brown and fell in luxuriant soft curls to her shoulders.

"Come and meet the others," said Jane, taking Julia by the arm and guiding her towards the sound of laughter echoing from a room off the large hallway. The two women entered a large, minimally, but tastefully furnished reception room. A group of five people stood in the centre of the room. They were all talking animatedly. One always knows when one is two drinks behind everybody else at a party, thought Julia. Jane took her to the group, three of whom she already knew.

There was the Reverend Denholme Theynard, an Anglican priest whom Jim had met when commissioned to do a mezzotint of a local church. Theynard was very voluble and an expert on esoteric literature. William Hope Hodgson, Edgar Allen Poe and Sheridan Le Fanu were his heroes. He loved nothing more than to carry on an animated discourse on the joys of being buried alive or vampirism; all conducted in a thin reedy voice. He was also rumoured to have conducted exorcisms in haunted houses. Although that was the one subject he was reticent to discuss. He was tall, cadaverous and had a thinning thatch of unruly white hair.

"How are you this evening?" he said.

"Very well, thank you, Denholme," she replied, turning to the second man present. "How goes it, Jim? I believe congratulations are in order."

"Yes, indeed. By the way, this is Sam Plaid who has purchased my latest work."

Jim turned to the other man in the group, a tall blond haired individual. He reminded Julia of Robert Shaw's killer in the film version of *From Russia With Love.*

"Pleased to meet you...you must be Julia Davenport, the famous expert on the occult."

The drawl spoke of a southern states upbringing, a "Good ole boy" made even better by the acquisition of considerable wealth. She laughed modestly and said that a spot on daytime TV hardly qualified her for the epithet 'famous'.

Jim Flagg led Julia to the drinks table and poured her a generous splash of Glenmorangie whisky, before returning her to the others in the party. A short, tubby lady in a long dress smiled an affectionate greeting. This was Miriam Brock, a Harley Street specialist in neurology and a mutual friend of Julia, Jim and Jane's. Miriam and Julia exchanged a kiss and the former gestured towards the final member of the party, Letitia Preece, a biologist who worked with the Oxford Film Unit.

"Call me Letty. Everyone does," she said.

Miss Preece was a young be-jeaned willowy blond who leaned against the back of a chair. Miriam had met Letty on holiday and apparently romance had blossomed. They now shared Miriam's house in Hampstead together with a Labrador and four cats.

Just then the door bell rang and a moment later a man appeared accompanied by Jane. Julia stared at the latecomer. He was introduced as David Linde, a research chemist at Imperial College. She studied him as he murmured apologies for his lateness. Julia liked the dark brooding type and found him attractive. She thought this was so because he had no idea that he had this effect on the opposite sex. If he did – he kept the knowledge well hidden.

Jane announced that dinner was served in the dining room. The assembled company filed through into the room adjoining the reception room, where the decoration had been designed by Jane Flagg. It was therefore not surprising that the taste was impeccable since Jane was one of the country's most prominent interior decorators. She was a strong believer in the principle that 'less is more'.

"David...you sit over there next to Julia...that's it," said Jane.

David Linde could not conceal a smile as he moved round the table to his indicated place. There was always an available bachelor girl placed next to him at Jane's dinners. Denholme Theynard was seated to Linde's right. He turned to his left and began to make small talk with Julia.

"How did you meet Jane and Jim?"

"I was originally a friend of Jane – in fact I was at school with her." said Julia, "What about you, how do you know them?"

"Initially Jane worked with my ex wife, Annie, after meeting her at an Ideal Home Exhibition five years ago," explained Linde. "They became friends while working on a project, which had developed from their first meeting. Jane had long admired Annie's work as an architect and it was therefore not surprising that they hit it off. Since then we have dined socially as a foursome many times until Annie and I split up. Annie has left the UK for India now – something I took very badly. The Flaggs have been very supportive of me ever since."

Dinner progressed and was delicious. Conversation round the table continued in a half-hearted manner until coffee and brandy arrived. The imbibing of the strong spirit seemed to add lubrication to the proceedings and laughter became less inhibited.

Denholme Theynard, in particular, was more voluble than anyone and had turned the conversation to the paranormal and books of fiction associated with it.

Jim Flagg added: "Henry James' *The Turn of the Screw* frightened me half to death."

"I remember seeing The Innocents, the Jack Clayton film version of that story made in the sixties and that was understatedly frightening," interjected Miriam Brock.

Letty Preece joined in the excited conversation: "*The Haunting of Hill House* was a terrifying piece in the same low key way. I think Shirley Jackson was a much—underrated writer in the genre."

Linde's quietly spoken statement came unexpectedly and caused everyone to turn in his direction.

"I may have a ghostly entity in my garden!"

Chapter 4

The Ghost at the Table

Sam Plaid was the first to speak. "Gee...are you kiddin'?"

Linde in a quiet, controlled voice described the woman in the garden.

"I thought I may have been working too hard and I was also absolutely famished. It may be that I had been hallucinating but I don't think so for a number of reasons. The first time I saw her was from a bedroom window. She was in a corner of the garden but I found nothing when I searched the place. The second time I was in the kitchen when I heard a deep sigh. I searched the house and garden again but having fruitlessly done so turned to re-enter through the back door and she was there in front of me. When I recovered I followed her in but she had vanished again. I also remember something else. On both occasions I was aware of an intense cold and a deep, deep silence. There was no traffic noise and not a dog barked. All the everyday neighbourhood sounds were muted. It was as though the whole world held its breath."

"Come on David, you are a scientist and this all sounds excessively melodramatic for a man with your background," said Jim.

"Yes, and at the time I had rationalised it in my head. It was cold because the autumn twilight was approaching on both occasions. It was quiet because I was in a garden enclosed within a wall seven feet high. Neither the cold nor the silence completely describe how I felt. I experienced something more."

"That something more may have been a mere illusion because of the state you were in. Your wife had left and you were in a new environment both emotionally and physically. You were tired and your sugar level was low." Miriam Brock was a reassuring voice.

"I have been a practising scientist and sceptic for 15 years," retorted Linde. "I make observations, I draw conclusions and I have had to do so for long hours working in poor conditions in a laboratory. I have also been hungry at the same time. My conclusions and judgement have always been fine when compared with those of colleagues present in the same situation. When this phenomenon had first happened I thought on exactly the same lines as you have done, Miriam. Since that time I have realised that there is more to this than meets the eye."

Julia Davenport then broke in. "I have a suggestion. Maybe this entity will appear again and a corroborative witness may be useful. I am, if I may say so, sensitive to these things. Maybe I could visit your house and get the feel of the place and we will see what we shall see. What do you say, David?"

Linde studied her face for a moment, smiled and agreed.

The others, particularly Theynard, were very keen to know the outcome of the visit. It was agreed that another dinner would be arranged at the same venue with the same group, very soon after the investigation. Jane Flagg suppressed a grin as she realised that maybe a romance would grow from this encounter.

Linde guessed what she was thinking and said as much when he was leaving and the others were out of earshot.

"Jane, you are incorrigible."

It was as the party broke up at just after eleven that Linde spoke to Julia as they walked up the drive: "May I buy you dinner before your visit?"

"Thank you David, I would like that very much."

The date was fixed for the following Tuesday at 7pm, and the two of them shared a taxi home, leaving Jane Flagg at the house, grinning like the eponymous Cheshire Cat.

Jim put an arm round Sam Plaid's shoulder. "Well we didn't discuss the painting much, Sam. Come inside for a nightcap and we can discuss final delivery arrangements."

"No problem. This ghost stuff is fascinating. I lived for some time in New England, the ghost centre of the United States. All I will say is that Dave needs to tread very carefully. I have seen some strange goings–on back there and folks should take the kind of thing he has experienced very seriously."

*****

Linde returned home and pondered on the night's events. He strolled into his living room and poured himself a stiff whisky. Was this all a storm in a teacup, after all? Dr Brock could be correct in her theory. Perhaps it is all down to brain chemistry. He settled back into his armchair and sipped his whisky. He thought about Julia Davenport and wondered how she had become involved in all this astrological hocus-pocus. She looked very conventional, not eccentric at all.

He felt very cold and moved to turn on the gas fire. The timer must have switched the central heating off. The gas lit with a comforting "woomph." Linde returned to his armchair and his musings on the people at the party. Dr Brock was a strange lady but she has a sharp intellect, no doubt about that.

There was certainly a melange of people at the party. He'd known Jim and Jane for five years and yet, bizarrely, he had never met any of the others. He could not recall them ever being mentioned. Theynard was the weirdest of all. Linde smiled as he imagined him being brought before the bishop to be defrocked for sacrificing the local virgins on the altar – a closet Satanist and a follower of 'the left-hand path' perhaps. These thoughts were what came of reading too much Dennis Wheatley in his youth, he mused.

It was now after midnight and he slipped deeper into his armchair. His eyelids grew heavy and he fell into the oblivion of sleep.

What woke him he did not know. A sound, a presence? All he knew was that he was now wide awake. Only the light from the coal effect fire flickered across the room.

He felt increasingly cold. He also felt a coil of fear in his stomach. His eyes moved round the room. The wavering shadows of the chairs in the room danced on the walls. He should have felt cosy but he felt cold enough to feel goosebumps rising.

The woman stood with her back towards him, her hair pulled back. He watched fascinated, his eyes riveted on her. His mouth dried like moisture on the hotplate of an oven. The firelight scintillated on her black beaded, long dress and he noted the bustle at its rear. She moved towards the door of the room. Linde leapt to his feet and rushed across the room. He reached her just as her hand closed on the door handle. He grabbed her shoulder and he felt the yielding flesh under his hand. The thought flashed through his mind that this spectre had an all too real solid form.

He turned her round and stared horrified into a featureless face. There were no eyes, no nose, no mouth, just smooth, horrifically blank skin.

He was overwhelmed by a sense of fear. This creature meant him harm – some primeval feeling deep within his soul told him so. Linde backed away and as he did so the backs of his knees struck against the armchair and he fell into it. His head fell forward. When he forced his head up again he expected to see the creature upon him, but it had gone. He realised having raised his head that he was emerging from sleep. He was alone in the armchair in the empty room. The whisky glass had dropped from his hand.

Jesus, a psychologist would have a field day with me; what a dream, he thought.

Linde mopped up the whisky from the carpet and went to bed. He could not sleep. He kept seeing that frightening faceless woman. What did she want from him? Maybe Julia would have some answers when he saw her next week. He tried to think of something other than the ghostly woman, such as work, but sleep would not come. He was reminded of his childhood. Having been tucked up in bed and the lights extinguished a partly opened wardrobe door could hide the devil and all his works within that dimly seen black rectangular space. Invisible yellow eyes watched from the stygian depths of the cupboard waiting for him to close his eyes. As soon as the lids descended the horrors of hell would emerge to claim his soul.

"This is bloody hopeless," he said out loud. "I give up!"

Linde rose and went downstairs very gingerly. He started at every creak, expecting to see the woman step from the shadowy alcoves and from around every corner. He tried to calm himself down with the thought that it had only been a nightmare and he had had those before.

All was quiet. He placed a saucepan of milk on the oven hob in his bright cheery kitchen and the irrational, primeval fears began to dissolve. He drank the hot chocolate he made with some relish. It was a happier man who ascended the stairs and, with thoughts of what work would bring tomorrow, he slipped into bed and very soon fell into a deep and dreamless sleep.

Linde woke refreshed. He showered, shaved, dressed and breakfasted. After breakfast he wandered into the living room searching for his briefcase. He found it beside the armchair. He bent to pick up the case, turned and headed for the door. As he moved forward the glitter of a shiny object caught his eye on the floor. He bent forward, picked it up and examined it. It was a small black, shiny bead rather like those found on dresses worn by ladies in old Victorian sepia prints.

Chapter 5

Uneasy Freehold

It was 7.25pm before David Linde arrived at L'Escargot restaurant. He was hot, ruffled and very apologetic as he entered the restaurant bar where Julia Davenport unconcernedly sipped a Martini. "Sorry Julia. I was tied up in a funding meeting at the faculty and could not get away. I could not reach a phone in the building and the battery on my mobile was rock bottom low."

"You left out the fact that your dog had a broken leg."

"Ok, I'm pathetic, but my department needs the money to complete our present agenda of projects... let's eat, you must be hungry?"

"Starved, but do you want a drink before we go in?"

"I've kept you waiting long enough," he said, signalling to the maitre d'. "Let's go to our table and order."

They were immediately led to a quiet corner table.

"Mademoiselle...monsieur," said the maitre d' in a strong French accent. "Your table is here. I will send over Michel to take your order. Bon appetite."

"Thank you Jean," said Linde.

After the maitre d' had departed, Linde suggested

to Julia that Jean was probably born in Stepney and ate jellied eels. This broke the ice and they laughed heartily together. Julia was still chuckling when they were interrupted by the waiter.

"Bon soir, Michel," said Linde.

"Mademoiselle et monsieur David, what is your pleasure, ce soir?"

They asked for time and concentrated on the menu and the joys of good food and wines. The meal was excellent. They started with Escargots au Beurre d'ail, which they washed down with a bottle of La baume – Cabernet Sauvignon. They then moved on to eat Carre D'agneau,Tomate au four, Demi-glace au Poivre Blanc. By the time the lamb had arrived they were talking like old friends and laughing uproariously. They derived considerable amusement from discussing the Reverend Theynard and his eccentricities.

Linde could not eat a sweet course but Julia had Mousse au Chocolat Noir and they quaffed more wine, this time a bottle of Muscat de Venise. At which point any hunger pangs had long since disappeared.

Eventually the talk turned to the reason for their meeting. "How did you get into this line of work, Julia?"

"That is a long story but I suppose I was conscious of certain forces or vibrations, call them what you will, of which others seemed unaware. It started at a very early age and I suppose, as a child, one thinks that one's view of life is the same as everyone else's. However, at 16, something happened which threw these 'powers' into sharp relief. I was at a wedding reception sitting at a table watching couples dancing. My attention was drawn to the Best Man and a girl who were waltzing down the room towards me. As the couple rotated the man turned to face me and as he did so I saw something." She paused.

"What did you see?"

"I saw he was going to die. I knew without a shadow of doubt that this young man before me, so full of life, had reached the end of his life."

"What did you see specifically?"

"I would rather not say."

Julia flushed a deep crimson and her eyes brimmed with tears. It was clear even after all these years that the emotional impact of what she had seen had not lessened one iota.

"Did what you see come true?"

"Yes," she said. "He died two days later in a motorcycle crash. He was killed outright."

Linde ordered her a brandy and apologised for pressing her on the subject.

"No, I'm sorry. We Irish are excessively emotional. It's our hot Celtic blood. The Celt in me is probably the source of this sixth sense. I went on to study psychology at university and did further research in parapsychology...and the rest is history. Now I read tea–leaves for old ladies who are dripping with diamonds and charge them huge amounts of money."

Linde raised the subject of his ghost and described the new event, which had left him somewhat nonplussed. He told her the story of his Victorian lady in the beaded dress.

"I came home and was sat in my armchair. I thought I had fallen asleep and was dreaming that she stood before me in a black-beaded dress with her back towards me. I leapt from the chair and grabbed her arm. I swear that the arm I felt was yielding flesh. The woman turned to me at this point and I was confronted by a horrific featureless face. I fell back into my chair and when I looked up; she was gone.

"I swear that I was not asleep and this was borne out later when I discovered this on the carpet near where I sat."

Linde took an envelope from his inside pocket and handed it to her. Julia opened the envelope and tipped the bead into the palm of her hand. She examined the sphere closely. Next she fondled the bead in her hand, closed her eyes and turned her head up to the ceiling.

"I can sense nothing, but that may not be significant...but...wait...!"

She looked puzzled and her brow furrowed. She remained in this state for some moments before handing the bead back to him.

"There is something there, something dark and shadowy but I cannot pierce the veil to see it. It is rather like when you are trying to remember something that you should know. Every now and then your memory allows you a glimpse of what it is you are searching for, but not enough to allow you to see and recognise it. Do you understand?"

Linde nodded although, up to now, he had always been sceptical of this clairvoyant mumbo jumbo. "You think my dream may in fact have been reality. What really stirred me up was that the woman was susceptible to touch. I felt her arm!"

"Dreaming and being awake are not totally separate, you know. For example, we all daydream sometimes. As for your bead, I think we need more data in order to eliminate the possibility that it is a mere coincidence. As for your very solid lady; well dreams do seem real sometimes."

Linde agreed and suggested that perhaps, if Julia was ready, they could go to the house. Julia acquiesced and they left the restaurant after paying the bill and generously tipping the staff for a delicious meal.

It was a short taxi ride to Rill Place and Linde led the way to the front door. Neither of them spoke as they entered the house. Julia felt as if the oxygen had been drained out of the air around her. She said nothing but she knew there was something there...and that it was not good.

"What's the matter, Julia? Come through."

Julia blinked, shook her head and followed Linde into the kitchen.

"How do you want to play this?"

"Show me a cold spot and we will go from there."

"Ok, I will switch on the security light and we will be able to see the corner in question."

He switched on the light, which he had fitted during the previous weekend. They made their way into the illuminated garden and over to the corner where the woman had first appeared. Julia approached the area with some trepidation.

Linde watched her with interest then followed her. It was as Julia reached the very corner where the two sections of garden wall met at right angles that she turned suddenly. Linde pulled up sharply as he stared at her face. Her countenance had taken on a look of abject horror. Her mouth dropped open and her eyes widened in terror as she stared into his face. Linde was about to speak when the security light was extinguished. He turned but before he could speak she rushed past him, a choking scream issuing from her lips. She ran for the light streaming from the back door. Linde, horrified, could only gape at her rapidly receding silhouette.

"Julia...wait!"

The words had barely left his lips when the light from the kitchen died. Julia tripped over an exposed root in the soil. She lay moaning, but quickly pulled herself up on to her knees and then to her feet. Her eyes became accustomed to the darkness and she saw the dark rectangle of the kitchen doorway ahead. She ran for it, through the house and out of the front door. David caught up with her halfway down the drive.

"Please come back. What did you see?"

Julia spoke with all the vehemence she could muster. "David, you have to leave this house. There is something here that is totally malevolent. I have never met anything like it. I must go!"

Just then light flooded the drive from the house. Linde turned to look back at the house but Julia was through the gate and away down the road. Linde hesitated. He could not decide whether to follow her or go back to the house. In the time taken for him to make up his mind and advance to the gate, Julia had reached the main road. She hailed a passing taxi and the car disappeared in the direction of the city.

Linde was left to go indoors, horrified by her behaviour and not a little frightened of what he would find in the house and garden. He closed the front door and walked through into the kitchen. He stepped tentatively into the garden. It was silent, empty and peaceful; he turned back into the kitchen. His hand reached up just inside the back door to switch off the security light. He felt an icy draught on the back of his neck. At the same time he heard the rustle of clothing behind him. He turned back, his eyes wide with fear. There was, however, nothing to see, no female figure, no horror. He closed the back door, locked it and headed towards a stiff, large whisky.

Chapter 6

A Deadly Prediction

Linde sat sipping his whisky and thought about Julia Davenport's behaviour that night. Decidedly unprofessional for someone who earned their living by contacting spirits. She seemed, in normal circumstances, a very lucid, articulate and logical girl. During their initial encounters he had been impressed by her demeanour. In fact he had thought that his generally jaundiced view of clairvoyants had been misplaced in her case. He could imagine that her clients would be impressed and feel better for her ministrations, despite the fact that, in his opinion, they may have experienced manifestations in the form of a placebo effect. In other words, people felt better because they expected to do so.

Whatever Julia had seen in the garden had been very real to her. She had been badly frightened. In fact he had not seen such naked fear before. He had also been aware of something strange. Why had the lights in the house been extinguished at such a key moment in the proceedings? Had there been a power cut? Perhaps it would be worth checking with the electricity supply people.

His mind turned back to Julia. They must meet again to discuss what had happened and to decide how they should play the meeting of the 'occult dinner group' at the Flagg's home. He had arranged with Jim Flagg that the dinner would take place on Thursday, in two days time. He would contact Julia in the morning.

The ringing of the telephone broke in on his thoughts. He placed the glass down on the table by his armchair and picked up the phone.

"Hello, Linde here."

"Hello David, this is Julia. I had to ring you to apologise. I behaved very badly; I should not have eaten or drunk alcohol before we went to your house."

"I was very worried about you. I tried to catch up with you but I had left all the doors open and...." She interrupted him with an urgent, breathless quality in her voice: "I know, I must see you; we need to talk about what I saw and sensed. There is something... and I think you may be in some danger."

Linde suggested: "Look, why don't we meet tomorrow afternoon for tea at Montpelier's in town at, say, three? We can talk it all through then."

"Yes, let's – I know where you mean. I am so sorry about my behaviour last night. I cannot apologise enough for what I did; it was unforgiveable and unprofessional. I will see you tomorrow."

Linde did not sleep well that night. He was plagued by dreams of Julia and him being chased by the faceless woman. Whatever they did they could not escape her. Eventually the woman caught up with them, whereupon her face transformed into the features of Denholme Theynard. When he awoke next morning he felt decidedly jaded. He showered, shaved and breakfasted. He rang work and told them he did not feel well and would take the day off. He dressed and walked to a local newsagent shop for a paper.

When he returned home Linde rang the local electricity service provider. When he eventually spoke to a human being he asked: "Was there a power cut last evening at approximately ten o'clock in the Rill Place area of Blackheath?"

There was a pause from the man on the help desk but eventually he spoke: "There have been no cuts in your area for more than three months."

*****

That afternoon he arrived at the tearoom almost at the same time as Julia. She looked pale and worried. He guessed that she had not slept well either. Linde opened the door to allow Julia into the tearoom first. They chose a table near the window and Linde ordered coffee for two.

She was still very apologetic about her behaviour. Linde told her not to dwell on it because he too had been frightened by the event. It was more important to discuss what had happened to cause her to react as she did, rather than the reaction itself.

Julia sipped her coffee and said: "I think I will start by explaining what I saw at that wedding all those years ago. You deserve that at least."

Linde shrugged and Julia continued.

"Where I reached the point in my story where the Best Man had turned to face me, for an instant his face had changed. In the blink of an eye I was aware that his features had transformed into a death's head. At the same time my whole body had been seized by a cold chill. I was transfixed where I sat. The music and the sounds of the party faded from my consciousness. Then he turned his face away and the normal sounds of the party penetrated my consciousness. In that moment I knew that his days were numbered. When he turned to face me again he was the same laughing boy I had seen before."

Linde realised the tragedy of this "gift" she possessed. "At first I put it down to imagination but it could not be ignored because, after all, the boy did actually die. I had indeed seen the grinning rictus of the death's head for what it was – a premonition of death. Since then it has happened a number of times and the dreadful confirmation has always followed. Not necessarily in a day or two but certainly within a month."

Linde listened with interest but wondered as to its relevance to the previous evening's events. Linde and Julia sipped their coffees for a minute or so longer before Julia continued.

"When we arrived at your house last night a feeling of utter dread and despair engulfed me. I felt this as soon as I crossed the threshold. There have been events in the house, that have left a dreadful mark on it. When we entered the garden and approached the corner. I turned towards you. I was immediately aware of two figures silhouetted against the glare of the security floodlight. There was you and close behind you a second figure, a woman. Even in silhouette I could see that she was dressed in the fashion of the late Victorian period, and there was something else…"

Julia paused and fiddled with her teaspoon.

Linde waited and then broke the tense silence. "Yes, Julia. What did you see?"

"No, I cannot say. It is too awful. I thought I could but I cannot."

Linde rose and moved round the table. He took her hands: "If it is about my future then it is only fair that I know what I am up against."

People in the tearoom had turned to look.

"Please, Julia. I must know."

"Very well," she whispered, a tear trickling down her cheek. "Your face was glowing and it had assumed the aspect of a grinning death's head."

Linde looked away from her face and down to the floor. He slumped in his chair and said: "You foresaw my death?"

There was a pause before she uttered the one word. "Yes."

They both sat silently. She eyed him with some concern as he stared unseeingly at a point on the floor 20 feet in front of him. Neither spoke for some minutes, then Linde broke the silence.

"Did the woman have a face?"

"I could not see her face because both of you were silhouetted against the light," explained Julia.

"How could you see my face?" asked Linde.

"Your face, as I said, was glowing as though you were holding a candle below and in front of you," said Julia.

"I held no light. How the hell do you explain that?"

"I can't. Look, David you must get away from that house. The cause must be there and if you are not around maybe it can be avoided."

"From what you said there is no way to avoid this end. It is my fate."

They sat, silent again for some moments. Linde spoke first.

"This defies all logic. If we can find out what has caused this haunting?"

"David, you must get away."

"Julia, I am a scientist. We are like children being afraid of the dark or being frightened by fairy tales. I am damned if I am going to be frightened off by the Big Bad Wolf."

Further protests by Julia were in vain. Linde had made up his mind. They agreed to share their experiences with the others at the Flagg's dinner party the following night.

"Think positively, Julia. I have found that to be a good axiom in life. It will probably be carved on my tombstone. Oh dear…sorry."

Their eyes met and despite their worries Linde and Julia laughed. They decided to end the rendezvous and meet again at the Flagg's house.

"Don't worry, Julia," said Linde, reassuringly. "I will survive and we will get to the bottom of this.

Chapter 7

Seen by Candlelight

Linde was very cautious in the lead up to the evening of the dinner. All was quiet in the house. He felt, however, that it was a queasy, oppressive quiet and not the still silence of peace.

He went to work the next morning but he found that the chemical element mendelevium could not command his whole attention. His mind kept returning to Julia Davenport's warning. He was tetchy with colleagues and his assistant, John Driver, maintained a discrete distance, especially after a particularly sharp altercation at the beginning of the day.

At 7.15pm Linde walked up the drive again to the Flagg's front door. All but Julia had arrived and Jane Flagg took him through to the reception room to join the party. After an exchange of pleasantries Linde was subjected to a barrage of questions as to what had happened in the house. He parried these by saying that it would only be fair to defer any discussion of the subject until Julia appeared.

Linde accepted a 'kir de cassis', a very tasty French aperitif, as the party engaged in small talk. Sam Plaid had taken delivery of the Flagg painting and as a result exuded self–satisfaction.

Discussing Lucien Freud's portrait work, Linde

said to Flagg: "Freud's portraits always look as though his sitters are 110 years old no matter how old they really are." An argument then took place which only ceased when Letitia Preece spoke: "I'm worried about Julia, look at the time, she is extremely late."

"I agree, I think we should try to contact her now," added Jane Flagg as she glanced at the art deco clock on the wall.

Jim picked up the telephone and punched in Julia's home number. A silence followed as they waited for the change in Jim's face, which would indicate that she had answered. No such change occurred and, after consulting his personal phone list, he keyed her mobile number into his machine and again drew a blank.

"That's odd," he said, staring down at the instrument with a puzzled look on his face. "She told me once that any client, if requiring her services, could get hold of her at any time because she never switched her mobile off!"

There followed a discussion as to why anyone would want their tea leaves read at three in the morning but the hubbub soon died down.

Denholme Theynard piped up: "Maybe Julia's soul has been claimed by some ghostly entity – no, you may snigger but these things do happen. I think that you should tell us everything that occurred last night, David. I see no point in waiting."

Linde frowned and spoke with a hint of impatience: "I disagree. Julia could still turn up but perhaps we should not delay having your delicious dinner, Jane."

"I think it will probably spoil if we don't eat soon. Let's go through to the dining room."

There was little talk over dinner until the party

were tucking in to the sweet course.

Miriam Brock broke a particularly long silence: "David, I think you should tell us what happened at your house now. Julia is obviously not coming and you cannot keep us on tenterhooks any longer."

The others voiced their agreement with Dr Brock and so Linde began his tale: "We went to my house after we had dinner. Julia seemed uncomfortable from the moment we crossed the threshold. I asked her what the matter was but she denied there was anything wrong. Nothing further happened until we approached the corner of the garden where I had seen the woman. Julia looked at me with a facial expression evincing such horror that it will haunt me forever. The garden security light failed at that point, Julia screamed and ran through the house and out into the road before I could stop her. The kitchen light extinguished as she entered the back door. I later established that the failure of the lights was not caused by a power cut. The lights came on again a short while after Julia had left.

"The only other strange phenomenon occurred as I was shutting the back door. It was a distinct rustling noise like the sound silken dress material makes when someone wearing it walks along. I immediately thought of the woman wearing that long silk, beaded dress. The sound came from the garden, but although I looked hard and long; I could see no one out there.

"Later that night Julia rang me. She said that I was in some danger and we agreed to meet in a tea-room the following afternoon. At that meeting she told me that I was marked for death and she had seen it in my face."

The dinner group greeted these revelations with a shocked silence and Jim Flagg decided to try phoning

Julia one more time. There was, however, still no answer from her mobile or landline.

Linde spoke, his voice filled with emotion:
"Something has happened to her, I know it. She
would not have missed this evening. When I left her
yesterday afternoon she was very keen to discuss
what we had seen with the rest of you."

"I told you that this is no game, Jim," said Sam
Plaid, shaking his head and stroking his chin thoughtfully. "Take it from me, it is dangerous territory...
particularly for someone who is as sensitive as Miss
Davenport."

Linde stood up.

"I'm going round to Julia's house. Will you come
with me, Jim? You know the area better than I do. We
may pick up a clue and at least we won't be sitting
on our hands."

"Ok, I'll get the car out of the garage. Won't be
long."

On the journey Linde spoke further of his concern
for Julia: "I am very afraid for her Jim, especially
after her reaction in my garden. She was completely
unnerved; desperately so."

"Understandable David," said Jim. "Although it
sounds as though you are in a more worrying position
than Julia. Anyway this is her road. I'll park near that
cedar tree over on the left there."

Flagg's car pulled into a mews courtyard in
London's dockland.

Linde observed: "This tea-leaf reading must pay.
These houses must cost the earth."

Jim Flagg agreed with a grunt as he stared at the
darkened windows in the flat. Linde stepped up to the
front door, knocked and waited. He knocked again
but the sound echoed eerily round the courtyard.

Nothing stirred in the house and as the echoes of the knock died he pressed his face against a front window, a hand cupped above his eyes to eliminate stray light from the lamp illuminating the court.

He waited for his eyes to grow accustomed to the darkness in the room he was peering into. He could make out a small table under the window. On it stood a small figure of the many-armed god Kali. As he stared at the outline of the god he became aware that the shape of it was gradually standing out against the background. He realised that a pallid orange glow was entering the room from the doorway, towards the back of the room and to the left. He felt the hairs on the back of his neck rise and his lips parted.

The light grew stronger as the bearer of the light approached the door of the room. Linde moved his head to one side in an effort to see round the door jamb. The light flickered in the illuminated rectangle of the doorway.

He caught his breath as a figure appeared, carrying before it a candle. The figure turned into the room and as it did so Linde caught sight of the face. The flickering light leapt for a moment revealing a faceless visage with its hair pulled back in a bun. That awful, featureless figure moved to approach the window. At that moment Linde's nerve broke and he backed away, inadvertently crashing into Flagg who had taken time to lock the car and approach the house. They both lost their balance for a moment and they struggled to remain upright.

Choking out an apology, Linde looked at the window expecting to see the phantom. A black, sightless window greeted his stare and he moved forward to confirm that he had not been imagining that faceless horror.

A dark cavern greeted his eyes. A room empty of ghosts was all he could see. No flickering light, not even from the doorway to at least announce its presence in the hall outside the room.

"Jim, did you see that. Did you see her?"

"Did I see what?" exclaimed Flagg in astonishment.

"I saw the woman...the ghostly woman from my house...in that room."

Flagg ran to the window but could see nothing. He turned and was about to speak when Linde burst out: "We must find a way into the house."

Chapter 8

The Julia Mystery Deepens

"Is there a back way into these places?" said Linde.

"I believe there is a passage through this door in the wall over here," said Flagg.

The two men walked over to the door and tried it. It opened at their touch and they made their way inside to the back of the building where a wall enclosed the back yard of Julia's flat.

Linde tried a gate in the wall but it was bolted. Flagg, realising it would be hopeless to prevent Linde from making an entry to the flat, crouched and cupped his hands in front of him in order to act as a lifting jack for Linde to reach the top of the wall. The latter stepped into the offered hands and pushed down. He reached up to the top of the wall and scrambled over and down into the yard below. All was in darkness in the yard and in the house. He made his way over to the nearest back window. It was latched and the door into the flat was locked.

He looked in at the window but it was too dark to see anything more than dark shapes. There was, however, a minute orange glow in the centre of the floor of the room. Linde ran back to the wall and asked Flagg if he had a torch in the car. Flagg said that he would fetch it. A few minutes later Linde heard Flagg's tread on the far side of the wall.

"It's only a pencil torch," said Flagg. "I'll switch it on and throw it over so that you can see it to catch it."

Linde caught the small cylindrical torch and immediately ran back to the window. He shone it so that the beam played over the area where he had seen the faint glow.

In the centre of the room stood a candle in a single brass candlestick holder, a twisting wisp of smoke ascending from the wick. Linde stared at it. Transfixed, his eyes widened. A single trickle of sweat ran down his temple and followed the curvature of his cheek to sit in the dimple at the corner of his mouth. The beam from the torch shook, causing the shadows of the chairs in the room to dance eerily against the walls. He took a step back and stared sightlessly at the wall below the level of the window. His mind was racing trying to assess what was going on, but he could make no sense of it.

The phantom had been real; there was now no doubt of it. He could see in front of him inescapable evidence of its presence. He closed his eyes but he could still see that twisting rope of smoke from the candle. His thoughts switched to that frightening, faceless phantasm, as it turned into that front room and moved towards him.

He was shocked out of his reverie by Flagg's muffled voice. "What's going on, David? Is she there?"

"No..er...there is no sign of her. I am going to try to gain entry into the house. Wait there, I will see if there is an easy way into the flat."

Flagg fell silent, realising that his friend was in no mood to be dissuaded.

Linde, meanwhile, had tried every window he

could reach and found them all latched until he was examining the back door with the torch. The fanlight above the door was fractionally ajar. Having briefed Jim he set about finding a way up to the window.

He allowed the beam of the torch to travel all over the yard. In a corner, partly concealed by a japonica bush, he saw a wheelie-bin. He pulled it into a position by the door and carefully climbed on to it via a metal watering can. He gingerly reached up to the window to pull it open. It moved slightly but was very stiff and it required a supreme effort to pull it out to the maximum angle. At one stage he almost lost his balance.

Holding the window ledge in his hands and taking his weight on them he swung his body horizontally up to try and align his body, from the hips down, along the line of the window ledge. It took three attempts to do so but eventually he succeeded. He bent his knees and was able to roll through the gap. As he fell through, he twisted and grabbed the window ledge with his hands. He was now hanging from the ledge inside the door, his feet dangling two feet from the floor. He dropped to the floor and assessed the damage. His elbows and knees were sore but at least he was inside the flat. He gave his injury sites a rub, moved across the room and switched on the light. He waited for his eyes to adjust to the flood of light and then moved towards the door.

He pushed the door open and there the candle stood, no longer smouldering, but still a testament to the fact that his eyes had not deceived him. He turned and quickly moved from room to room switching on lights as he went, but no ghostly or any other presence revealed itself to him. He remembered his companion and made his way to the front door and out of the house to where Jim was waiting. The pair ventured back into the house and as they stepped into the hall Flagg grabbed Linde's arm.

"I still think our best course of action would be to go to the authorities," said Jim.

"What the hell would I say?" asked Linde. 'A woman may be missing, she has not been seen for 24 hours. We appreciate that is not a long time, but somehow we know something is wrong.' The police will not see it that way. All I want to do is have a quick look round. I owe that to myself after seeing that ghostly apparition or whatever it was and I think I owe it to Julia."

"Are you sure you really did see a ghost, David? The house was in complete darkness, you were pretty excited."

"Look, let's just have a quick look; do it for me!"

"Ok, but let's make it just that...quick."

Linde did not mention the candle in the back room. He felt that Jim would rail against that...one step too far. Jim began to look in all the ground floor rooms while Linde climbed the stairs. All was quiet and the only sounds came from them as they switched on lights and made their way round the house. Linde gingerly opened the door of the bathroom but all the soaps, towels and shampoos were neatly arranged on their shelves, a picture of ordinariness. Linde moved on to the front bedroom...Julia's bedroom.

He experienced a shock as her perfume invaded his senses. He pictured her hair swinging as she walked. He put these imaginings aside as he wandered round the bed and opened the lid of a jewellery box. He sniffed a perfume bottle and idly opened a dressing table drawer. He moved on to the bedside table and examined a book she had obviously chosen for bedtime reading. A book by Aleister Crowley called *The Book of Lies*, probably not an easy read. It was then that Linde noticed the computer in the corner of the room diagonally opposite to where he now stood. He went over and switched it on.

He waited as the machine made the 'throat clearing' sound of booting up and watched as the desktop program icons sprang on to the screen. There was no password protection and he clicked on the e-mail program and the hard disk drive murmured as it strove to contact the ISP server.

Linde watched as the list of emails stored in the in-box appeared on the screen. He rubbed his forehead as he stared at the VDU, feeling guilty at invading Julia's privacy. It was rather like reading her diary...private and containing recorded, innermost thoughts to close friends. But there could be a clue to her whereabouts locked within this machine. One email caught his eye and his heart missed a beat. He read the sender's name again. He was not mistaken. His mind raced but no obvious explanation came to him.

david.linde@gosmart.co.uk

The email address swam out of focus as his mind raced to understand what was going on. He did not know her email address and had never sent her an email.

He clicked open the message and read the words with baited breath.

"Hi Julia, could you come round to my house on the way to the Flagg's tonight (say 7pm)? I have something important to show you. It will not take long but it is very important. David."

Linde reread the message and the lines on his forehead deepened. Just then an expletive from downstairs reminded him that Flagg was still searching below.

"You ok, Jim?"

"Tripped over a bloody candlestick. Who the hell left that there?" came the reply.

With the minimum of thought he deleted the email and also deleted it from the 'Deleted File'. Linde powered down the computer and made his way downstairs, meeting Flagg in the hallway. They agreed that it was time to leave. Linde did not mention the computer issue because he needed to think about it first. Having ensured that the house was secure, they left.

Chapter 9

Cold Blood

"I don't know how you persuaded me to break into Julia's house."

"We did not 'break in'...there was an open window," argued Linde.

"Don't split hairs," continued Flagg. "After all, she has only been missing for 24 hours and she may have been called away to her mother or something."

"I explained before that all my instincts are telling me that there is something wrong," retorted Linde.

Flagg, however, continued to berate Linde but did admit that the faceless woman had been a strange incident. Especially as he had seen, or rather, tripped over a candlestick similar to the one held by the woman described by Linde. The car, meanwhile, drew into the drive of Flagg's home. Jane appeared at the door as they approached the porch.

"Anything?" she asked, her face a mask of concern.

"Let's get inside...and we will tell all of you what we found," said Flagg wearily.

"I have rung Julia's mother, her TV producer and her agent," said Jane, as she followed them in to join the waiting party. "None of them has seen her for two or three days."

Linde cast a knowing and somewhat self–righteous glance at Jim Flagg as he accepted the brandy offered by Letitia Preece.

"Hope you don't mind me offering your drink in your house, Jane, " said Letitia, thoughtfully. "But these two look as though they could do with some strong stimulants."

The two arrivals sat down in the comfortable chairs in the lounge. The remaining members of the group sat expectantly hushed while the two men collected their thoughts and sipped their drinks. David Linde opened by describing their arrival at the house and the appearance of the phantom female. He proceeded to explain how they had succeeded in entering the house but had found no sign of the missing woman or the phantom. While Linde told his tale, Flagg remained silent for the most part, only interjecting to affirm certain points. There was no mention of the email.

The assembled company said nothing for a short time until Miriam Brock broke the silence. "I still think that Julia may have had an appointment that no-one knows about. She has been missing only a short time. Before you say anything, David; I think we need a structured plan of campaign that makes Julia's whereabouts a priority but, importantly, also starts us on a research plan which leads us to an understanding of what is going on at The Eaves."

Animated discussion began with Jim Flagg speaking decisively: "I know most of Julia's friends and I will ring them to see if they have seen or made any sort of contact with her."

Sam Plaid leaned forward: "What do we do if you still cannot trace her?"

Flagg replied: "I will inform the police, of course."

David Linde came in. "That sounds sensible – I, meanwhile, will explore the history of The Eaves and Rill Place from documents such as deeds and census records.

"I am also quite keen to set up a camera in the garden to record any events. How I'm going to get the kit – I am not sure."

Letitia Preece spoke next, excitedly: "I can lay hands on instrumentation which will prove helpful, I am sure. We could, for example, measure temperature changes. The cameras could be triggered by motion sensors. My work at the Oxford Film Unit gives me access to all the equipment we will need. I will see what I can do and contact you in the next few days."

The excitement of this interchange galvanised Theynard: "I can do some research at the London Psychical Institute Library to ascertain if there is any record of The Eaves in Rill Place and any ghostly associations."

Miriam Brock volunteered: "Why don't we meet next at Rill Place where we could test the equipment and attempt to detect any phenomena at the house overnight. Always assuming Letty can acquire the equipment.

"The plans may need to change depending on what has happened to Julia. The investigation of The Eaves situation should still be pursued because no-one but us are interested. Anyway the disappearance of Julia may – and I say only may – be linked to it."

"It would make sense for me to be the link man here. I work from home and I am easily contacted. I can also keep you all informed of progress via e–mail," concluded Jim Flagg.

There followed an exchange of email addresses before the group separated at 11.45pm.

*****

Linde was very thoughtful as he drove home. It had been a very eventful night. He slowed down outside his home and slowly turned the vehicle into his drive. He stopped outside the front door. It was then that his eye caught sight of his mobile phone, which he had, absentmindedly, left on the seat of the car before going to the party. The display indicated that he had had a missed call.

He dialled the voicemail service. When the message played it shocked him into sitting upright in his seat. It was Julia. "Hello, David. I am at your house standing in the hall. It was very silly of you to leave the front door ajar. Anyway, you asked me to meet you here at seven and you're not...oh my God ...who are you? Help me...it's Drew...!"

The phone went dead at that point.

Linde sat in disbelief and then replayed the call. He had previously convinced himself that the email he had read on Julia's PC had been as a result of a virus on his computer, but this clearly could not be so. The fact that Julia had acted upon the request to meet and was now missing caused a rising panic within him. He looked out at the ground floor windows of the house. All was in darkness and his stomach muscles tensed into rigid knots as he exited the car and made his way around the vehicle. He approached the front door, a feeling of cold overcoming him. He turned his head sharply, expecting to see the ghostly presence he had seen before. No such phantasm was near but he became aware of something else and that was...the silence. There was no traffic noise, no dogs barking, no wind; just this feeling of cold cloying stillness, as though something was awaiting him inside the house. He looked through the front door windows but all was in darkness. However, the windows stared back at him and it seemed to him that it was a malign stare. It took him all his strength to summon the effort to approach the door and insert his latch-key. He was afraid, a fear that was primeval. It was the dark inside the child's wardrobe again.

He turned the key, pushed the door open and entered the hall. He switched on the light, all seemed quite normal and he began to gain some courage. He called out Julia's name but all he heard in return was the faint echo of his own voice reverberating from the walls. Linde stared at the phone in the hall. The receiver was off the hook lying on the floor by the hall table. He picked it up and felt a sticky area on the phone. He looked down and on the surface of the receiver was a smudged, bloody fingerprint. He dropped the phone.

He called Julia's name again. It was to no avail. He thought about what was threatening Julia and whether it was still in the house waiting in the shadows. Linde called her name again, this time with desperation in his voice. With no answer he went into the lounge and his eyes lit upon a heavy brass candelabra on the mantelpiece, which he grabbed. He started to move around the ground floor rooms, his eyes darting this way and that as he searched, anticipating horrors. His attention at last switched to the stairs. He started to climb them, his eyes fixing on the landing as more of it came in view. It was dark up here because in his haste he had not switched on the light.

He turned the right-angled bend at the top and as he strode on to the landing his eye was caught by a flicker of light to his left. It came from the gap at the bottom of the closed door to his bedroom. At the same time he became aware of a very faint tapping sound which seemed to emanate from the direction of the flickering light. He approached the door.

Chapter 10

Enter Superintendent Kayne

A feeling like pins and needles crossed his forehead and the hairs on the nape of his neck rose. He raised the candlestick in his left hand. His right hand reached out to the door knob. Unnervingly, out of the corner of his eye, he glimpsed a dark figure move away into the stygian blackness to the left of the door. As it moved it made a faint rustling sound and he thought he glimpsed a frighteningly pallid face half turned away from him. A figure he recognised. Before he could turn and follow the shape his attention was arrested by the sound of a tattoo of tapping sounds from inside the bedroom before him. He reached gingerly forward and pushed the door ajar. The bedroom wall opposite him was bathed in an eerie flickering orange glow, which seemed to come from the window side of the bedroom out of his line of sight. He could not move – a strange paralysis gripped him and his eyes watered and widened in abject horror.

He forced himself forward and turned towards the bed, which was behind the door in the direction of the glow. The light was coming from a group of candles burning in orange glass tubes on his dressing table, backing on to the window beyond his bed. His stare fell to the bed itself and through the refracted light from his tears he saw only a vision of red. He cleared his eyes with his sleeve and beheld a sight causing them to bulge from their sockets. His hand released the candlestick, and it dropped with a clang to the floor and rolled under the bed.

The figure of a woman lay in the middle of the bed. Her shoulders were flat on the bed and her head was turned on the left cheek. Her left arm was flexed at the elbow across her abdomen. Her right arm lay on the bedclothes pulled back diagonally across the bed under the body. Her legs were wide apart and bent inwards from the knees down. It was the face that caused Linde's gaze to halt and he leaned forward to see it more clearly. It had been hacked out. There was no nose or eyes but the hair was shining in the candlelight and was spread out on the bed-clothes in a luxuriant curl. He knew it was a beautiful reddish chestnut colour, even though the roots were clearly caked in blood and the orange glow hid its true colour.

He could look no longer; he ran to the bathroom and vomited violently. He remembered the tapping sound and realised that it was the dripping of blood on to the floor. He retched again. He waited for the nausea to subside and staggered over to the washbasin. He splashed water in his face and as he reached for a towel looked at the drawn face in the mirror before him. He looked and felt very old.

The memory of the dark figure on the landing returned to him. Had he imagined it or was it real? Was it the murderer?

No, he knew who it was. It was her, that woman, the faceless creature which now haunted both his dreams and his waking hours. It had started with her and now it had led to a death, a horrible brutal murder. He would have to leave this house. It was a harbour for evil, but for the moment he was trapped.

Linde knew with absolute certainty that if he searched the house again for that dark figure; he would find nothing. He stumbled downstairs and phoned the police.

*****

The man with the dark complexion crossed the main Blackheath Road into Rill Place. He walked with the slightly stooped gait of a scholarly man. He had shiny elbows on the sleeves of his dark blue in-expensive suit. The hours of leaning on a desk poring over files or old books. He had a full head of hair. It had once been dark brown, almost black, but was now shot through with grey at the temples. On his arm he carried a raincoat. He approached the 'DO NOT CROSS' tape and raised his handsome but gaunt face to examine the road leading to the murder house.

Detective Superintendent David Kayne spoke to the constable standing in the road and ducked under the tape. He entered the van, which had been set up at the end of the road and donned the regulation white suit, gloves and overshoes and walked towards the house.

Detective Sergeant Collins, standing in the hall of The Eaves, looked up from his notebook as he heard the measured tread of his distinguished colleague. He was happy to work for this quiet man who had hunted violent murderers, with such success, for over 15 years.

Abel Collins was not an ambitious man with regard to climbing the ranks. He was 38-years-old, a bachelor and married to a job. He loved it deeply for its own sake. He was beginning to thicken at the waist and his hair to thin at the temples. The thickening waist was the result of a liking for Irish whiskey – he never said no to a Jameson or a Bushmills. He had intelligent dark brown eyes. He was nobody's fool and because of his undoubted intellect, he was an excellent sounding board for Kayne's ideas.

"Morning, sir. Pathologist is already in attendance."

"Who is it, Tom Bond?" asked Kayne, in a voice of deep bass tones.

"Yes, he was soon on the scene. Here he comes now...how goes it, Tom?"

A large, slightly overweight man descended the stairs and nodded a greeting to the two detectives.

"Messy up there. Looks like a frenzied attack at first glance but the body has actually been mutilated systematically. Woman, well nourished, aged between 25 and 30, I would guess. I am not yet sure of the cause of death but it was probably the severing of the carotid artery. All the incisions are very deep and the neck has been cut through to the vertebra. She also received a blow on the head prior to death and ..and, oh yes, both breasts have been removed and placed on the table by the bed. The thorax has been opened to reveal its contents. Time of death was sometime yesterday...evening or night."

"Bloody hell, Tom. Can't you be more precise than that?" said Kayne.

"Well, that's not bad, David, bearing in mind how much of the body has been opened up and hence cooled. You know as well as I do that if I give you a time of death accurate to the nearest hour, you could and should put the cuffs on me...because I would have been there. Oh and by the way, the sexual organs have been cut out and the heart is missing also. I'll be able to tell you more after the autopsy."

Tom Bond then moved past the two men and left. David Kayne was happy with the preliminary report. Bond was a good man to work with because he always confided as much information as he had. All of it was supported by hard fact.

Kayne turned to Collins and asked: "Is the person who found the body still here?"

"Yes, he is also the house owner and is in a considerable state of shock since the discovery. His name is Dr David Linde and he is in the dining room."

"Ok, I'll see him later. Let's take a look at the body first."

The two men made their way to the bedroom where the forensic team were working. The body was ready for removal. A body bag lay on the floor alongside the bed ready for its gruesome burden.

Kayne entered the bedroom; there were blood stains everywhere. At the periphery of the stains on the bedclothes, where the blood was drying, the redness was darkening to a deep maroon colour. He stared at the girl lying in the final position where her life had left her. Once he had rid himself of the initial effect of her revolting injuries and the awful smell, he felt a profound sense of sorrow for the loss of a young life.

Kayne advanced towards a young man bagging a candelabra.

"Anything interesting yet, Haymes?"

"Found this under the bed and there are traces of blood on it. I'll let you know if we find anything of further significance. By the way, sir, I have taken Dr Linde's fingerprints for elimination purposes."

Haymes was the Senior Crime Scene Investigator and he too was a longstanding colleague of Kayne.

Kayne moved round the room opening drawers and examining the heap of clothes, apparently belonging to the girl, lying haphazardly round the bed. With a deep sigh he turned to Collins and said that, bearing in mind it was approaching 2am, they had better have a word with Linde.

Chapter 11

The Aftermath

The two detectives entered the dining room where Linde sat brooding, staring straight ahead at the opposite wall.

"Dr Linde, may I disturb you please? I am Detective Superintendent Kayne and this is Detective Sergeant Collins. I realise this is very difficult for you, but we need to proceed with our investigations. In my experience this is a critical phase and the trail soon goes cold from here."

"I understand – what do you want to know?"

"Tell me what happened from the moment you arrived home."

Linde took a moment to compose himself, and then spoke softly.

"I noticed, as I left a dinner party at Jim Flagg's house, which Julia Davenport should have attended, that I had a missed phone call on my mobile from Julia. It came from this house, the phone in the hall. She said that the front door had been open when she arrived. I had definitely closed it. She said that she needed help and was cut off before she could say anything apart from mentioning a name."

"A name?" asked Kayne.

"It sounded like 'Drew' but I can't be totally sure. She was cut off immediately after that."

"Did you hear any other voices in the background?"

"No, there was only Julia's voice."

"Did you delete the message after you listened to it."

"Yes, I am afraid I did. Force of habit, I'm afraid. I don't like them to stack up."

Kayne wondered why anyone would delete a call at such a time but he remained silent on the matter. "Carry on with your story, please."

"I entered the house, found the phone off the hook. There was blood on it. I called her name with no result. I decided to search all the rooms. Although, it occurred to me that the thing she was afraid of could still be in the house. I started the search and eventually came upon...well, you know the rest."

"We will, of course, need to contact her family..." said Kayne. "...to officially identify the body, if that is possible. How did you know it was Julia Davenport?"

"She had a very distinctive hair colour. To be honest, after the phone call, who else could it be?"

"I think perhaps you had better get some sleep, Dr Linde," suggested Kayne. "I'm afraid you cannot stay here. Have you anywhere you can stay 'pro tem'?"

"Yes, Sergeant Collins allowed me to contact Jim Flagg, who was hosting the dinner party, and he and his wife have agreed to put me up for a while."

"Ok, if you could leave an address with my sergeant. That will be all until tomorrow – when we would appreciate further words, please."

As they were leaving the room Haymes appeared in the doorway. "Excuse me, sir, I thought you ought to see this. We found it clutched in the right hand of the victim."

He passed a plastic envelope to Kayne. In it was a chain with a small medallion attached: cut into its surface were the letters 'MJD'.

"Dr Linde, do you recognise this?"

"No, I've never seen it before in my life."

"Have you any idea whose initials they are?"

"No idea at all."

The detective passed the envelope back to Haymes and they all left the room. Linde drove away into the night.

*****

"Goodnight, Jim. See you in the morning."

David Linde closed his bedroom door, undressed, cleaned his teeth in the smart en-suite bathroom and climbed into bed. He switched off the light and lay staring sightlessly at the ceiling. He listened to the sounds of the house. Jim and Jane Flagg had been very supportive. They had waited in dressing gowns with hot chocolate until he arrived. He had briefly told them of events. Jane reacted very badly, understandably, since Julia was a friend of hers. Jim took her in his arms and led her to their bedroom upstairs. As he climbed the stairs he called back to Linde to go up to his bedroom when he was ready and bid him goodnight.

Linde now lay wide awake in bed, feeling that he was living through some Poe-like nightmare and that he would wake in the morning and all would be as it was before this hell began. It was all too difficult to believe; ghosts and mutilated corpses invading his world. He now wondered why he had ever bought

The Eaves. Ever since he had stepped over the threshold strange things had started to happen. It was as though the house itself held some evil. Perhaps that should be his next positive step; he would research the house and its past owners. Maybe he could make contact with some of them and find out if they too had seen or heard anything untoward. Nothing paranormal was going to convince Superintendent Kayne but the research may shed some light on what was going on. It was also one of the agreed actions of the group meeting at the Flaggs' earlier that evening. That meeting seemed to be an age ago.

As his mind drifted back to the earlier events of the day he heard a sound outside the door of his bedroom. It was a footfall and it sounded as though it was moving away down the landing towards the stairs. He swung his legs out of bed and headed towards the door. After opening the door, he listened and heard a sound coming from downstairs. It seemed to come from the kitchen area and he therefore headed in that direction.

It was Flagg. He now stood at the stove heating a saucepan of milk. He turned as Linde entered the kitchen and gave him a wry smile. "Can't sleep either, huh?"

"No, Jim. Too much going on in my head."

As Linde sat down wearily at the kitchen table he interlinked the fingers of his hands and stared at them. Flagg spoke first.

"Do you want me to tell the rest of the group about what has happened?"

"I don't know. Before this it was almost a game. Now someone has died and I feel responsible. After all, I dragged Julia into this mess."

"My dear boy, Julia never did anything Julia did

not want to do. Anyway, why are you so sure the body you found was Julia's? It was pretty badly mutilated from what you said." Linde put his head in his hands at this and after a moment or two he looked up and said; "It was her. I recognised her hair. It was quite distinctive, you know...how is Jane taking all this?"

"Very badly shaken and upset. I've given her a sleeping pill and she has at last gone off to sleep."

"Look, Jim, to make my statement I will go down to the station, then the police won't need to come here. That way Jane will not be disturbed any more than necessary."

At that point Flagg laid a friendly arm round Linde's shoulders and said, reassuringly: "That is not necessary. Come on, let's at least try to get some sleep, David."

Linde was too exhausted to argue and they both made their way upstairs.

*****

Superintendent Kayne sat in his office, having just arrived after a couple of hours sleep. He had made a comfortable office. On the walls were a Beardsley print (*A Repetition of Tristan und Isolde* taken from an 1896 edition of The Savoy magazine) and a poster advertising a local production of Henrik Ibsen's *The Dolls House.* There were, of course, the usual notice boards with paper notices pinned to them. One or two of these had been displayed for some time and were curling like brandy snaps.

Kayne sat, leaned back in his chair, talking on the telephone to Dr Bond who was speaking from the morgue. "OK, so your original statement about cause of death was accurate. Any further thoughts on time of death?"

He held the phone an inch or two away from his ear as Bond repeated his opinion expressed so eloquently when they had last met.

"When can I expect your final report?...ok, thanks, Tom."

Kayne rose and headed for the door.

"Come on, Collins. Let us go and see Dr Linde. Have you asked the forensic IT people to look at that computer at Julia Davenport's house? It may give us an insight as to who were her contacts. Among them may be the murderer. Mrs Davenport Senior gave her permission for us to search the place on her way to identify the body."

"Yes, sir, they are on to it now. We have a forensic team in there as well doing a general search."

The two men left the building.

Chapter 12

Two Women Gone

"Mr Flagg? I believe you have a Dr David Linde staying with you at the moment. I wonder if we might have a word with him, please?"

The visitor at the door, having already made his introductions and shown his warrant card, made to enter the house. Jim Flagg stood aside to let the two detectives pass into the hall. Linde appeared at the door of the reception room and everyone followed him into the room.

"Can we see Dr Linde alone please, Mr Flagg?" asked Kayne.

As Linde and the two detectives sat down, Jim nodded in assent and went into the kitchen to make some coffee.

"When did you originally meet Julia Davenport?" Kayne asked Linde.

"Is the dead woman definitely her?" asked Linde, forlornly.

"Yes, her mother came in and identified her body a short time ago. Can you answer my question, please?"

Linde proceeded to tell the story of his original arrival at the house in Rill Place and of the ghostly inhabitant residing there. He moved on to the dinner party where he had met several of the Flagg's friends, including Julia who had turned out to be a clairvoyant.

"I was fascinated to discover that all the attendees at the party were interested in paranormal phenomena," he explained. "The story of my ghostly house guest started a lively discussion. Julia Davenport volunteered to come to the house in order to assess the atmosphere of the place. This was agreed and a date was set for the following Tuesday. The party would reconvene two days later on the Thursday at the Flaggs' house – earlier this evening in fact – that is; yesterday.

"Julia and I duly met and she fled in panic after entering my garden. We met up on the next day for tea. At that meeting she said that I was in mortal danger – life threatening peril."

Kayne listened intently, asking the odd question and prompting here and there. Collins made notes throughout the discussion.

Linde then described the events when he had met Julia in the teashop the day after she had fled the house. He finally arrived at the night of the murder.

"What happened next, Dr Linde?" probed Kayne.

"I went to the Flagg house on Thursday evening."

"At what time did you leave home to go to the party that evening?"

"Just before seven, I think. I know I arrived at the Flagg house at 7.15pm, because I looked at my watch as I walked up to the front door."

"Who was there that evening?"

"The same group of people as at the earlier dinner except, of course, for Julia. We talked about the happenings at my house and eventually dined without her."

"Did anyone attempt to make any contact with her?"

"Yes. I think Jim rang her on her mobile but it was turned off."

Just then Jim Flagg appeared with coffee. He left the room and Kayne turned to David Linde once more.

"What happened after dinner?" he asked.

Linde went on to describe the events at Julia Davenport's flat. He described the ghostly woman he had seen and how he had found a way into the building but could find nothing. He did not discuss the email and was pleased he had deleted it.

"Did Mr Flagg see the ghostly presence at the flat?" asked Kayne.

"No."

"I left for home at about 11.45pm...and you know the rest."

"Were you sexually attracted to Miss Davenport?" asked Kayne, examining his coffee cup intently.

"I liked her and I was worried about her when she did not appear."

"Were you aware of any other men at the first meeting at the Flagg house who might have been attracted to Miss Davenport?"

"No."

"One more thing. We will be examining the rest of your house during our investigations. I trust you have no objection?"

"No, not at all."

Kayne asked Linde to write and sign a statement. Linde agreed and, having completed the task, handed back the signed papers.

"Thank you Dr Linde. That will be all for now."

*****

Kayne and Collins interviewed Jim Flagg next. He echoed much of the story told by Linde. One piece of information given by Flagg, however, caused Kayne to raise an eyebrow.

"It is all a great shame. We had great hopes that David would make a new life when he moved into this new house."

"What happened previously to warrant that hope, Mr Flagg?"

"He split up with his wife, who was a great friend of my wife."

"Where is Mrs Linde now?"

"In the north of India, near the Pakistani border, I believe. My wife was very upset because the two women had worked together for some time and we had been out together as a foursome many times. It was through her that we had befriended David. A purely professional relationship had blossomed into a personal bond."

"Have you heard from Mrs Linde since she left?"

"No. Jane received a note from Annie just before she left. In it she said that she was going to make a complete break and take up nursing with the Red Cross. The letter was posted, believe it or not. We had no personal contact."

"Had you any idea that the marriage was in any kind of trouble before the event?"

"I think you would do better to speak to my wife on that subject. I believe she was aware of some problems."

After Flagg had left the room Kayne turned to Collins.

"What do you think?"

"There are two things that bother me," mused Collins. "The precipitous way the wife left and where she went."

"There are quite a number of things which do not quite gel here," agreed Kayne. "After this next interview I think we need to marshal our facts including the forensic data. We need to get the team together and make a systematic plan of action."

Just then Jane Flagg appeared in the doorway. The two men caught their breath; she had that effect on men. She had the high cheekbones of a timeless beauty. The events of the last 24 hours, however, had left their mark on her. Her face was somewhat drawn and her eyes were red-rimmed from the tears she had shed for her dead friend. She fidgeted with a hand-kerchief.

Kayne rose to greet her and asked if she was feeling better. She replied that she was still in shock but understood that the superintendent had his job to do. Her voice was slightly husky. As the questioning began she made the supreme effort of a woman well used to making her own way in the business world. Jane could shed very little new light on the events that had occurred during the two dinner parties in question. Kayne then changed tack.

"What happened to David and Annie Linde's marriage?"

"What do you mean?"

"Your husband told us that they became estranged. What do you know of the causes of that estrange-ment?"

"I think that they grew apart. David was diverted by his work."

"There was no one else who had become part of the problem?"

Jane's eyes no longer met the unwavering gaze of the detective.

"Mrs Flagg, I shall find out one way or another. I do not give up easily."

"Annie was having an affair."

"With whom?"

"With Stephen Murray. Annie had been designing a house for him. David was spending more and more time at work. The relationship between Stephen and Annie grew because she felt neglected. David spotted them together one day and realised what was going on."

"How did Linde react to this relationship?" asked Kayne.

"Not well. Not violently, though. He became morose and silent. Annie said that he frightened her because his silence was more accusatory than any screaming, banshee reaction could be. I understood how Annie felt. David spent up to 18 hours a day at work and she had a lively mind. She was an attractive woman and what happened was inevitable."

"Things came to a head presumably?" asked Kayne.

"I assume so, although I do not know the details. The first I knew of a complete break between David and Annie was the arrival of a letter from her. It said that her relationship with Stephen was over and so it was, also, with David. She was joining a Red Cross expedition to northern India. The decision to go had to be made within days because the expedition was to leave within the week."

"Have you the original letter in your possession Mrs Flagg?" Asked Collins.

"I may have. I will need to search for it."

"Very well, Mrs Flagg, I think that is enough. We

will leave you now but please contact me as soon as you locate the letter." Jane Flagg agreed as she led the detectives to the door.

At the door Kayne hesitated, turned and asked Jane: "Could you provide me with a list of telephone numbers and addresses of people at the dinner party?" Jane agreed and the two detectives left the house.

Kayne was stooping to enter the car when his eye was caught by the shadowy figure of a man in an upper window. He recognised the figure as Linde. This was no surprise but it was the look on Linde's face that disturbed Kayne; there was the trace of a smile.

The car pulled out of the drive..

"Get on to the Red Cross. Ask them if they have a record of Annie Linde as a nurse working for them in India?"

Chapter 13

Above Suspicion

Kayne riffled through the papers on his desk. He looked across at the photograph of his wife and wondered what she was doing at that moment. Samantha Kayne was a marine biologist working at this moment on South Georgia, an isolated rock in the South Atlantic inhabited mostly by penguins. She had been away for three months now and would not be back until the winter returned to the Southern Ocean. He missed her. This feeling was particularly acute at the moment. Not for any real reason, it seemed to depend on his body chemistry. The pain returned cyclically.

He did not want to go home yet and so he decided to drive out to The Eaves. Thinking the case through at the site of the murder often helped to clarify things for him. He stood up, donned his coat and headed for the door, which opened at his touch because WPC Rawlins was on the other side of it, as if lying in wait. "Dr Bond's report has just arrived. Shall I leave it on your desk, sir?"

"Let me have a quick look at it now, thanks."

Kayne retreated to his desk and sat down, opening the file as he did so. He turned to the cause of death, which Bond gave as, "severance of the carotid artery at the right hand side. She would have bled to death in a very short space of time with a wound of that nature, ignoring the remaining lacerations. The position of the cuts in the body would also indicate that the perpetrator was most likely left-handed." Kayne raised his grey eyes and stared straight ahead. He was lost in thought for some minutes. Eventually he shook his head out of its reverie. He placed the file in his briefcase and made his way out of the building to his car.

When he arrived at Rill Place he noted that the barriers had been removed and at The Eaves the police 'DO NOT CROSS' tape had been set up at the front gate. A sturdy PC stood at the door. Kayne produced his warrant card and entered the house wearing protective clothing from the parked caravan in the driveway. The last of the forensic team were packing their kit and leaving for the day. Kayne made his way upstairs to the murder bedroom. He walked over to a chair in the corner of the room and sat down.

The body had gone now. The linen and mattress had been removed from the bed for forensic analysis. Kayne began to think. Interviews with neighbours had yielded little information on the murder itself. Little was known about Linde as he had only recently moved into the house.

A neighbour living next door but one to The Eaves had lived there for many years. He said that he could not remember any single inhabitant living in the house for longer than a six-month period. Many had left inside one month. In the seventies the house had stood empty for a full decade. How did this relate to the murder, if at all? As he pondered the case, Kayne stood up and wandered over to the window.

He was thinking that the night was growing foggy outside when he realised that the window was misting over before him. He shivered and felt very cold. He turned and noticed that a cloud of his condensed breath had launched itself into the air, dissolving into tendrils and fading to nothingness.

The light from the single pendant bulb hanging from the ceiling grabbed Kayne's attention. Did it appear duller than a few moments ago? He stared in disbelief but it was definitely not as bright as before. The action was so slow he felt that his eyes must be deceiving him. He looked round the room and watched as the shadow thrown by the wardrobe lengthened. The centre of the ceiling became a dusky patch. Soundlessly and stealthily that dark shadow on the ceiling was growing. He ran to the door of the bedroom and called out but all was silent and so, so cold. There was no traffic sound, no dogs barking, no murmurs from neighbouring houses – just profound, utter, blanketing silence.

He turned back into the room and looked down at the bed expecting to see the faceless ghost of Julia rise from the bed. He could just see, in the gathering gloom, the dull whiteness of the wooden slats of the bed. He became aware of a familiar perfume pervading the air. It was sweet, intoxicating and caused him to turn his head, but there was no sign of anyone. The filament of the bulb was now just a pale orange glow and it was at this point that he heard a faint, but definite, sound. It sounded like the hiss of some reptile and it came from the ceiling. Silence fell again but it was only for a short period because he soon became aware of the hissing sound once more – this time much louder. It ended with a dull thump. There was silence again as though, whatever was up there, had gathered itself. A few seconds later the process repeated with a hiss followed by a louder thump. The sounds were moving across the ceiling. Kayne was transfixed staring up at the bland emulsion painted surface above him. His mouth had dried and he was freezing. Despite the cold he felt beads of perspiration form on his forehead.

He forced himself to contemplate what was causing the sounds; there were no rooms above this bedroom, only a loft space. He wiped his sleeve across his forehead, rubbed his chin and turned to move out on to the landing. He looked up at the hatch–way door which led to the loft space, wondered if there was a loft ladder and turning back, entered the bedroom. He fetched the chair he had vacated earlier.

He stopped in his tracks as he realised that the lighting level was back to normal. A car passed by and somewhere in the murmur of evening the familiar opening theme of *EastEnders* could be heard. He no longer felt cold.

Kayne, you are developing an over-active imagination, he mused.

It was still worth a look in the loft. Imagination could not have conjured up those sounds. He placed the chair beneath the hatch and climbed up, but even stretching as far as he could it was not possible to reach far enough. The high Victorian ceiling was too far above. He looked round to see if there was anything else that could help him reach up and as he did so came face to face with a very rubicund visage. Kayne's eyes widened and he shuddered from the shock of this unexpected arrival.

"Excuse me, sir. There is a man outside who would appreciate a word. I said that you were busy but he insisted."

"Very well, constable. I will come out to see him. Don't let him in; we don't want to contaminate the crime scene. By the way, did he give a name?"

"Said he was the Reverend Denholme Theynard."

Kayne replaced the chair in the bedroom and made his way downstairs to meet the waiting churchman. Theynard advanced to meet him as the detective stepped out into the cold night air. The priest extended a hand of long bony fingers in a sleeve. Kayne removed his gloves and noted that the proffered hand felt like a handful of dried leaves and twigs. The Superintendent could not help thinking that Theynard reminded him of Pagets drawings of Professor Moriarty of Sherlock Holmes fame. He remembered the opening line of the Professor when the two men met; "You have less frontal development than I should have expected." Theynard's opening words were in fact much more mundane than that.

"Good evening, Superintendent. I am sorry to disturb you but I felt that I must speak with you. Your office said that you would probably be here."

"Very well, Reverend Theynard. Let's sit in my car, it will be warmer there. I cannot let you into the house for obvious reasons." The two men made their way to the car. Kayne took off his protective suit and climbed in to the car next to Theynard.

"I believe you were at the dinner party at the Flaggs on Thursday evening last, Reverend Theynard?"

"Yes I was, and because of that dinner and the previous one, I am pretty sure that the murder is as a result of evil."

"You better believe it."

"No, you don't understand; I mean that this

murder is the result of evil residing in this house."

"Look, Mister Theynard, I have heard about the ghosts. Julia Davenport was killed by a human agency not a phantom and my investigation will continue along those lines. Now can you account for your movements immediately before the party on Thursday?"

"I spent the entire afternoon, up to the time when I showered and dressed, writing in my library."

"Did you go straight home after the dinner party?"

"I did, I was one of the first to leave and unfortunately I was alone for the rest of the night. There is therefore no-one who can verify this."

"How well did you know Julia Davenport, the murdered woman?"

"I knew her because she was a friend of the Flaggs and so am I. We met at dinner parties and had talked. We had a common interest in the occult."

"When did you last see Miss Davenport?"

"This is what I wanted to talk to you about and caused me to seek you out; she came to see me on Thursday morning, the day of the dinner party."

"Why did she come?"

"She said she was terrified because there was a presence in the house threatening the very soul of anyone who lived there."

Chapter 14

Theynard Proposes

Theynard turned his upper body towards Kayne in an earnest manner and his brow wrinkled. He began to gesticulate excitedly as he spoke; "You have to understand that I have made a thorough study of the occult and I am convinced that some houses, although not inherently evil, in their walls carry the history of evil events. One can think of it in terms of perhaps a video tape of happenings there. Some people are more sensitive to these video images than others. Julia Davenport was just such a person. In fact, I have known only one other person as sensitive as her."

Theynard's eyes shone brightly as he continued.

"While in the house, Julia had become aware of a presence which was so diabolical that she had to flee. There was something else too."

"Well, Mr Theynard?"

"She saw a sign that death was waiting while she was standing in the garden and interpreted it as being a portent of the death of David Linde."

"You think, however, that she was mistaken and in fact had forseen her own death?"

"Yes," said Theynard, staring ahead into the night.

A silence followed as the two men sat deep in thought. Then Kayne broke in upon that quiet. "What do you want from me, Reverend Theynard?"

The priest slowly turned his head towards the detective.

"I do not think that this is a 'run of the mill' murder. I believe that there are forces operating here way beyond the normal. This house is like an undiscovered country and there is only one way to find clues as to what is going on."

"How do we do that?"

"I want you to give me permission to hold a séance in the house. I know a medium of impeccable reputation and she is prepared to help me conduct this procedure."

"I am sorry but I cannot do that. This is a crime scene and, although we will soon complete our forensic investigations, it must remain sealed for some time."

Theynard brightened appreciably.

"I will wait until you have completed your work. After that I would advise you to allow me to do this."

He stared earnestly at the Superintendent who was remembering his recent experience within the walls of The Eaves. He looked out of the car window and his eyes travelled up the house frontage. The moon was full and high in the sky, its light eerily reflected from brick surfaces. The windows were black sight-less eyes and it was as though the house was waiting for Kayne to make his reply. He was non-committal.

"We will see. Now I must get on. I will be in touch, Reverend Theynard. Can you leave me your address and telephone number, please?"

Theynard was about to protest but had second thoughts. He took a card from his pocket and passed it to the Superintendent. The two men climbed out of the car and the priest headed towards the road calling over his shoulder, "Goodnight Superintendent."

Kayne replied: "Goodnight, sir," and stared again at the house. His thoughts turned to something They-nard had said about the house being an "undiscovered country". When Shakespeare had used the phrase in Hamlet's famous "To be or not to be" soliloquy he was referring to death. "The undiscover'd country, from whose bourn no traveller returns."

Kayne felt tired and after having a word with the officer on duty at the house, he walked to his car and left for home.

*****

At ten the following morning Kayne stood before his team of detectives in the Squad Room. On a cork notice board were photographs of the corpse as seen from various angles. On a white board was a list of names of people who had attended the final dinner party. Kayne was reviewing progress and setting out the plans for further work.

"Any progress with tracing the whereabouts of Linde's wife, Collins?" asked Kayne.

"There is still no sign of that letter which she apparently wrote to Mrs Flagg," replied Collins. "I will ring her again this morning."

"Ask her about the names and addresses I requested," added Kayne. "I have Denholme Theynard's details. I saw him last night."

"I have talked to the British Red Cross and there is certainly evidence that Annie Linde had applied to join a group in India," continued Collins. "But there is no evidence that she actually went, which is strange."

The two men agreed that this required further effort. Collins had made an appointment to see one of the British Red Cross co-ordinators at Grosvenor Crescent in London on the following Monday. Kayne made a note of this on the white board. Just then Gabriel Haymes, the Senior Crime Scene Investigator, entered the room with John Garth, a forensic IT man. They asked if they could discuss the computer in Julia's flat.

Kayne spoke to his team: "OK guys, off you go. Let's have a review meeting here at 10am tomorrow."

Kayne, Collins and the two new arrivals made their way to Kayne's office. "Better make this quick, I have a press conference at eleven. What have you got, Gabriel?"

"Garth here has been looking at the computer as you requested. We decided that we would take the hard disk apart to check for stuff which may have been deleted."

Haymes nodded to Garth.

"It is a pretty laborious job but I made a particular effort to reinstate any deleted emails. I found one particularly interesting item, which I have printed out for you."

He passed the paper to Kayne who stared at it for some time. He did a mild double-take and passed the print-out to Collins who, after reading it, gave a long low whistle.

"The water around Dr Linde is deepening fast," observed Kayne.

"I think that we should take a look at Dr Linde's computer. Let me know if you find anything concerning emails, websites visited, etc, which relate to this case. The sort of sites I am thinking about are those featuring sado-masochism and the like."

Garth nodded in assent and left the office, leaving Haymes who had further business to discuss with

Kayne and Collins.

The door closed and Haymes moved to sit in a chair by the desk. He cleared his throat before he spoke: "I found a bloody set of fingerprints on the candlestick holder which lay under the bed in the murder room. They matched those from the left hand of David Linde as did dabs on the telephone receiver in the hall downstairs."

"Dr Bond reported that the killer of Julia Davenport was left-handed, judging by the angles of wounds on her body."

Kayne took a deep breath and said: "Summarising the situation; we have a left-handed killer, the candle holder was held in the bloody left hand of David Linde and there were blunt instrument wounds on the head of Julia Davenport."

Kayne reached down for his briefcase which contained Dr Bond's report. He leaned against the desk as he thumbed through the pages. Eventually he found the relevant section; "Large contusion on the left hand frontal eminence of the skull caused by a blow from a blunt instrument administered prior to death."

"Can you do me a favour, Gabriel? Have a word with Tom and ask him if the wound could have been caused by the candlestick holder."

Haymes nodded and made to leave the office together with Collins.

"And Haymes, can you ask one of your men to get me access to the loft at The Eaves?" added Kayne, making no mention of the sounds of movement he had heard so mysteriously the previous evening. "I don't want anyone going up into that loft space until I get to the house, which will not be until this afternoon. Good hunting, guys."

The press conference was short and relatively sweet. The newshounds wanted, as usual in cases of this kind, more information than Kayne was prepared to give them.

He held them off with a short statement: "We are investigating the murder of a young woman. Her name was Julia Davenport and she was found in the bedroom of The Eaves, Rill Place. Her face had been badly mutilated. She had received, ante-mortem, a blow on the head and the latter had then been almost severed from the thorax. Both breasts had been removed and the abdomen had been laid open. A terrible crime and we are following up a series of significant clues found at the scene. That is all I have to say for the moment, ladies and gentlemen."

Kayne then left for a progress meeting with the Assistant Chief Constable. It was not until late afternoon when dark was beginning to fall that he entered The Eaves. The house was relatively quiet and only Haymes was present up in the murder bedroom. Carrying a torch, Kayne led Haymes up the ladder into the loft space. They found that the joists had been boarded over but there were no lights fitted. The two men stared as the torch beam played over the loft floor. The dust particles in the air whirled and danced in the shaft of torch light.

They could see nothing in the dark, dank space. They descended the ladder and Kayne asked: "Did you make contact with Dr Bond today?"

"Yes, he said he had come to the conclusion that the contusions had certainly been made by the candleholder."

Haymes left the house at that point and Kayne was about to follow him when he hesitated. Still carrying the torch he turned and climbed the stairs again. Something nagged at him and he thought that he would have just one more look in the loft. He climbed the ladder and his head entered the darkness above the loft hatchway.

Chapter 15

A Mysterious Trunk Revealed

It was during the Saturday afternoon when Kayne was briefing the Assistant Chief Constable that the phone rang in the reception room of the Flagg household. Jim Flagg picked up the receiver and heard the voice of Denholme Theynard. The latter seemed very excited and he spoke rapidly. "I hope Jane is ok after this dreadful business. I have been talking to Miss Preece and Dr Brock. We would like to come round to your house to speak to you and your wife."

"She is somewhat shocked and upset. Julia was an old friend and it was not only her death but obviously the circumstances of her demise. What do you want to talk about? asked Flagg.

"Is Dr Linde staying with you?"

"Yes, but he is moving to a hotel tonight. I have tried to persuade him to stay but he says that Jane and I need time and space to recover."

Denholme Theynard realised the difficulty of the situation but persisted. "It is quite important that we talk to all three of you. Can we come, please?"

"Let me speak to Jane and Linde. I will ring you back."

Jim Flagg frowned as he replaced the receiver and walked through to the kitchen where his wife and

Linde sat drinking coffee.

He poured himself a cup of coffee, "Theynard just rang and he, Miss Preece and Dr Brock would like to come round to talk to us. He says that it is of the utmost importance." Jane pulled a face and Linde sighed deeply.

After some discussion Jane said: "Well, I don't like it but perhaps it will do no harm."

Linde finally agreed and Flagg rang Theynard and agreed that they would assemble at 8pm, after dinner.

Abruptly there was a ring at the doorbell. Sergeant Collins, refusing coffee, walked into the room. "Good afternoon, everyone. I came to collect the letter you said that you had received from Annie Linde, Mrs Flagg."

Jane Flagg reddened noticeably and apologised, saying that she had so far been unable to locate the letter.

"I don't understand it because I know I placed it in my dressing table drawer. I am particularly worried because I saw it only a week or so ago."

"You are sure you returned it to that drawer, darling?" asked her husband.

"Yes, I distinctly remember doing so," continued Jane, flustered and somewhat embarrassed.

"Don't worry ma'am, it may turn up later. The other outstanding item is a list of addresses and telephone numbers of people who attended dinner on Thursday night."

Jane Flagg fetched the list from a small table in the hall. She returned as David Linde appeared struggling with a suitcase.

"Are you on the move, sir?"

"Yes Sergeant, I'm moving into a hotel."

"Can I have your new address please?"

"Certainly, it's The House Hotel on Rosslyn Hill in Hampstead. When can I go back to The Eaves?"

"I'm afraid it won't be for a while yet. I will let you have more definite news soon.

"I have a question for you, sir," said Collins. "I am having difficulty locating Mrs Linde. Are you sure she went to India with a British Red Cross group?"

"That was the plan. Unfortunately I do not know all the details as we were estranged by the time she organised it and left."

"Thank you, sir, that will be all for the moment. If you do locate the letter Mrs Flagg, please let us know immediately. Good afternoon all."

Collins took his leave of the house feeling that the atmosphere had changed between the Flaggs and Linde. There was tension that had not been there before. Linde moving was also significant.

Collins phoned the office and learned that his chief was at Rill Place. He turned his car in that direction and thought about the visit he had just made. When he had asked Jane Flagg if she had found Annie Linde's letter he had happened to notice that the look on David Linde's face had also changed, for a second the mask of calm had slipped revealing a slight, but perceptible start. The mask was back in place so quickly that Collins wondered whether he was just imagining what he saw. There was something else significant he had noticed which now eluded him. He was turning into Rill Place before he realised what it was; when he had arrived David Linde was about to return his empty coffee cup to the draining board by the sink in the kitchen before fetching his suitcase. On returning with the case he struggled somewhat and most people in that situation would use their strongest arm and hand. In both instances he used his left hand.

*****

Kayne raised his head through the hatchway into the loft at The Eaves. He stared into the darkness and switched on his torch. A shaft of light pierced the gloom. He pulled himself through the square-shaped opening above him and scrambled to his feet and stared around. It was freezing cold, the mist of his breath could be seen in the beam of the torch.

The same heady perfume he had noticed the night before in the murder room attacked his senses. He took a step forward but immediately spun round as a sound broke in. Kayne turned to the dark corner of the loft. Out of the ominous blackness in that corner came the sound of a familiar hiss and thump. The beam of the torch moved slowly round towards the sound.

Kayne's eyes widened and it seemed to him that just ahead of the beam, in the area of the penumbra, he could see a black area of shadow. He moved the torch more rapidly and it was as if the area of blackness now stood in the direct path of the light-beam.

Kayne focussed his eyes to try to make out the shape of the shadow. The torch failed at this point. Kayne cursed aloud but as he did so a new light source flickered into life. The gentle glow from a candle flame appeared at a point three feet above the floor of the loft where his torch had been pointing. The flickering light glistened on the brass body of a holder, resting on the lid of an old leather trunk approximately two feet by four feet by two feet high. Kayne stared transfixed at this new sight.

"Who's there?" he whispered in a croaking voice, which echoed round the roof chamber and then died away into a numbing silence.

"I don't believe this, pull yourself together man," he told himself out loud. "Now why did we not see this trunk before?"

His rhetorical question was left hanging in the air as he moved towards the trunk and lifted the candle and its holder from the lid. He examined the outside of the pale brown leather surface. The top was grey with dust. There was little doubt that it was old, probably Victorian, and it had been lodged in the loft, unopened, for a long time.

Kayne knelt and lifted the candle and holder; he examined the latter as best he could in the dim light but saw nothing unusual. He then lifted it high in the air in order to illuminate the loft. Someone must have ignited it and placed it on the trunk. The loft was a black chasm... no-one was there. He turned his attention back to the trunk. The lid was secured by a hasp and small padlock. Just below the padlock two letters were embossed on the trunk, 'AH', presumably the initials of the original owner of the trunk. Kayne attempted to lift the trunk but found that it was quite heavy.

Just then he heard a sound from below and a head appeared above the hatchway.

"Hello, is that you, Superintendent Kayne?" came Collins' familiar dulcet tones.

"Yes Collins. I wonder if you could give me a hand with this trunk. It's quite heavy and I would like to take a look inside it. Have you a torch handy, mine has failed?" Collins drew his mobile phone from his pocket, switched on the torch app and Kayne blew out the candle flame after a further long stare at the brass body of the holder in the stronger light. The superintendent placed the candle and holder on the floor of the loft and shook his head, mystified. He said nothing to Collins.

Collins pulled his beefy frame through the hatch and together the two detectives managed to lift the trunk to a point close to the loft exit. Collins climbed down the ladder to take the weight of the trunk as Kayne pivoted it on the edge of the opening before lowering it through. With further effort the container was eventually manhandled on to the landing floor.

The two detectives slumped on top of the chest and breathed hard. A full minute passed before Collins summoned up enough energy to say: "I think we have enough to pull Linde in, sir."

He updated Kayne on the events of the afternoon. The latter raised an eyebrow during Collins' discourse, but did not comment until he had finished.

"Let's get more information on Mrs Linde from the British Red Cross before we make any formal moves to arrest him. I think there may be a skeleton in the cupboard there...and I am being literal."

Kayne turned his attention to the chest and looking across at Collins he said "Have you got a screwdriver or anything that will open this lock?"

"There might be one in the boot of my car."

After a hunt in their vehicles, Kayne located a short crowbar in the boot of his car and the two men returned to the house. The hasp on the chest resisted for a while but age and rust proved its undoing, and it gave way with a loud 'thung' sound.

The Superintendent lifted the lid, the hinges of which groaned in protest. He stared down into the interior of the old container.

Chapter 16

Enter Lucinda Randolph

Letitia Preece kissed Miriam Brock lightly on the forehead as she passed her chair in their flat in Hampstead. "Time to go, Mim, I wonder what that old stoat Theynard is going to propose?

"He seemed to have a bee in his bonnet about the evil in Linde's house when we spoke earlier."

"Probably wants another chance to slip his hand up your skirt, Letty."

The two women put their coats on and made their way out of the front door. Miriam Brock was a rather plain, buxom woman in her forties. She made a striking contrast to her partner who was slim, shapely and beautiful. Letitia Preece was in her late twenties and today wore a charcoal grey jacket and skirt. Men lusted after her and she had had numerous short–lived affairs before she met Miriam while on holiday in Greece. It had been a meeting of minds initially as both women were highly intelligent and well read. Their friendship had developed and they had slept together on the last night of their holiday. Letitia had been very uncertain of their relationship at first; she was confused about her own sexuality. They parted at Gatwick Airport, each promising to ring the other but expecting nothing. Miriam had been the first to break radio silence with a message left on Letty's answerphone. They had met and their affair had begun. They had moved in together three months later.

Miriam had no doubts about the relationship. From the beginning she had been in love with Letitia and considered that, as far as she was concerned, it was a relationship for life.

Miriam Brock had never had any doubts about her sexuality. She had been a lesbian from the time of her first crush on a gym mistress at school. She had come to terms with her preference after reading that paean to lesbian love, *The Well of Loneliness* by Radcliffe Hall. Miriam marvelled at the bravery of its author bearing in mind Hall had written it in 1928 when lesbianism, although not illegal, was not socially acceptable.

From then on Miriam was determined to realise her destiny. Her academic career had blossomed and she had cut a swathe through her examinations; qualifying as a doctor when she was only 25–years–old and becoming a consultant at 35. Her single–mindedness was what endeared her to Letitia.

"Penny for them, darling" said Letitia, as they drove out of their drive.

"I was wondering when those detectives will come to interview us. Theynard seemed to think, when he phoned this afternoon, that things look black for David Linde."

Letitia adopted a quizzical expression. "Don't you think that it's a bit obvious to accuse him of the murder? The only evidence is that it happened in his house. What was the motive for the killing?"

"It could be a purely sexual motive." As soon as she had said this she felt her lover's eyes boring into the side of her head and she glanced back at her before returning her gaze to the road ahead. It was some moments before Miriam Brock spoke.

"I wonder...."

Letitia did not disturb her after that because Miriam seemed so lost in thought. The two women sat in silence until they arrived at the Flaggs' house. They parked their car just as Theynard's taxi appeared in the drive and pulled up beside them.

"Good evening, ladies. How are you?"

Theynard appeared from the car together with a rather large, middle–aged woman dressed in a long black coat and wearing a paisley patterned shawl round her shoulders.

"May I introduce Lucinda Randolph?" said Theynard.

The women shook hands and they all approached the front door. Jim Flagg answered the knock and after taking their coats, led the group into the reception room where David Linde and Jane Flagg stood, drinks in hand. Linde, it seemed to all of them, had changed overnight. He was pale, drawn and nervously rotating the glass in his hand.

"What has happened to Sam Plaid?" asked Theynard.

"He is out of town on business," replied Jim. "I will update him when he is back."

Introductions were made and Theynard told them about Lucinda Randolph.

"I took the liberty of bringing Miss Randolph with me, I hope you don't mind. She is an old friend and an experienced medium. She has carried out much good work for The Society for Psychical Research and also knew Julia Davenport."

The company murmured a guarded but collective

approval and turned to the visitor who, having removed her top–coat, was dressed rather tweedily in a suit. She spoke with a high, reedy voice.

"I hope I am not intruding but having spoken at length with Denholme, I am convinced that we are dealing with the paranormal here."

"Forgive me, but what leads you to that conclusion? People have seen some strange things I grant you but all that may be the product of overactive imaginations," said Jim Flagg, playing devil's advocate. "Where does it fit in with the murder anyway?"

"I saw what I saw, and Julia certainly saw something in the garden at Rill Place," interjected David Linde, who became more agitated as he spoke. "At the moment, the way things are shaping up, I need all the help I can get." Linde's pallor increased, and he swallowed down his whisky in one gulp.

Theynard's calm voice brought the atmosphere back to an even keel. "I see it this way: if we can persuade the police to allow Lucinda to perform a séance in the house it may give us a clue as to the nature of the entity which walks there."

Jane Flagg walked up to her husband and facing him said: "What have we got to lose, darling? If we learn nothing from it then that leaves us exactly where we are now."

Before Jim Flagg could react Theynard spoke. "Unfortunately Superintendent Kayne will not allow us to enter the house yet because it is a crime scene. I think that if we pressure him, as a group and individually, he may give in when the forensic team have finished their work."

Miriam Brock seemed prepared to let a non-scientific view come to the fore. "Miss Randolph, what do you think is going on paranormally there?"

"From what I have learned from Denholme it would seem that past events have left an indelible mark on its atmosphere. I need to talk to Dr Linde about what he has seen and felt first hand. I gather that you were going to examine the history of the house. It is a good idea and it may yield useful information."

"Maybe a chat with some of the neighbours may also prove fruitful," suggested Linde, warming a little to this energetic woman.

"Excellent," enthused Miss Randolph. "That is a good idea, although the damage may have been done a long time ago and before their time. The visible entities described sound as though they originated from the late 19th century. Would you agree, Dr Linde?"

"Yes Lucinda. If I may call you that?" checked Linde. "Certainly the skirts were long and appeared to be from the 1880s or 90s. The woman I saw in the house wore a beaded dress. I remember that because I found a bead on the floor."

The assembled company turned towards him and took a sharp intake of breath. Lucinda Randolph spoke first. "You found a solid object originating from an entity?"

"You mean a bloody ghost, Lucinda," added Jim Flagg, still sceptical.

Letitia Preece now spoke up. "Where is it David, do you still have it?"

The scientist's brow creased as he tried to remember where he had put it. So much had happened since he had found it. Nothing came to mind and he told the others that he thought that it must be back in the house.

"This is very worrying, Denholme," said Lucinda. "A solid artefact means that this entity is very powerful. If the death of Julia resulted from it then we are dealing with a presence possessing the sort of evil power occurring once in a century. There have been many powerful entities reported in the literature, many of them representing good as well as evil. Two thousand years ago such a force for good appeared in the Middle East. That appearance, in the form of a simple carpenter, changed the world forever."

"Are you saying that this ghost may be representing the devil himself? Come on, Miss Randolph this is the 21st century not the 17th," said Jim Flagg, far from convinced.

"Do you believe that Christ existed...exists?" asked Miss Randolph.

"Yes."

"If you believe in a force for good then how can you dispute that there must be a reverse?"

"Where there is matter then logic dictates that the presence of anti-matter must follow," said Linde. "If there is a positive then there must be a negative. The north pole of a magnet is always accompanied by a south pole. Is that what you mean?"

"Yes indeed, *quod erat demonstrandum*."

The room erupted into discussion. The majority present felt that this was not a case of QED but it did provide much food for thought.

Miriam Brock spoke above the resulting chatter: "I think that the murder may have been indirectly caused, or inspired, by the presence but that a human agency was the most likely perpetrator."

"Intense cold..."

The voice of David Linde cut through the general hubbub like the honed edge of a razor. Lucinda broke the fallen silence. "What did you say, David?"

"Whenever I was about to witness any of these phantoms I felt an intense cold. The day I worked in the garden; I was working towards a corner of the yard when I felt a rapid drop in temperature and something more. I felt a terrible feeling of dread and melancholy. It was almost a physical ache that filled me. The woman I saw carried with her an air of great unhappiness."

"When I opened the door to the murder room, at the time I found the body, I became aware of the woman again. I saw a shadow flit across my peripheral vision and I now realise that it was her."

He paused for a moment and then said "I think that Theynard is right: we need to put pressure on the Superintendent to hold this séance. You may think that I would say that; but arrest is not my only worry. I believe my life may be in danger from whatever walks my house."

Chapter 17

Victoriana and Tragedy

Kayne and Collins stared into the trunk, now standing on the landing of The Eaves. Kayne reached into the container and drew out a garment, which was black and covered in shiny beads. There had been some deterioration in the state of the material where some damp had entered the box but, for the most part, it was in reasonable condition. Kayne unfolded it and laid it out on the landing. It was a full-length dress and padded. He realised that the padding was a bustle at the back of a late Victorian garment. He folded it and placed it aside.

Meanwhile, Collins was examining the remaining contents of the trunk. They seemed to be of the same vintage as the dress. Collins next brought out two faded sepia photographs. The first he selected depicted the image of a young, dark, moustached male seated at a table. On the table sat two books, one upon the other. The volume on the top was open and the man appeared to be reading it. He sported a full head of hair, parted in the centre. He was probably in his late twenties or early thirties and was leaning on one elbow with his forehead resting on his fist.

Kayne stared at the image and thought that the

figure looked familiar. Collins passed him the second photograph, which showed two women photographed in a garden. One of the women was in her late fifties and was smiling. There was something about that face; it was the eyes. They stared out at him across 120 years and conveyed something uncomfortable.

He turned to the second of the two women. She was young, probably in her twenties, quite pretty in a careworn sort of way. Both women were dressed in the style of the late Victorian period. Kayne looked at the reverse of the first photograph: written in pencil were the letters 'MJD'. The back of the second photograph indicated the identities of the women it depicted: 'Mother and Annie'.

Collins, meanwhile, had discovered a book beneath the photographs. He opened its foxed pages and realised it was a diary. He passed it to Kayne and then lifted the next item out of the trunk. It was a long envelope containing a large set of folded documents tied together with a stained pink ribbon. On the envelope were written the words 'Deeds to 9 Eliot Place'.

In the bottom of the chest was a black leather satchel. On the flap of the satchel the letters 'MJD' were embossed in gold. Collins lifted the satchel out of the chest and proceeded to release the catch on the flap. It took some effort because the catch had rusted in the closed position. Collins eventually lifted the flap and gazed inside. It contained an oilcloth pouch stained by some dark substance.

"Oh my God, sir!"

Collins gingerly unwrapped the pouch and inside was a bloody mass. They both recoiled as they stared down at what could only be the missing remains of Julia Elizabeth Annie Davenport.

Kayne was the first to regain some kind of composure and he took the pouch from Collins. "Have you an evidence bag, Collins?"

"How the hell do you think it got here, sir?"

Kayne wondered how it could have got into a box with a lock rusted in the closed position. "I want each item bagged carefully and taken to the laboratory. I want to know if these are the organs of Julia Davenport and is there any evidence present to indicate who handled any of these articles?"

Just then sounds of movement came from downstairs. Voices could be heard and a few moments later the ample figure of Chief Superintendent Townshend made his way upstairs. He was flushed and had a very anxious expression on his face. "Kayne; there you are, I need to have an urgent word with you, please."

"Ok, sir. You have a job to do, Collins. I will see you tomorrow. Tell forensics to make this lot top priority please."

Kayne and Townshend made their way into the room next to the murder room. Townshend insisted that Kayne sit down.

"What's up, Bill?"

"David, I have some bad news. We tried to get hold of you but your mobile either does not work or is switched off."

Kayne ignored what he saw as the implied censure: "Out with it, Bill."

"It's Samantha, David. She is missing. A message has come through from South Georgia. Apparently she was out with a colleague in a boat researching krill shoal movement when their vessel capsized in a storm."

David Kayne stared down at his feet. He sighed

deeply and said nothing. He raised himself from the chair and walked over to the window. He stared into the garden, which was now shrouded in darkness, and he stared sightlessly. The chief was saying how sorry he was but Kayne did not hear. There was no pain, no tears, just a weary numbness that was worse because it was accompanied by guilt for not feeling agony. He wanted to be alone; alone with this emptiness; alone to think.

"I must go, sir."

"Yes, of course. Take as much time as you need. I will talk to you later and don't worry about the case; I will assign someone else to it."

Kayne made his way out of the house past a surprised Collins. He divested himself of his plastic gloves and protective suit and headed for his car.

"Are you ok to drive?" called Townshend after him.

"Yes, I am fine. I will call you later."

*****

Kayne garaged his car and unlocked his front door with the action of an automaton. He picked up the mail from the hall floor and made his way into the kitchen. He poured the whisky twice before he placed the bottle down and carried the third full tumbler into the lounge. He felt very tired and alone. Sam would not be coming home and he would never see her beautiful face again.

He thought about what he would do and it quickly occurred to him that the chief had said she was missing: not dead. He stood up suddenly so that a dizziness almost caused him to fall back into the armchair. He bent and steadied himself by holding on to the arm of the chair. When his head cleared he moved towards the phone. He rang the expedition headquarters in Oxford.

"Hello, is that Simon? David Kayne here. I have heard the news, yes, but have they found the…the body?"

Dr Simon Hogg was the expedition co-ordinator in the UK. He had said that there was no chance of any survivors after the boat capsized. No-one could have survived for longer than a few minutes in the water at the current temperatures of the Southern Ocean. Simon had also said that he would be in touch when they found her body and that he was very sorry.

"I suppose that is true," replied Kayne. "Please don't hesitate to ring me, you have my mobile number."

Kayne remembered what his father had always said; the sea always gave up its dead. He drained the whisky glass and slumped back in his armchair and he stared sightlessly up to the ceiling.

Samantha's face swam before his eyes. Her features were out of focus and he panicked. Sitting bolt upright he desperately searched his memory for the details of her features, then spoke aloud.

"Christ, I can't remember what she looks like. My own wife and I have forgotten her five minutes after her death."

He stood up and went across to the piano: her piano. He picked up a framed photograph from its flat shiny surface. Samantha smiled up at him, her face peeping from inside the hood of her parka. She was breathtaking and she looked very young.

Why couldn't he cry…why did his eyes remain dry?

Kayne felt he needed to be near her. He made his

way up to their bedroom and sat at her dressing table. Before him were her lotions and perfumes still as she had left them; after all there is not much need for large quantities of makeup in South Georgia.

He idly picked up a perfume bottle and on the label was the single word 'Longing'. He removed the lid breathed in the fragrance and felt the pain of her presence in that odour. He put his head in his hands. He immediately slowly raised his head, however, as a new significance flashed into his mind: this was the perfume he had smelled in the murder room and in the loft at Rill Place. Why had he not realised this before?

All lingering thoughts that she might still be alive left him. He knew with absolute certainty that Samantha was dead. He could also hazard a guess as to the moment when death had claimed her.

Chapter 18

A DNA Surprise

At 9pm Detective Sergeant Collins entered the communal office where, that morning, Kayne had addressed the team. He sat down at his desk and stared at the cork board in front of him. He thought about the bloody remains and the other items found in the trunk, now in the Forensic Laboratory. His mind wandered to the tragedy of Kayne's wife. David Kayne was a very private man who kept his own counsel in the matter of his private life. Collins knew as much about Kayne's life outside the force now as he had on the first day he had been assigned to him. Nonetheless he liked the quietly spoken detective, his tenacity and unassuming intelligence. Now Kayne was alone with his grief. Collins would ring him in a day or so and in the meantime Chief Supt Townshend had assumed command of the case. This was not a happy development for Collins who disliked the man. He saw Townshend as a social climber: a member of the local golf club; probably a freemason. He was not in the same league of investigators as Kayne, although the two men were of a similar age.

Gabriel Haymes entered, his face wreathed in smiles.

"Is Kayne in?"

"No, not at the moment. What have you got?"

"I have the results of the examination of Linde's computer. The email to the murdered girl was definitely sent from that machine, not unexpectedly.

"What about the websites he has visited recently; any luck there?"

"Garth has prepared a list. He has cross-referenced site addresses to the dates Linde accessed each of them. Garth still has a bit more work to do."

"Thanks, Gabriel." Haymes left the room leaving Collins with his chin resting on his hands. He stared down at the list and, taking a highlighter pen, he marked any that seemed of significance. Some of the sites had addresses that did not clearly indicate their content. Collins made a separate list of these in order to check them on the Web later.

On Monday morning the Director of the British Red Cross rang him: "I can save you a journey here Mr Collins. Annie Linde was definitely listed as going to India in a group. She never joined the party and, although we have unsuccessfully tried to contact her husband, we haven't received any information as to why she never came."

Collins rang Chief Supt Townshend and told him the news. Half-an-hour later the two detectives entered the House Hotel in Hampstead and took David Linde in for questioning.

*****

David Linde sat in one of the interrogation rooms at the police station. He looked tired and pale. The two detectives before him were quite merciless in their questioning and he looked as if he had entered a nightmare world where nothing made sense.

The questions came in quick succession.

Townshend: "Why did you e–mail Julia asking her to meet you at the house on the night of the murder?"

Linde: I didn't email her; I don't even have her email address."

Collins: "There is no point in denying that you sent that email because we have found evidence on both of the computers.

"Tell us from the beginning what happened when you met her at The Eaves that night?"

Linde: "I've told you before – I never met her at the house on the night she was killed. She was already dead when I came back from the Flaggs' house late that evening."

Townshend: "Did you intend to kill her when you arranged the meeting?"

Linde: "I did not arrange the meeting and I did not kill her I tell you. I just don't understand how all this has happened."

Collins continued: "We have examined the candlestick holder under the bed in the murder room and we found some finger prints on it. The fingerprints from your left hand were lifted from it."

"I was afraid that somebody might be in the house other than Julia and I picked the candlestick up from the lounge in order to defend myself."

"The fingerprints on the candlestick holder were bloody; how do you account for that?" Townshend was taking no prisoners at this stage in the proceedings.

"When I arrived at my house I noticed that the telephone receiver was on the floor, I picked it up to replace it and there was blood on it. I must have transferred some of it on to my hand then. Anyway there was blood everywhere in that bedroom. That blood could have come from anywhere in that room."

"The pathologist has confirmed that Julia Daven-port had been struck on the head with a blunt instru-ment similar to the candlestick holder. The position of the resulting head wound also indicated that it had been made by a blow administered using the left hand. Your prints on the holder were those from the fingers of your left hand and you are left handed Dr Linde: are you not?" This last question from Collins was the last straw and Linde broke down completely, sobbing into his hands.

"Denholme Theynard believes that there is an evil entity within the walls of that house. It was this mon-strosity that did the killing."

Townshend frowned: "An awful thing with your fingerprints and left-handed like you, Linde. No, I think the murderer is a little more substantial than a ghost.

"David Ernest Linde, I charge you with the wilful murder of Julia Elizabeth Annie Davenport. You do not have to say anything. But it may harm your defence if you do not mention, when questioned, something which you rely on in court. Anything you do say can be given in evidence."

Linde spoke quietly with a break in his voice: "I would like to ring my solicitor please."

"OK, get him a phone, Collins, and after that let's take him to a cell please."

The questioning had lasted some hours now and it was late into Monday evening. Townshend sum-moned a uniformed constable and Linde was led away to the cells.

*****

The phone rang in David Kayne's lounge. On the

other end of the line was Simon Hogg, his wife's expedition co-ordinator: "Hello David – I'm sorry but Samantha's body has been washed up on the shore between Husvik and Stromness on South Georgia. I need to know what you want us to do about the body. Whatever you want I will arrange it."

Kayne was silent for a few seconds and then the words finally came in a rush: "I want her to be flown back home, please."

"That's fine, David. I will contact you again when arrangements have been made."

David Kayne wearily replaced the receiver and sank back in the armchair.

His eyes stared unseeingly ahead of him. He reached for a glass of whisky, which sat on a small table at his right hand, and sipped it thoughtfully. His whisky stock had been much reduced in the past 24 hours.

He stared at a photograph of his wife on that same table and a line from Romeo and Juliet came into his mind: *Death, that hath suck'd the honey of thy breath, Hath had no power yet upon thy beauty.*

He decided the only thing to do was to snap out of it and bury himself into his work.

Kayne's thoughts returned to the murder and for several minutes he turned the problems of the case over in his mind. He made his mind up as to what to do next and stood up. He put his coat on, left the house and drove to the Forensic Laboratory. Surprised faces greeted him as he entered the building and presented his warrant card to the bored security man. He walked with a determined air through the corridors to Dr Tom Bond's office and laboratory area.

Bond was washing his hands in the laboratory and

turned in surprise as Kayne entered the room. "Did Collins bring you some items from the loft at Rill Place?"

"Yes, David, he did. But what are you doing here? We were all very sorry to hear about your wife."

"I need to see the papers that accompanied the body parts. By the way, did the organs belong to the body of Julia Davenport?"

Kayne ignored the reference to his wife; he wanted to avoid that issue for a while. Tom Bond gestured to Kayne to accompany him into his office attached to the laboratory. In one corner of the room was a large table. On it was a group of labelled plastic envelopes containing the papers. The two men stood before the table, Bond turning to Kayne with a rather worried look on his face.

"I was going to talk to Townshend about that particular subject, David," said Bond.

"Tell me, Tom," urged Kayne. "I am back on the case."

Bond turned and walked over to his desk and slumped into his chair. There was obviously a problem of some magnitude on his mind.

"First of all there were no discernible fingerprints on the oil cloth," explained Bond. "Oil cloth, by the way, is an interesting choice of material. It was used a lot before plastics in the 19th century. There were two body parts, the heart and vagina, and both are identical to the organs missing from the body. I also discovered that, like a jigsaw, the cuts where the organs were attached to the body matched exactly in both cases."

"Well, there is a surprise," said Kayne.

"I did not leave it there, though, David. Before I examined the organs in relation to how they fitted to the corpse I sent samples of the organ tissue for DNA sequencing."

Bond turned his worried gaze on to Kayne.

"The DNA sequences on the samples did not match those from the body. In other words the organs do not come from Julia Davenport's corpse!"

"That does not make sense, Tom. You said that the excision lines on the organs and the body match."

Hesitantly Bond uttered the one word which, when spoken, sat between the two men like the splash of a pebble on a pond.

"Yes."

Neither of them spoke as the ripples from that pebble spread through Kayne's mind.

Chapter 19

The Diary

Kayne sat on the chair in his office and stared out of the window into the darkness and focussed on the lights of the town. Before him were the documents from the old chest out of the loft at The Eaves. The forensic team had taken fingerprints from them but that had proved nothing as none corresponded with records. They had certainly not been handled by Linde.

Kayne felt very lonely and it frightened him. He felt like a character in an Edward Hopper painting. He remembered a particular piece called *Office in a Small City*, which depicted a man seated at an office desk staring out of a window overlooking a stark cityscape. The loneliness in that man's face, he was sure, was reflected in his own features. His mind dwelt on his wife and the fact that he would never see her again. Never feel her touch...and yet he was sure that she had been with him at Rill Place; in the loft and earlier in the murder room. He remembered her perfume and wondered why her presence was there. Could she have been directing him to the chest in the loft?

His brow furrowed deeply as he considered issues running counter to everything his logical mind believed in. Yet here before him was the evidence;

the contents of that chest which had lain untouched for a century or so. He would not have found it had he not been led there by his wife. A wife who had died only hours before the event and that was why he knew that she had died before the discovery and was intervening in the case. It was all so strange and, although he would not admit it, rather frightening.

Kayne stood up and paced the room in agony. The agony of having lost the woman he loved and the mystery of her intervention in a murder more terrible than almost any he had seen in his career. There was also the puzzle of the body parts found in the chest. Organs not belonging to the corpse in the room below but with severance lines exactly matching those on the body. In fact, this chest was a complete enigma.

Kayne fingered the grey and white marbled covers of the diary and he opened its leaves. Maybe there was a clue to the mystery of The Eaves therein. He turned over the pages of the diary; they were yellow and foxed with age. The edges of the pages crumbled to powder in some places. The first few pages were unreadable as they had been badly water-damaged but he found that after a dozen sheets the handwriting was legible. It was written in a bold hand and, judging by the language, executed by an educated person.

January 7th
Mother will not listen because she is concerned about the girl, Annie. The pregnancy is not going well and she has a terrible ache in her back. Gull called again today; he said that we must not speak of the girl to the neighbours.

January 10th
Mother was better today, did not fret so much,
even though Annie has gone downhill considerably.

January 12th
Gull called and said that Annie is near her time.
Mother is beside herself with worry. Since she
started caring for Annie she has become more like
a daughter to her; more so than Ethel, Edith and
Georgiana.

January 13th
Terrible day.
Annie has given birth to a daughter. She, Annie, is
very ill and also very low in herself. Mother is in
a black mood and I am afraid.

January 16th
God help us all. Annie has a fever and is likely
to die. It is childbed fever and the life is leaving
her. Mother is a black shadow and she talks only
of seeking revenge against those who caused this.

January 17th
Annie has passed on to a more peaceful world and
Gull has taken the poor motherless mite of a child
away. Mother calls upon me to avenge my 'sister'.
She says she will help me but it is I who must do
the deed. The women who must pay are known to
her. I must obey her for she is my mother and I
love her. I can do it – I know how and the revenge
must be bloody.

January 18th
Gull has paid us for doing our duty and tonight I

must go to the city. Mother has kept the instruments father used and I will take them in his bag.

The next few pages were stuck together and stained a dark coloured brown. Kayne attempted to separate them but the paper had undergone decomposition during the adhesion process and the separate pages had lost their integrity. Kayne turned to the next group of clean pages later in the diary but the writing had been lost to the contaminating moisture – all that is but one. The date recorded was February 25th. The ink was smudged and faded but with the aid of a magnifying glass he was able to make out the following...

Found the woman and used my metal on her. Found out later...(not legible) name of Annie Millwood. Came home to mother who did not speak and turned away. Saw her later reflected in the lounge mirror and her eyes turned heavenward and she smiled. I worry about that smile.

Kayne raised his eyes from the magnifying glass in his hand. He wondered at the meaning of the entries; there was certainly a sinister aspect to them. He made some notes in his notebook and then stood up, walked out of his office to a water cooler in the large, now dark, general office area. He drank deeply from the plastic cup as he stood in the darkness and stared back through the windows of his office. Light from his desk lamp illuminated his blotter and the strange tome he had been reading. The words haunted him: they spoke of tortured souls and even insanity reaching forward to envelope him many decades later.

Kayne threw the cup into the nearest waste bin. He

propelled himself forward to his office and, putting his coat on, headed for the door and out of the building. When he desisted from thinking about the work; the pain of his loss found a crack in the door of his mind to make its presence felt.

The lights of Blackheath reflected in the wet roads. Kayne stared ahead of him through the rain-spattered windscreen as he sped his car towards the house in Rill Place. It was there that the case had started and, more importantly, he would feel closer to his dead wife. Despite the horrific nature of the murder there, that last fact somehow did not matter. At least he might experience her presence there and that was all that mattered in the agony that he now felt. This pain was much worse than any physical pang and there was no relief, no analgesia, no let up and it was expanding to fill his field of view, his whole mind. It no longer left any room in his consciousness for other rational thinking. A line from Poe jumped into his tortured brain.

And Darkness and Decay and the Red Death held illimitable dominion over all.

Poe's brand of despair was a fitting accompaniment to his current feelings and another line snapped into sharp relief in his mind.

There are moments when, even to the sober eye of Reason, the world of our sad Humanity may assume the semblance of a Hell.

He gripped the wheel and stared resolutely into the rain-soaked gloom. His lips were set in a grim line and his brows were drawn together, they cast deep shadows over his slit-like eyes. His car slithered to a halt by the side of a heath and he scrambled from the car and crashed into the gorse to a piece of open ground 100 metres from the road.

There he stood, the rain splashing over his face, the rivulets of water running down his cheeks. He could not cry but nature was weeping for him and raising both fists in the air and his face to the sky, he shouted his pain into the night like a wounded animal.

Chapter 20

Kayne Gets Too Close

The car turned into the driveway at The Eaves and hissed to a stop on the gravel. The duty constable approached Kayne and examined his warrant card: "You can go in without protective clothing, sir. The forensic and SOCO people have completed their work."

Kayne entered the front door and switched on the hall light. The silence was palpable as he made his way through to the dining room. He looked around aimlessly and then headed towards the stairs. Rain dripped off him on to the floor but he no longer cared and so, leaving an aqueous trail, he solemnly climbed.

It was as he began his ascent that he became aware of the clinking sound from above. He stopped in his tracks and listened. The sound ceased at the same time but continued a moment later. Kayne recommenced his climb and as he reached the top of the stairs he noticed a light issuing from the back bedroom. He turned into the doorway. A figure was seated before Linde's computer; it was John Garth, the forensic computer man.

"Good evening, sir. I wondered who it was down there. Can I help you at all?"

"What are you doing here?" asked Kayne. "Does the duty officer know that you are here and, if not, why not?"

"He wasn't about," said Garth. "I had a key and I had been told by Gabriel Haymes that the house was now cleared forensically. I have returned the machine, having lifted the contents from the hard disk. I thought I had better check that all was well with it before I left for home."

"Have a word with the duty officer before you leave. Have you found anything interesting?"

"I'm about to go through the data with a fine tooth comb but as yet there is nothing to report. I'm off now. See you later, sir."

Garth's ample form disappeared down the stairs and Kayne listened to the crunch of the gravel in the drive as he left the house. Kayne turned to the window as he heard the wind hurl the rain against it. Droplets of water slanted their way across the glass. He turned on his heel, closed the door of the bedroom and walked through to the murder room. The stripped bed stood before him once again. His eyes turned upwards to the ceiling, and he expected to hear that thud which he remembered from before. No such sound greeted his ears. The anonymous white surface of the ceiling was all that he could discern. He did not know what he expected to see; perhaps the dead face of his wife staring down at him through the ceiling from the darkness of that dusty loft.

His thoughts turned back to the day that his wife had bid him farewell at the beginning of her fatal journey to the South Atlantic. It had been a grey, rainy day then and he could still see that beautiful pale face as she turned to wave him farewell.

At that moment something made him turn to look

towards the doorway.

There was no light outside the bedroom; the hall light bulb must have failed. The only illumination came from the pale reflected light of a street lamp in the road entering the landing via a window at the top of the stairs. He caught his breath as he beheld against this pale light the silhouette of a female standing at the threshold of the room. The figure turned as he looked and moved to one side towards the room where the computer resided. Kayne watched in disbelief as the figure turned again towards him as though beckoning him to follow before it disappeared beyond the door jamb. For a moment Kayne was unable to move but, summoning his strength, he lurched forward in the direction of the door. He re-alised that the figure was that of Samantha even though he could not make out her features. She was here.

He stared along the landing as he stood trembling at the threshold. His eyes widened, wondering what he would see. The closed door of the back bedroom housing the computer was now before him but of Samantha, there was no sign. Kayne stepped on to the landing and it was then he became aware of the per-fume. 'Longing' – his wife's perfume. The door of the room slowly and silently swung open before him. He ran forward into the room. He gazed around. It felt incredibly cold but empty and before he could stop himself he called out his wife's name in anguish. He registered the dull thump as the door of the com-puter room closed behind him.

A sudden gust of wind shook the windowpane. He turned to look at it. The coldness in the room had caused a film of condensation to form on the inner surface. As he watched, a distant light from a nearby house allowed him to see that a break of clear glass was opening up within the film of moisture on the surface of the glass. He stared fascinated as the break in the condensation formed itself into four clear characters, numbers in fact. He heard himself muttering them as each of them formed in turn across the glass: "One, eight, eight, eight."

As soon as they were formed the tiny condensation droplets coalesced into globules of water. They ran down the glass obliterating the numbers. Kayne turned back towards the computer, which coughed back into life. Garth must have left the machine on. Running across the screen were the numbers "one, eight, eight, eight...one, eight, eight, eight...one, eight, eight, eight" with a space between each group of four digits. This continued until the screen was full of numbers. Kayne scribbled them down on a pad of paper on the computer table.

Suddenly all the characters vanished from the monitor as the computer died. Silence reigned throughout the house together with total darkness. Only the wind and rain could be heard, still battering the windows with increased ferocity.

Kayne stood quietly for some time assessing what was happening. Bells were ringing inside his head now; he had a series of jigsaw puzzle pieces, all beginning to fit together. He knew now at least part of what was going on here. Nobody would believe him; particularly as he felt that one or two of the puzzle pieces were supplied by his dead wife. He needed to sit down and write out what he had and do a little historical research.

The words of Denholme Theynard came back to him – "I am convinced that some houses, although not inherently evil, carry in their walls a history of evil events occurring within them."

"Well, Reverend Theynard, I think you are correct," muttered Kayne to himself. "Maybe we will have that séance you wanted after all."

The cloying atmosphere of the house broke in upon his thoughts. He realised that he was not alone in this dark place. Kayne desperately tried to walk out of the room but he could not move. What is more, he had become aware of something moving up the stairs. A primeval sense inside him was aware of the presence. The door of the bedroom, which had closed behind him when he had entered the room, now began to shake within its doorframe. It was as if a giant fist was smashing against the wood.

The crashing noise ceased after what seemed to Kayne like minutes. It was followed by what sounded like a hand working its way round the outside of the door. It was accompanied by the sound of something breathing heavily, each breath ending in a grunting noise. Whatever the thing was it was trying to find a way in – a way to him.

Kayne could feel the cold now biting into his extremities and he could also feel a pounding inside his head as the terrible fear of this unknown presence began to affect his mind. He listened in horror to the sound of the spring in the handle of the door as it resisted the force trying to turn it. The thing was coming in here and he would be powerless.

Kayne summoned all his strength and lurched forwards to the door to hold it shut. His hand reached down to grasp the door handle but as he did so, the door was flung open with tremendous force. Kayne was hurled backwards across the room so hard that his feet left the ground. The backs of his knees struck the window ledge. His head, carried back by his momentum, crashed through the window and his whole body followed it through the disintegrating pane. To him this was all happening in slow motion.

The last thing Kayne saw before his head struck the path below the window was a woman watching him from the centre of the garden. She appeared to be wearing a long black dress and the pale light from the street lamps reflected from what looked like small black beads sewn on to her dress.

*****

Denholme Theynard emerged from behind the shed in the garden of The Eaves, a look of horror on his face. He had seen Superintendent Kayne fall. He ran forward to try to help him. One glance at the staring eyes and the spreading pool of blood beneath the head told him that David Kayne was beyond any earthly aid.

Theynard looked up from where he knelt beside the body. He stared up at the shattered window, which looked emptily down at him. He dropped his gaze back to Kayne's lifeless body but something drew his eyes back to the window. He thought he heard a sound from above. It was a deep sigh. For a moment he thought he saw a shadow disappear back into the room away from the window.

Chapter 21

After the Fact

"Why were you in the garden on this particular night?"

"I had been driving home from the house of a sick parishioner when I spotted Superintendent Kayne walking back to his car from the heath," said Denholm Theynard, wiping his forehead with a red--and-white spotted handkerchief. "He was soaking wet and, to my mind, looking rather distressed. I pulled over to have a word with him but before I could do so he had driven off. I decided, on impulse, to follow him."

"Why do that?"

"As I said, he looked very distressed and I thought he might need my help. He drove to Rill Place and entered the house. I could not get past the officer stationed at the front of the house immediately, so I waited."

Chief Superintendent Townshend stood up from where he sat at the table in the dining room at The Eaves. He was worried, as only a senior officer would be, when he had lost one of his men. Denholme Theynard sat on the other side of the table. He was worried too because he felt that his explanation for the death of Kayne would be totally indigestible to this man. He regarded him as a plodder. Not a lateral thinker and certainly not a believer in the occult.

"I remained out of sight until I saw the constable disappear round to the rear of the house via the garden gate," continued Theynard. "I took my chance, and entered the drive and hid behind a bush near the gate. When the officer returned, as he was moving away from the gate, I slipped through the gateway behind his back. You may think that my behaviour was strange but I sensed that there was something very seriously wrong with Kayne and this house is not the place to be when one is in a delicate mental state."

"What the hell does that mean?" snorted the irritated detective, as he disengaged an indigestion tablet from its foil wrapper.

"There are things going on in this house which go way beyond a simple case of murder. I told Kayne that at our first meeting and he was as sceptical as you are."

"Leaving that aside and returning to the more mundane; what did you do next?"

"I crept round to the back of the house. The back door was locked, as was the French window, but I caught sight of the back of Kayne in an upper storey window. He was talking to a second person in the room who I could not see."

"Were they talking normally or did they seem to be arguing?"

Before Theynard could answer the question Sergeant Collins appeared in the doorway. He looked flushed and was still obviously trying to come to terms with the death of his boss. "Are you ok, Collins? You can go home if you wish; I do understand."

"No, sir. I am alright and we need to make our next moves quickly before the trail goes cold. I have been talking to Constable Reade who was on duty. He said that there was another man here during the evening, John Garth, the IT man. He had brought back Linde's computer. He was still here when Mr Kayne arrived."

"When did Garth leave?"

"He had logged out half-an-hour before Reade reported the death of Mr Kayne, sir."

Collins voice trailed off at the end of this statement. It was obviously an emotional barrier even mentioning his boss' name.

Just then, Tom Bond appeared at Collins' shoulder. In a hurry as usual, he too looked less matter-of-fact than usual. As he spoke he laid a supportive hand on Collin's arm. "I have finished for now and I thought you should hear my preliminary findings," he explained.

"Of course, Tom. What have you found?"

"Mr Kayne was killed outright by the fall. He sustained a fractured skull and the brain damage would have caused instant death."

The Chief Superintendent pondered this and then asked: "Is there any evidence to suggest that Kayne's death could have been suicide?"

"None whatsoever. He fell from the window backwards probably by the application of a hefty push. I noted that there were abrasions on the backs of his knees obviously acquired striking the window ledge as he fell backwards. This was no accident. You need to look for a killer."

Denholme Theynard's quiet voice broke in. "There was no other person inside the house, Chief Superintendent. I think you need to investigate outside of the normal. May I suggest that you start by following the trail that Superintendent Kayne has lately travelled. It could be that he had discovered the secret which lurks within the walls of this house and that, as a result, he had to be killed."

For several moments silence reigned and all four men present stared into the space in front of them. Townshend was the first to say something. He moved round the table.

"Wait here a moment please, Reverend Theynard."

Townshend ushered Bond and Collins into the hall and closed the door of the dining room. He spoke to Bond first.

"I think, despite the clergyman's pleas, I shall avoid the paranormal for a while. Did you find anything unusual on the body, Tom?"

"Only the look of horror on his face," said Bond.

"That could have been caused by the realisation his impending death was close at hand?" suggested Townshend.

"Well possibly, but it's useless to speculate. I will have the body moved and get the autopsy underway, then I may be able to secure you more substantial facts."

Tom Bond turned on his heel and walked out in the direction of the garden.

"Can you check with the SOCO/CSI team to see how they are faring?" said Townshend, turning his attention to Collins. "After that collate all of Mr Kayne's papers, including Tom Bond's reports. We will go through them together. Fit some sleep in between the two and we will have a team meeting at eight in the morning. I will finish off here with our ghost hunter friend. See you later."

Townshend turned back to the dining room,

leaving Collins rubbing his chin thoughtfully. He followed Tom Bond out into the garden. A tent stood over the place where the body had lain. Two men were carrying a zipped, body bag out through the door in the tent. Gabriel Haymes, the Senior Crime Scene Investigator, followed them and seeing Collins walked towards him.

"Ah! Abel, there you are. I thought you ought to have Mr Kayne's notebook. It was in his pocket. Have you been upstairs yet? We have found one or two things."

Haymes led the way into the building and up to the back bedroom. Pausing at the threshold, he said: "We found some bloody handprints on the outside of the door–frame and the handle. We will confirm that it is blood and attempt to identify the owner."

The two men entered the room. Two others were present; one over by the window brushing a white powder on to the frame. Another man was carefully examining the floor near the computer. He was holding a slip of paper in his hand, which had fallen from the computer table. He spoke to Collins.

"What do you make of this?"

Collins, wearing protective suit and gloves, took the paper and examined it, then said: "One, eight, eight, eight. This was written by Mr Kayne. I recognise it from the foot included on the number one and the upper crossed loop on the eight. They are unmistakeable."

The note was placed in a labelled plastic envelope as Collins crossed to the window and stared out into the garden. The blue-grey steel of dawn was creeping into the sky in the east. He was tired again and decided to go home to sleep...if he could.

Chapter 22

A New Face on the Scene

The hands on the clock stood at ten minutes to six and Abel Collins' gaze drifted around the office. Sleep had not come at all and he had given up the struggle at five that morning.

He took in the small personal details that made it the workplace of Mr Kayne: the Beardsley print, a coffee mug bearing a picture of St Pauls Cathedral and, poignantly, a two day old dried dribble of coffee down the outside of it. It was strange how such a trivial item could send a cold steel shaft of pain through his body.

Collins sat down at the desk and looked at the book, which lay in the centre of the old-fashioned blotter. He opened the marbled cover of the diary and began to read. Soon he was lost in its tale and his brow became more and more furrowed the longer he read. He stroked his lower lip. Next, Collins retrieved Kayne's notebook from his pocket and read the final relevant pages with growing interest.

Time passed and as it did so the office began to wake up. Collins at last closed the books, leaned back in the chair and, with his hands clasped behind his head, stared up at the ceiling. He pondered on the meaning of what he had seen and read. The final sentence on the last completed page of the notebook still swam before his eyes.

The DNA of the tissue from the chest in the loft does not match that of Julia Davenport.

Just at that moment, a very tired looking Chief Superintendent Townshend jarred him out of his reverie. "Can you spare me a moment in my office, please?"

Collins made his way after Townshend's retreating back and as he entered the CS' office he became aware of a second man seated before the desk. CS Townshend introduced the other man as Superintendent Thomas Dumairt. Collins was aware of a very oily handshake and the penetrating unwavering stare of this stranger:

"I have bought in Mr Dumairt to replace Mr Kayne. I also wish to change the shape of the investigation," explained Townshend. "We will have a team meeting in a few minutes. I thought you ought to meet Mr Dumairt before that happens."

"Thank you, sir."

"I would like you and I to follow up on the Linde case, in particular the disappearance of his wife. Mr Dumairt will proceed to examine the circumstances associated with the death of Mr Kayne. It would be as well for us, you and I that is, to keep that issue at arm's length. An objective approach is required and our closeness to Kayne would jeopardise that."

"Let's go through to see the troops now. Can you bring Mr Kayne's papers through with you, Collins?"

"Yes, sir."

Collins examined the stranger during the team meeting. Dumairt was a tall dark man with a clipped moustache. His luxuriant hair was brushed back from his forehead. His deep-set eyes, invisible beneath hooded brows for much of the time, were never still and had the same effect as a gimlet when he spoke or looked at someone. He had a deep sepulchral voice of about the same timbre as the actor Christopher Lee. When he spoke, he enunciated each word separately and clearly, as though much thought had gone into each syllable. He emphasised his arguments with a wave of his left hand. His hands had long, smooth digits.

He was impeccably dressed in a dark blue, well-tailored Savile Row suit. His shirt was blue silk with a red patterned tie. Collins took an instant dislike to him. If you asked him specifically what he did not like, he would be at a loss. Dumairt made him feel uneasy.

One could argue that Kayne had been a hard act to follow and Collins accepted that. However, there was something more than that. He hoped that his initial impression was erroneous and that the man was a professional detective who would do a good job. He had done well to reach the rank of Superintendent at such a young age. That was another thing; Collins found it very difficult to guess the age of the man. His hair showed not a trace of grey and yet his face had the look of a much older man.

Townshend started the meeting. "Since the unfortunate death of Superintendent Kayne a review of the command structure has taken place. To begin with, this is Superintendent Dumairt who will effectively replace Mr Kayne." The hooded eyes of Dumairt scanned the group of officers before him.

Townshend continued: "Mr Collins will now give us an overview of the case thus far."

Collins brought in the boards, still carrying pho-tographs and notes of the case from earlier meetings. He outlined details of the initial murder and all the information up to the death of Superintendent Kayne. This included referencing the ghoulish findings in the trunk, the diary and photographs.

Townshend took over at this point: "I interviewed Theynard at the scene of Mr Kayne's murder. I am convinced he was not involved in the commission of that crime at all.

"On the subject of Linde, who is in custody – charged with the murder of Julia Davenport. I spoke to him this morning about the whereabouts of his wife. He continues to maintain that she is in India. I told him there was no record of her going to the sub-continent. Linde still maintains he has no idea where she is."

Collins told the group of the DNA mismatch between the organs found in the trunk and those miss-ing from the body of Julia Davenport. This statement was greeted with shocked silence.

"I will discuss this further with Dr Bond. I think the two groups should go to work now. There will be daily review meetings to discuss progress." Town-shend turned away and left the room with Dumairt.

*****

Collins and DC Gillingham stepped out of the car they had parked in Vale Road, Epsom. Linde had moved from a house in this road in November. Mrs Linde was now officially registered as a missing person. Collins had agreed with Townshend as a first step that he would ask the neighbours if they had observed any strange behaviour in the Linde household.

They drew a blank at number 17, to one side of the house in question, but a diminutive, elderly woman answered the door at number 21.

Collins produced his warrant card. "I am Detective Sergeant Collins, this is Detective Constable Gillingham and we are investigating the disappearance of one of your former neighbours, a Mrs Annie Linde. First of all could I have your name please?"

"Yes, certainly. My name is Barbara Eade and I have lived here for 30-odd years. I do remember the Lindes. They were a very quiet couple who kept themselves to themselves."

Collins asked: "Do you remember anything unusual happening during the period prior to Dr Linde moving out?"

Mrs Eade warmed to the task as she continued: "I do remember an argument about a month before the house was sold. I happened to hear raised voices next door when I was in my garden. The argument had been quite heated and concerned Mrs Linde's decision to work with the Red Cross in Asia. There was also mention by Dr Linde of another man in her life. Mrs Linde declared that the affair was at an end."

With some regret Mrs Eade continued: "Dr Linde ushered his wife into the house at that point but raised voices could still be heard. The row ended with a crash. It was very quiet after that. Strangely enough I never saw Mrs Linde again. He told me that she had gone to work in India for a while.

"I think he was very lonely after that because he spent a lot of time in the garden. He worked for long hours out there. I presumed he did not have her at home to talk to and therefore he concentrated on the garden.

It was later explained by the fact that he put the house on the market. He was obviously making it presentable for potential buyers to view."

The two detectives thanked Mrs Eade and walked out into the roadway.

"Thank heavens for nosy neighbours," mused Collins, as the two men moved on to the next house. The woman there did not remember any arguments but she had noticed Dr Linde's recent interest in gardening.

Collins climbed into the car and remarked to Gillingham: "I think we may need to take a look in, around and possibly under the garden at number 19."

Chapter 23

Randolph and Theynard
Take the Initiative

Denholme Theynard sat at the table in his library. Before him were two books. His long fingers turned the pages carefully as he perused one of them. They were both important works for anyone investigating the occult. One was *The Clavicule of Solomon* and the other was *The Kabala*. Theynard had the version of 'the Clavicule' translated by Colorno. He regarded this version as closer to the original text than the Mather translation. He frowned as he raised his eyes.

His companion, Lucinda Randolph spoke quietly to the old man.

"You warned Kayne about the house and he chose to ignore you," she said. "There was nothing you could have done to prevent his death."

Theynard was tired and ran his fingers through his thin hair.

"I am certain that the entity within that house sensed that Kayne was too close and that he had to die," reasoned Theynard.

He paused and then continued.

"I need to know what he was working on immediately prior to his death. That may give me a clue as to the nature of this beast. That house is the portal for some entity to enter this world. If I could get you inside the house, I am convinced that you may be able to sense the strength of this being. Julia Davenport realised something evil had come that way and paid for it with her life. That is why we must arm ourselves against whatever walks there before we go anywhere near it, hence my reading these ancient texts."

Lucinda Randolph stroked her chin thoughtfully.

"You told the Flaggs and David Linde that we would try to persuade the police to allow us to perform a séance."

"Yes, but the situation has moved on apace. I still intend to ask them but at my last meeting with them it was neither the time nor the place."

Lucinda struggled to her feet, her ample form somewhat of a hindrance to her progress. She turned at the door to face him.

"Take me to the house. We can ask to see the detective in charge on some pretext. All I need is a glimpse inside, just a sample of the atmosphere."

"I must read these texts further before I go..."

"Denholme, you know 'the Clavicule' by heart. Come with me. Nothing will happen in daylight in front of several hard-headed policemen."

Theynard looked down at the books and was lost in thought for a few moments. He slapped both his hands down on the table in a decisive manner.

"Very well, we will do it. After all, they can only throw us off the site and you might have enough time to get a feel for the place. You may then be able to tell me if you think I'm barking up the wrong tree."

"After what you have already told me I do not think that. No, there is something serious at work there. This visit may give me an idea of the strength of the presence."

She put on a voluminous imitation fur coat and a large pattern paisley scarf. Theynard pulled on a three–quarter length thick black overcoat. There was a decided chill in the air. As the two friends left the house Theynard slipped a carved ivory crucifix into his pocket. They climbed into her car, an old Morris Traveller, which had had its fair share of buffeting over the years. The Morris lurched forward. It left a cloud of blue smoke in its wake.

Some time later the old Morris murmured to a halt about 100 metres from The Eaves. A police car stood in the drive and two burly officers were talking beside it.

Theynard opened the car door. "Stay in the car, Lucinda, until I signal you to come."

He strode along the road towards The Eaves and crossed in front of the entrance to the drive without stopping. He glanced up the drive as he did so. The policemen had climbed into the car.

Theynard walked on. The police car overtook him as he reached the corner of Rill Place and the main Blackheath Road. As it disappeared he turned back towards the house. On reaching the entrance, he again looked up the drive. All was quiet and he gestured to Lucinda to join him.

The two friends approached the house, ducked under the police tape, and skirted the driveway courtesy of a narrow strip of grass at its edge. The front door stood ajar and Theynard saw his opportunity. He turned to his companion. "Let's enter the hallway. We'll probably be spotted and ejected on the spot but it may give you enough time to make a judgement. Is that ok?"

Lucinda nodded and they tiptoed up to the door. Theynard gingerly pushed the door back and Lucinda stepped forward. She crossed the threshold and entered the hallway. A low babble of voices came from the floor above. Facing her at the end of the hall was a long mirror and, as she moved forward, she raised her eyes to the mirror. Lucinda caught her breath, just as the front door opened behind them.

Theynard and Lucinda turned and beheld the angry face of Superintendent Thomas Dumairt, his voice a roll of thunder. "What are you two doing in here...and where is the bloody officer on duty?"

A rather flushed Constable appeared on the stairs: "Got a weak bladder, sir."

Dumairt turned on the man: "Get back to your post – idiot." He then turned to the two unwelcome visitors.

"I am Superintendent Dumairt and I asked you two a question."

Theynard was somewhat taken aback by the explosive entry of the detective: "I am Denholme Theynard and this is Lucinda Randolph. We are here to explore the psychic phenomena associated with this house. Both of us are experts in the field."

Dumairt's face adopted a sneer. "I hope you are not here to tamper with evidence. That is a serious offence. You, Reverend Theynard, were here at the time of the murder of Superintendent Kayne, were you not?"

"Yes, I was. I am convinced that he was killed by an agency not of this world. Miss Randolph here is a medium and I wanted her to experience the atmosphere in this building first hand."

"This is a crime scene and as such must remain uncontaminated. I will speak to you both later. In the mean time please be good enough to leave. Constable, escort these two from the premises."

Theynard and Lucinda made their way out of the house. Neither of them spoke a word until they were in the car driving out of Rill Place. Lucinda spoke first: "Denholme, I think I need to consult works in the British Museum and your copy of *The Clavicule of Solomon*. If I enter that house again I shall be carrying holy wafers and holy water."

Theynard turned to his companion before returning his attention to the road; her face was ashen and her hands shook.

Chapter 24

Everything in the Garden

"Has this house got a cellar, Mrs Bryant?" Abel Collins posed the question while sipping tea in the kitchen of 19 Vale Road, the former house of David and Annie Linde. Gayle Bryant was a pretty woman in her mid-thirties. She was in a state of shock as she stared through the kitchen window at half a dozen burly police officers wielding spades in her garden.

"No, it has not. Do they really need to demolish the garden like that?" asked Mrs Bryant, before standing up and shouting: "Be careful of the roses, we are very proud of those."

"I'm sorry about that," said Collins. "You will be recompensed for any damage, I assure you."

Collins felt sorry for the woman but, unfortunately, this was unavoidable. Evidence had accumulated which suggested that Annie Linde had been murdered by her husband and her body might well be on these premises. CS Townshend had had no difficulty obtaining a search warrant. The team had assembled this morning to commence the hunt. CS Townshend had also confided in Collins the results of the inquest on the death of Julia Davenport. The Coroner had brought in a verdict of unlawful killing. This was as expected and the Coroner had also agreed to give the police time to investigate the death of David Kayne further before conducting an inquest on his death.

Collins stood up and laid his cup on the draining board. As he did so, a rubicund DC Gillingham appeared at the kitchen door.

"Constable, do we need to dig holes all over the garden? Let's be a bit more..."

Dr Bond appeared in the doorway at that moment and interrupted Collins in full flow. "Ah, here you are. DCS Townshend said that you would be digging up most of Greater London in order to find a corpse. I may be able to help."

"Thanks Tom. Any news on the bloody finger-prints at the scene of Kayne's death? I thought you did your bit when we had found the body."

Dr Bond responded: "In answer to your question – they are not on record. As for your second point, I spent last summer in Tennessee at the so-called 'Body Farm'. While I was there, I met an extraordinary guy called Dr Arpad Vass. He had discovered and successfully used a technique for finding subterranean bodies and it works unfailingly. The method involves the use of a metal coat hanger and two lengths of plastic tube. I kid you not, I successfully used it myself while I was over there."

Dr Bond produced two lengths of wire from a coat hanger, each bent into an 'L' shape and two tubes. He inserted an arm of each wire into each of the tubes so that the wire pieces could rotate freely in the tubes. He walked out into the garden holding the tubes vertically, one in each hand.

"Now watch," he said.

Bond proceeded to walk up and down the garden. The wires remained pointing away from his body on each side. He continued his sweep until he came close to a bay tree; whereupon the wires rotated sharply towards the central point between the tubes.

"Gentlemen, I think you may dig here."

The voice of Bond dragged Collins back to reality. He had been staring in disbelief at the antics of the doctor and at first he thought that it must be some kind of joke. Dr Bond was not a very jocular man, and when the detective saw how the wires reacted he immediately ordered his men into action.

"Ok men, let's get on with it. We will need to lift that bay tree."

It was some time before they found anything. Collins scepticism of the method of detection was beginning to surface when a cry went up from one of the men in the newly dug pit: "I think we may have something here, Sergeant."

Collins scrambled down into the hole and the men moved aside to allow him through. Half submerged in the sandy soil was a white object approximately 30 centimetres in length. It was caked in dirt but it looked very much like a human limb.

"Tom, I think this is your area of expertise."

Bond made his way to the hole and slid down the slippery walls. He scraped some of the dirt away and then signalled to his team to commence the delicate task of unearthing the find. Further gentle excavation over a period of more than two hours revealed a corpse in an advanced state of decomposition.

"I think I will send a bottle of Bolly over to Dr Vass," said Tom Bond, looking very pleased with himself. "His crude corpse detector certainly works."

Bond then began a closer examination of the body *in situ*. After a further period of half an hour, he declared. "I would say that we are looking at a stage five state of decomposition," he continued. "There is some odour of butanoic acid and I would therefore say that this lady has been dead for between one and two months. Presumably this means that your suspect is a double murderer?"

*****

Letitia Preece made her way along the hall of her house towards the front door. Whoever was knocking was decidedly impatient. The wizened Reverend Denholme Theynard stood before her on the doorstep. She invited him in and followed his slightly stooped figure through to the drawing room.

"I'm sorry to bother you, Miss Preece, but there have been developments in the Julia Davenport case."

Letitia noticed that the old man looked very tired and somewhat drawn. There was, however, excitement in his eyes.

"Did you know that Superintendent Kayne has been killed and in most mysterious circumstances?"

Theynard went on to explain what he had seen from the garden of The Eaves on the night Kayne had died. Miss Preece listened with widening eyes.

"I think that he was pushed from the window and not by any human agency. After he fell, I saw a shape in the window and something about it caused me to feel chilled through to the bone. It could not have been David Linde, could it? He was in custody at the time so his alibi is watertight?"

Theynard paused for a moment as he remembered the shape and shivered. Miss Preece spoke. "What do you think is going on there and what do you want from me?"

Theynard was jolted from his thoughts and turned

to her. "I want to reconvene our little group. Is Dr Brock here?"

"No, she is at work but I will tell her. I am intrigued by your story and I am sure she will be keen to get involved, as I am."

"I will arrange a date and time with the others," agreed Theynard.

At this point diaries were consulted and times and dates were pencilled in. Theynard did not move to leave: "There was something else. At one of our dinner meetings at the Flaggs' house you said that you could acquire some equipment, is that still so?"

"You mean the time lapse cameras, infra–red cameras, motion detectors and temperature recorders?"

"Yes, we discussed it, if you remember."

Miss Preece nodded and strolled across to an elegant wooden bureau. She took a notebook from one of the drawers and made a note.

"How do you propose that we use the kit when I have collected it together?"

"I think that should be an item on the agenda of our meeting. I will confirm the date and the time. If you could start things rolling with the kit I would be very grateful."

Theynard made to leave. He made no mention of his visit to The Eaves with Lucinda Randolph. He had been unable to cajole the latter into telling him what had so frightened her there.

Chapter 25

Burned Epistles

Jim Flagg shovelled the heap of leaves towards his bonfire area. He turned and gazed at his wife who was busy pruning a rose bush. She looked drawn and pale as if she had aged ten years in the last few days. Jane was still as beautiful as the day he had seen her on Woolacombe beach in Devon. She had been happy then; carefree, full of hope; eighteen and fancy-free.

Jim picked up the rake and moved towards a collation of leaves and broken branches. As he did so he disturbed a white object. It seemed to have been part of a previous bonfire because it was scorched at the edges. Jim moved more ashes aside in order to uncover it. He realised it was a screwed-up ball of papers and picking it up, he shook the remaining ash from it. He carefully proceeded to straighten out one of the papers, and began to read.

I have told David about my affair with Stephen and his reaction was terrifying. I expected him to be angry but he has become a narrow-eyed silent shadow. Jane, he frightens me. He told me that if I leave him, he will kill me. I will leave him...

The rest of the paper was burned away and the

writing illegible. There were other sheets in the ball and Jim flattened them into a readable form.

"Jane," called out Jim Flagg. "I think I have found the letter you lost."

The two carefully read all the sheets, which amounted to two or more letters. Jane had seen only one of the notes. The others had been written a day or so later by Annie. They appeared to be the writings of a woman half out of her mind with fear.

Jim Flagg raised his eyes from the papers and he said huskily: "David Linde must have stolen the letter from our bedroom and found the later letters before Annie could send them. He burned them here on the bonfire just before he was arrested. He killed her...he killed Annie."

Jane collapsed at his feet in tears and she choked out: "Oh, poor Annie. I stood by and did nothing while my best friend was being mentally tortured and then murdered."

Jim Flagg took her in his arms. Over her shoulder, he stared thoughtfully ahead. He would need to contact the police. He lifted his wife to her feet and led her into the house. She was shaking in his arms and sobbing. He sat her down and gently talked to her. He told her that she was not responsible for Annie's disappearance and there was a chance she might not be dead anyway.

Jim frowned as he filled the kettle in order to make tea. He had just turned the kettle on when the phone began to ring.

It was Denholme Theynard on the line: "Hello Jim, the dinner group are meeting to talk about the events at The Eaves. Are you and Jane free to come?"

"Look Denholme, David Linde is behind all this not some paranormal evil. Don't look for what isn't there and no, we will not attend your meeting." He slammed the phone down just as his wife appeared:

"Who was that, Jim?" She said, her eyes reddened by crying.

"Nothing to worry about, Jane. It's only Denholme Theynard trying to organise some sort of bloody exorcism."

*****

"The body is that of a well–nourished female of approximately 30 to 35 years of age. Cause of death was a blow to the right frontal eminence of the head followed by severance of the carotid artery. The blow would have rendered her unconscious and the cutting of the artery would have caused her to bleed to death very quickly. Her body had been mutilated after death. The mutilations had been carried out in order to remove her heart and sexual organs post-mortem. These have not been found in the vicinity of the body despite a search of the garden and the shed."

Tom Bond addressed Chief Superintendent Townshend in his office with Detective Superintendent Dumairt and Detective Sergeant Collins present. Tom had interrupted a review meeting early on the day following the finding of the body at Vale Road. It was now two days since the death of Kayne and barely six days since the finding of the body of Julia Davenport.

Collins was amazed how time had flown. His whole life felt like it had been turned upside down. He had to admit, however, that the finding of this particular body had been no surprise at all.

"Are you going to try to do tests to check that the heart found in the loft at Rill Place belongs to this body?" asked Collins, staring down at case papers held in his hand.

"Yes, I will check the DNA profile," confirmed Bond. "I have to say that the geometry of the excisions are a good match with those from the Davenport body. Has Mrs Linde any family? If so, I could use DNA from them to confirm the identity of the body."

"No, she was an orphan," said Collins.

C. S. Townshend broke in. "We need to talk to Linde. We can find out who his wife's dentist was and then check dental records. More importantly, I think we can try and break Linde as a result of finding his wife and get a confession. Unfortunately I am addressing a press conference this morning concerning the Kayne case. Can you handle Linde, Dumairt? Take Collins with you."

Collins shifted uncomfortably in his seat.

"Yes, sir, I will do that. I think perhaps we could take him back to Vale Road, show him the grave and the morgue photographs of his wife. That might shake him up enough to elicit a confession."

"Good idea Dumairt, but you had better contact Coldwell, his solicitor, SOCO at Vale Road, the remand centre authorities and also Mrs Bryant. The visit of a murderer to her house is a lot to take in. Any further news on the Kayne autopsy, Dr Bond."

"Death was caused by extensive brain damage precipitated by the fall. I did also find bruising to the backs of the knees. This is consistent with him having been given a violent push, causing him to topple backwards and his legs to strike the windowsill. The impact would have tipped him backwards and out through the window. An act of murder not suicide; Kayne was deliberately pushed."

Dr Bond had almost finished speaking when the telephone rang. Townshend answered it and listened intently as the caller spoke. He merely offered the odd "yes" or "aha" until the final stages of the conversation: "Ok, Mr Flagg, I will ask someone to pick them up. In the meantime handle them as little as possible."

The Chief Superintendent replaced the receiver and rubbed his forehead: "It appears Flagg has found the lost letters. They had been partially burned in the back garden. Their contents indicate that Annie Linde was having an affair and when she told Linde; he threatened to kill her."

Dumairt let out a long, low whistle before saying: "Well that certainly has cooked David Linde's goose...and for a second time."

The meeting broke up. Dumairt and Collins left for the remand centre housing Dr Linde. Securing a confession looked to be a mere formality. Fate, however, had not read the police's version of the script.

Chapter 26

Bird Has Flown

Lucinda Randolph paused on the steps of the Bodleian Library, among the dreaming spires of Oxford. She felt tired and somewhat frightened. She had been reading dusty tomes for the majority of the day. She loved the Bodleian because of its ancient majesty. She mused on its history as one of the oldest libraries in Europe and was founded in 1602, the year before Queen Elizabeth the First died. It was not the first library to be established in Oxford. That honour went to the congregation house at the church of St Mary the Virgin and contained books donated by Thomas Cobham, Bishop of Worcester between 1317 and 1327. The books were dispersed after his death to pay for his debts and funeral expenses, but later redeemed and deposited in Oriel College. Around 1337 the Commissary of the University declared the library the property of the university and arranged for the removal of the books back to St Mary's.

By the middle of the 16th century the university was in financial crisis and according to Sir Thomas Bodley the library "in every part lay in ruined and waste". Much of the book collection had again been dispersed. It was Bodley and other benefactors who had the building refitted and restocked with books. It re-opened on the 8th November 1602.

Lucinda had been studying books from the early 14th century stock. Her understanding was that Thomas Bodley had collected ancient texts from the old religion. Books which described so-called "leprous dwellings" and if treated they may be made "fitte" to inhabit again. Much of this ancient knowledge would have been lost had Oriel not owned the books. They were rare, priceless and unencumbered by the interference of modern Renaissance thinking. Written at a time when men believed in possession by evil spirits and greatly feared the latter. Monks actively sought the means to defeat evil and learned the ways now lost to the minds of men submerged in the modern material world.

Lucinda thought that the ancient libraries of the world are the only source of this knowledge. She believed the power of ancient evil has grown in strength because no one believes that it exists. Any manifestations of this power were explained away by the actions of physical forces; as a result, dark forces can grow unhindered under a cloak of anonymity. Modern man regarded them as the provinces of the primitive and ignorant.

But Lucinda knew that she had to protect herself. She had not revealed to Denholme Theynard what she had seen at the house. She knew, however, that the evil there was much older than the bricks of the building. She had felt it and, having taken three steps beyond the threshold, seen it in that hall mirror. What she had seen, she was convinced, was not a mere reflection. It was a window into the soul of the ground on which the house was built. She believed that soul was as black as pitch.

Her first reaction was to consult the texts in the

Bodleian on the matter, in order to familiarise herself with the powers they were probably going to face. A friend who worked in the library had directed her to the most useful sources. Her second action was to elicit from the writings what protection she needed. She was on her way to the third which was to study the history of the ground on which the house was built and a history of the house itself. This information was available at the Blackheath area Records Office.

Having armed herself effectively she would talk to Theynard and together they could formulate a plan to destroy the evil. Denholme Theynard was already in possession of the necessary knowledge of the old religion but was not possessed of the gift to see into the other world. Together, however, they would be a formidable team again and ready to face what had to be done.

*****

Collins and Dumairt drove in silence to the remand centre in Southwark where David Linde was being held. Having completed the formalities for the release of the prisoner to them, they were joined by a burly prison officer, and Linde's solicitor.

David Linde looked haggard and grey. An office was put at their disposal for interview before the journey to Vale Road.

Linde was handcuffed to the prison officer. The prisoner was silent as he waited for chairs to be placed on the opposite side of the table for the interviewers.

Dumairt opened proceedings: "My name is Superintendent Dumairt and I think you know Detective

Sergeant Collins.

"We have discovered a body in the garden of your former home. We think it is your wife and you killed her, didn't you?" Linde's face assumed the colour of marble before he replied: "My wife is dead...oh my God!"

"You killed her, didn't you?"

"No, I did not. This is a nightmare."

Dumairt continued to press: "We know you killed her. We have written evidence that your wife was frightened of you and that you had made death threats towards her. A neighbour has also heard you use violent language towards her."

"I tell you I love my wife, I would not kill her, There has been some awful mistake."

Linde fell silent, as though in a trance, and refused to respond to any further questions on the advice of his solicitor. Eventually Dumairt decided that the time had come to take Linde to Vale Road. They left the remand centre with Linde sitting in the back seat of Dumairt's car. He was sandwiched between the prison officer and Mr Coldwell. Collins drove with Dumairt beside him in the front passenger seat.

They drew up at the house 30 minutes later. Dumairt instructed Collins: "Go to the house and make sure all is ready for us to take Dr Linde in there."

Collins made his way into the garden under the tape stretched across the front gateway. A police constable stood on the front step of the house and Collins proffered his warrant card. The officer moved aside to allow him through saying: "Mr Haymes says that it is no longer a crime scene and there is no need for you to put on protective clothing and gloves."

Gabriel Haymes was in the kitchen filling his case

with his instruments, brushes, dusting powder etc.

"Hi, Abel. You are bringing Linde into the house and garden, I believe?"

"Yes, do you have the photographs of the body here?"

Haymes took an envelope from his case. He passed it to Collins and closed the case with a snap. He was about to speak when a sound resembling corks popping and a cry came from the hall area.

"Probably my lads clearing up out front. We are finished here now and I think I can leave you to it."

Collins turned and was about to go back to the car when the constable appeared in the front doorway. "Mr Collins, you'd better come quick," he said, looking flushed and worried.

Collins and Haymes raced past him, down the garden path and out into the road. The sight that met their eyes was, at first, beyond comprehension. Mr Coldwell lay sprawled across the pavement, his feet and lower legs were still in the car through the open rear door. A pool of blood was spreading across the path from a wound in his chest. Superintendent Dumairt lay across the two front seats bleeding from a head wound. The bullet that hit Dumairt had penetrated the windscreen.

The other occupant of the car had been shot in the face and was slumped in the far corner of the rear seat of the car. A neat round hole had formed a third eye in his right hand cheek. The bullet had continued through the top of his skull to the window which had shattered. The prison officer had escorted his last prisoner. His handcuffs remained attached to his arm but of his prisoner, there was no sign.

Collins took off towards the main road, guessing that was the probable direction taken by Linde. He yelled back to the constable to check in the opposite direction. Collins ran to the main road where he saw a woman walking her dog. He asked her if she had seen anyone running in that direction. The surprised female answered in the negative. Collins could see no one answering Linde's description in either direction on the main road. The fugitive had completely disappeared.

Chapter 27

Mr Roylance's Strange Tale

The meeting of Theynard's ghost-hunting group was more formal than previous ones had been. It took place in the library of Theynard's vicarage in Hampstead. Attending were Theynard, Lucinda Randolph, Dr Brock, Letitia Preece and Jim and Jane Flagg. It was now three and seven days respectively since the murders of Kayne and Miss Davenport.

It was four o'clock on a dull December afternoon and the light was failing fast. The imminent prospect of Christmas did not feature in the minds of this group as they sat silently waiting for Theynard to open proceedings. An atmosphere of gloom pervaded the scene, which would have taken a turn for the worse had they been aware of recent events in Vale Road.

Denholme Theynard addressed the attendees seated around the table.

"Thank you for coming," he said, filling cups of tea as he spoke, and passing them around the table. "I am particularly grateful to you, Jim and Jane. I am glad that you changed your minds, especially as I know that you were particularly upset after hearing from the police that poor Annie Linde had been found."

"What can we do that the police are not already doing?" said Jim Flagg, filling the pause Denholme had left. He was clearly still unconvinced about the necessity for this meeting, particularly after Annie Linde's murder, which to his mind had obviously been perpetrated by her husband.

"I wanted this 'get together' because I have made some rather significant discoveries about the house in Rill Place," stressed Theynard. "My research has led me into very murky water indeed. I shall tell you my tale and then you must judge whether you think that there are any supernatural phenomena involved." He glanced round the table and all nodded to indicate that they were at least prepared to listen.

"In the last 40 years there have been a series of owners. Not one of them has lived there for longer than six months. It stood empty for a full ten years throughout the seventies."

Jim Flagg still looked quizzical. "What does that prove?"

"Nothing in isolation, but I decided to follow–up on it," explained Theynard. "I managed to track down the estate agent who sold the house to Linde. I told him that I was trying to contact a friend who I thought had lived there about six months ago. Mister Tayt, the agent, said that a Mr Roylance had lived at The Eaves for the six-month period before selling. I told him that the name of my friend was, indeed, Roylance and I asked if a forwarding address had been communicated to his office. Tayt gave me that address...a dog collar has its uses and still engenders trust in people. I think that I was justified in the white lie since this business has cost lives."

Miriam Brock spoke up. "We ought to speak to this, Mr Roylance."

"I have already done so, Dr Brock, and with fascinating results," said Theynard, pausing to sip his tea and reach for a chocolate biscuit. The assembled company were now silent and one or two leaned forward in their seats as they waited for the outcome of the story. Theynard cleared his throat. He was taking his time and enjoying the dramatic effect he was creating.

"Mr Roylance is a bookseller and a bachelor," continued Theynard. "He now lives in a flat in Harlow. I visited him yesterday and he was very helpful. He was shocked but not astounded with the events at The Eaves. He takes little note of the world outside of his books and had not heard about the murders. I asked him about his time at Rill Place and he immediately became more diffident. I eventually persuaded him to tell me of his experiences there."

At this point Theynard stood up and went out of the room. He returned accompanied by a short, plump man with sparse hair, longish at the temples. He wore large unfashionably thick black-framed spectacles, which lent him an owlish appearance. This conclusion was borne out by his habit of blinking nervously at the group. Theynard led him to a vacant chair next to him.

"This is John Roylance. I invited him along to tell his story in person."

Theynard made individual introductions before requesting that his guest reveal his tale.

"I moved into The Eaves last March," began Mr Roylance. "I was particularly pleased with the purchase of the house. This was because it is Victorian and retains much of its original character. The problems began within a week of my having moved in."

Theynard prompted Roylance to continue.

"I was in my bedroom standing before a full length mirror. I was adjusting my tie. Some movement behind me caught my eye. Disappearing from view past the open door of my room, I saw the figure of a woman. It was only a glimpse but it was enough for me to turn and run out on to the landing. There was no–one there. I fruitlessly searched the house from top to bottom, in the end convincing myself that it was illusory. After I completed the search I went out and would have thought nothing more of it but for subsequent events."

Lucinda Randolph broke in at this point and asked: "Did you notice how the woman was dressed?"

"As I said it was only a glimpse. If pressed I would say that her dress was late-Victorian. It was long, black and may have had a bustle at the back."

Murmurings filled the room, as each person turned to their neighbour in some excitement. It affected even the most cynical such as Jim Flagg who felt the hairs on the back of his neck rise as he listened to John Roylance's story.

"I saw the woman a number of times after that. Well, saw is a slight exaggeration; I glimpsed her at the periphery of my vision. Whenever I took a good look, there was no sign. I would see the back of her or the hem of her dress disappearing round a corner and out of my sight. Whenever I followed there would be nothing to see.

"Did anything else happen?" asked Lucinda Randolph excitedly.

"There were noises."

"What kind of noises and when did you hear them?" asked Theynard.

"Late at night or in the early hours of the morning I would be asleep and dreaming. I could never remember the details of the dream only that it would end with a huge scream in my ears. It would wake me and realisation would dawn that I had been dreaming. Except that after waking, I became aware of the residual echoes of the scream in the walls of the house for a second or two. Does that make sense?"

"You mean the scream was not dreamed at all but was real?' interposed Lucinda Randolph, quietly. "What kind of scream was it?"

"It was the scream of a woman; a woman who was suffering the tortures of hell."

"Did you ever hear the scream when you were fully awake?" asked Lucinda.

"No, I only ever heard it when coming out of a deep sleep...and always at night."

For a moment or two, the group sat quietly, each one pondering the story of this house. A house with a troubled past and in the present tense; the story had not improved.

Lucinda Randolph was about to speak when she was interrupted by a sound in the room. It was an insistent knocking on the French window overlooking the garden. The long curtains were open. There, pressed against the glass, was a terrified face. Rivulets of water streamed down the pane and rain also dripped from the livid visage. The bloodless lips worked frantically, desperately seeking attention.

Jim Flagg broke the silence first. "Oh my God, it's David Linde."

The sound of a bell at the front of the house caused them all to turn. At the same time, the face at the window vanished. Denholme Theynard moved towards the library door.

"Go to the back, Jim...to Linde, while I see who it is at the front door."

Flagg did so and meanwhile the front door was opened, to reveal the rain soaked figure of Abel Collins and an equally damp constable.

"Good evening, sir. We are here to ask if you have seen anything of Dr David Linde today. He has escaped from custody and there has been a report of him having been in this neighbourhood."

Chapter 28

The Crossroads at The Eaves

A commotion at the back of the house interrupted proceedings at the front. Collins did not stand on ceremony but burst in past the astonished Theynard. He ran past Flagg at the back door and out into the garden. He was just in time to see a dark figure, silhouetted against distant street lamps, climbing the wall at the bottom of the garden. Collins turned and shouted to the three officers now gathered at the front door. "It's Linde, he's gone over the back wall. Go round via the street and cut him off…and hurry."

Collins ran down the garden and shinned up on top of the wall. Beyond were the gardens of other houses. There was no sign of Linde and although Collins waited quietly on his perch, no sound came to his ears except eventually the sound of his men arriving in front of those houses.

A uniformed Sergeant rang Collins on his mobile. "We can't find him at the moment but I have sent men to scour the surrounding area, sir."

"Ok, sergeant, continue the search. Ask one or two neighbours if they have seen or heard anything. I will speak further with the people here at the vicarage. Call me back in half-an-hour."

Detective Inspector Collins turned and climbed down from the wall and strode back towards the luminous rectangle of the open back door.

Townshend had confirmed Collins' promotion that very day, just after Dumairt had been removed to the infirmary. He grabbed the opportunity. He should have felt some elation but all he could feel was a profound tiredness and the fear that this case was out of control. He also missed his old boss both as a man and mentor. He could no longer rely on Kayne's innate wisdom and the result was loneliness, loss of confidence and the sense that if something could kill Kayne…what chance did he, Collins, stand? Linde was not the only killer here. He could sense a second, much more dangerous, shadowy presence.

Two silhouettes stood framed in the doorway and Collins addressed them: "I wonder if I might have a word inside, please?"

Flagg and Theynard turned and Collins followed them into the library. The others stood by the window. Theynard introduced Lucinda Randolph and John Roylance. They all resumed their seats and raised their eyes to Collins who stood with his hands resting on the table.

"A number of events have occurred since I last saw you. First, however, Mr Flagg, I should like to know if David Linde said anything to you earlier."

"He said that he was on the run and needed money. I told him that I had none to give him. He then said something rather strange…that the Devil himself had arranged his escape. Your appearance at the front door then caused him to panic and run for it."

"What has happened, Inspector Collins? That is your new title, isn't it? At least according to one of the officers with you tonight?" Denholme Theynard looked at the nodding policeman and reached for another chocolate biscuit.

"Linde escaped from a police car on the way to his old Vale Road address. During the escape, he killed a prison officer, his solicitor and wounded Superintendent Dumairt, who was in charge of the investigation of the murder of Mr Kayne. Somehow Linde had got hold of a silenced gun while in prison."

For a few moments the group were stunned. Jane Flagg broke in. "You mean he has killed my two best friends and now you have allowed him to kill twice more and escape," she said emotionally.

"Darling, I don't think that Inspector Collins has *allowed* David to do these things," said Jim Flagg, standing up and putting a sheltering arm round his distraught wife. "Why do you think David Linde has become this monster, Mr Collins?"

"There are aspects of this case which baffle me. There is something about Rill Place that remains an enigma. Remember, however, there is persuasive evidence to suggest David Linde murdered his wife before he moved to The Eaves."

"Maybe you should hear what Mr Roylance told us before you came," said Dr Brock.

John Roylance explained how he came to be present and told the story of his experiences while owning the house. Collins listened politely and then sat down at the table, rubbing his chin studiously.

Denholme Theynard spoke up excitedly. "That house is evil and that evil has transmitted itself to David Linde."

Collins retorted: "As I said before; Linde murdered his wife before he had even heard of The Eaves."

The quiet voice of Lucinda Randolph entered the

fray. "His evil entering that house could have unlocked a door and released something of far greater significance. Denholme and some others here think it is imperative we hold a séance at The Eaves as soon as possible." There were nods from around the table, as Lucinda continued. "I know that you are a hard–headed policeman but, believe me, there are paranormal entities which are also a fact of life."

"I know that you asked this of Superintendent Kayne and were dismissed out of hand," said Collins as he stood up. "I cannot promise but I will see what I can do."

"Before the séance we would like to install some sensing equipment," said Theynard. "Would you consider that also, please?"

"I will get back to you on these matters," said Collins. "I must go now to check on the pursuit of Linde. For now I will bid you all goodnight, but I can see you have active plans as a group. Please leave this murder investigation to the police."

Lucinda Randolph spoke, again very quietly. "We are only considering the psychic phenomena involved here. Before you go, Inspector, I have been engaged in some research and there are some more strange tales to be told about the ground upon which the house is built. It may influence your final decision on the holding of a séance. In any case, my story will not take long."

Collins hesitated and then sat down. "Very well, Miss Randolph, I will listen."

"In the 11th century a monastery existed on the site of The Eaves. In 1098 the quiet, contemplative monastic life of the monks was shattered by one of the monks becoming homicidally insane. He ran amok in the scriptorium of the monastery. He took a knife and killed three brothers. He finally threw himself from a parapet of the monastery building and his brains were dashed out on the stone flags beneath. The monks later abandoned the monastery because they wrote that thereafter, 'God has forsaken this place.'"

Inspector Collins half raised himself to his feet but Miss Randolph continued: "The Public Records Office then revealed that the monastery had subsequently been demolished and the need for communication routes had caused a road to be built in the area. In the place where The Eaves now stands was a crossroads with strange superstitions associated with it."

"I, however, was in pursuit of facts and further reading revealed a story which astounded me. Not because, on its own, it is amazing but because it is a link in a chain stretching forwards."

"The crossroads existed from the 14th to the early 19th centuries and had been the favourite haunt of highwaymen during the early to mid-18th century. In 1735 one Thomas Rowden, from a well-known gang of cutthroats known as the Gregory Gang which included Dick Turpin in its ranks, held up a mail coach at this crossroads. The coachman had drawn a weapon and was shot in the face for his pains. Before he left the coach Rowden raped and mutilated a woman, Elizabeth Rayner, who was travelling as a passenger in the coach. She subsequently died of her injuries. Rowden also stole a bag containing 50 gold sovereigns. The hue and cry raised was immense. Two months later Rowden was captured near his birthplace of Hempstead in Essex. He was brought back to Blackheath, tried, found guilty and hanged at the very crossroads where he had robbed, and raped."

"It is said that as he was led to execution he swore

that his spirit would remain in the area and would "stain the very air of this God forsaken place". His body was left to rot on the gibbet as was customary at the time. Local people would not go near it because of the awful stare of his open eyes, which "froze thy very soul". People talked for a century afterwards of a baleful light issuing from the now empty eye-sockets of his fleshless skull. His skeleton had also been seen plunging and clawing the air even on windless nights."

"Eventually his body was taken down and buried beneath the gibbet. Rowden's ghost is said to have haunted the crossroads up until the area was redeveloped in the early 1850s."

A quiet voice intruded on the proceedings. "My experience of frightening events in the recent past within the walls of The Eaves was not the first in the last few years either."

Chapter 29

The Cardews

It is amazing how, in a tense situation, a quiet voice with a contribution can, in an instant, create huge drama. Such was the case with John Roylance, seemingly on the periphery of the story. All eyes in the library turned to him as he began to elaborate.

"When I left The Eaves I moved to my present house. The events I recently related to you had become too much for me. I decided to move in the hope that a new start would clear my mind. No more strange happenings occurred after the move and I began to slip into old routines of work and leisure I had formerly enjoyed. My memories of events at my former address persisted. The horrors had now gone away, however, and my previous ghostly experiences must have been linked with The Eaves itself. This came as a considerable relief because at one stage I had thought that I was on the verge of madness.

"It also occurred to me that I might not be the only one who had seen things," continued Roylance. "Like you, Reverend Theynard, it occurred to me to contact a previous owner. I prevaricated for a while because it is quite an embarrassing subject to raise with strangers and I thought I could well be dismissed as, at best, an eccentric. As the days went by, however, I became more and more curious to find out whether my experiences had been unique.

"I decided to contact the people who had lived in the house immediately prior to me. I had their address in order to forward mail. They were a middle-aged couple, a Mr and Mrs Cardew, and they had owned the house for about a year. I wrote to them telling of my ghostly experiences and asked if they had seen anything untoward during their period of occupancy. Weeks passed after I sent the letter and I began to wonder if they had moved or maybe they did not wish to have anything to do with the matter. If you have a busy life, it is easy, with the passage of time, for old concerns to fade from one's mind. Three months passed, business was going well and the whole affair went out of my mind.

"One evening last summer I closed my shop and walked home through the warm evening streets. I was in a good mood, the weather had been idyllic and I had just completed quite a lucrative business deal. I had purchased, in a bulk lot, a batch of books as part of a house clearance. Every one of them was a rare first edition and the deal had been worth several thousands of pounds."

The room remained silent as Roylance continued.

"I bought a bottle of good red wine on the way home and it was with a light heart that I opened my front door, humming to myself. I enjoyed a good dinner and afterwards sat down to read the evening paper. It was then that the front doorbell sounded. At the door stood a man who introduced himself as Mr Cardew. I remembered him from the house sale.

"I did not remember him as looking as he did now. His hair was pure white; it had been barely iron-grey at the temples when last we met. It was his face, however, which particularly took my attention. His skin was lined with sadness and his eyes looked tired and filled with hopelessness. His head was bowed over rounded shoulders. He looked as if he had been brought down by worry and something else; fear."

"He spoke with a voice cracking with emotion."

I'm sorry I did not reply to your letter; it came at a very bad time for me.

"I invited him into my flat and he stumbled forward and slumped into the chair I offered him. He raised his eyes and spoke quietly and huskily."

You are OK then?

"I replied in the affirmative..." said Roylance. "...and offered him a scotch which he accepted gratefully. I sat down before him, took a pull from my glass and asked him to take his time and tell me all about his experiences. He laughed and at the end of it, he lost some control. His laughter turned to a choking cry of pain."

I have to go on with life but there does not seem much point. I have lost the one person that made my life worthwhile. She was cut down before her time.

She died because we stayed too long in that house. Your letter arrived on the day she died and it confirmed what I already knew: the house killed her. It killed her as surely, as if the bricks and masonry of it had tumbled down on top of her. It still stands there mocking me, while my beautiful Melissa has been taken from me.

"He bent his head and sobbed into his hands. His shoulders shook. I stood up rested a hand on his shoulder and asked him to tell me his story.

"Andrew Cardew swallowed another shot of whisky and wiped his face with a handkerchief. In two or three minutes, he was ready to tell what had happened."

It began when we moved into that house. All was well for a while then the nightmares began. Melissa would wake up in the middle of the night distressed. She dreamed that she had woken and, as her eyes became accustomed to the darkness, she became aware of a dark shape standing at the foot of our bed. The figure was that of a woman its back to Melissa and as my wife sat up it gestured to her, without turning round, to follow. It glided towards the bedroom door. Melissa watched, fascinated, and got out of bed quietly so as not to wake me. The woman opened the door and moved out on to the landing, disappearing from view round the door-jamb. Melissa made her way towards the door. The landing was half lit by light from the street.

Melissa turned to follow when she suddenly came face to face with the apparition. It appeared to rise up in front of her from below her eye-line. My wife jumped back with shock as the woman let out a wordless scream.

The head of the thing was thrown back and the mouth wide open. The horror of it was that the face was peeling and melting as though subjected to great heat, peelings of skin hung in festoons from the face. The lips did not exist. The eyes were bloody sockets. The horrific visage was a screaming, partly skinned skull. Even as she watched, the face was transformed into a horrific blankness, just a flat, featureless face of skin.

Melissa woke at that point to find herself sitting up in bed, shaking and perspiring. Her movements woke me and I tried to calm her down. Night after night this happened for several weeks.

I eventually persuaded her to go to the doctor who

prescribed Prozac. Nothing seemed to work and I was preparing to ask for a referral to a specialist when, as suddenly as they had begun, the nightmares stopped. For the first time in weeks, we slept through the night. We thought that it was over and Melissa successfully stopped the medication. I had begun to think that this unpleasant episode was behind us when something happened which completely reversed this view. We had dined at home with friends and were feeling particularly good. We climbed into bed and I kissed Melissa goodnight. Soon we were both fast asleep.

I dreamed that a movement in the bed had awakened me. I looked round to find that Melissa was not beside me. I looked up to see her walking towards the door and she beckoned to me to follow her. I slipped out of bed as she disappeared. I approached the door calling her name and asking if she was all right. I turned at the door and there she was; my beautiful Melissa hanging lifeless by the neck from the pendant light over the landing. Her head was pulled to one side at a frightening angle. Her tongue was black and hanging from between, partly open, bloodless lips. Her dead eyes stared at me accusingly, desperately, pleadingly.

I woke yelling, my wife desperately trying to calm me down this time. The nightmare came to me nightly after that and I became fearful that I was losing my grasp on my sanity. Melissa suggested that it was strange that both of us should experience similar dreams. We wondered if her description of her nightmare had affected me unconsciously. After a couple of weeks of hell, my dreaming ceased as suddenly as in Melissa's case.

We decided to dine out to celebrate the end of our

troubles. I booked us a table at Claridges and we enjoyed a delicious meal. The evening relaxed us and we arrived home laughing. I paid the taxi and we approached the house, crunching up the drive chatting merrily.

I was hunting for my key when I happened to look up. A light in one of the upper storey windows caught my eye. Melissa saw the light as soon as I did and reacted with a sharp intake of breath.

The light was a moving glow at the back of our bedroom. It began moving forward towards the window as we watched. A woman appeared in silhouette, her back to the window and as we looked, she turned to face us. She was carrying a Victorian oil lamp. To our horror, the lamplight revealed that awful face with no features. A flat stretch of skin was framed by a rather old–fashioned hairstyle. The hair was severely pulled back in a bun.

Jim Flagg broke in: "Oh my God, he was seeing what David Linde saw at home and in Julia Davenport's flat at the beginning of this bloody awful affair."

Just then the mobile phone in Collins' pocket began to ring again.

Chapter 30

Mr Roylance Finishes His Story

David Linde had completely eluded his pursuers. Collins was angry about it and told Sergeant Dove, clearly and directly, that he had better widen the search. Collins also contacted the local station for additional help. After further irritable exchanges with Dove, the Inspector returned to the library, keen to hear the final chapter of John Roylance's story.

*****

At that moment David Linde exited from a copse at the edge of a wooded area two and a half miles from Theynard's vicarage. He was frightened, wet, dirty and exhausted. He looked furtively about him before moving forward.

The dark silhouette of a tall figure detached itself from a tree in front of him. Linde paused and spoke. "Who are you...are you a policeman?"

The figure came towards him and Linde stared into the shadowed face as it approached. All that had happened to him made sense now.

"The time has come, David...for you to know all."

The voice entered his head like the tolling of a great bell. He knew that this meeting was inevitable.

From the moment he had closed the front door of Vale Road for the last time aeons ago...perhaps even before that.

*****

John Roylance raised his eyes as the Inspector re–entered the room.

"Apologies for the interruption, Mr Roylance. I am keen to hear the end of your story. Please continue."

Roylance cleared his throat.

"Andrew Cardew explained that after seeing the faceless woman they entered the house. He rushed upstairs but found no sign of the woman. The lamp she had held stood in the middle of the landing. It was unlit but still hot and the silence of the house was broken by the ticking sound of the lamp as it cooled. He pondered on the fact that there were no other lamps of this kind in the house. As he descended the stairs his ears caught the sound of his wife sobbing as she sank to her knees in the hall. He held her in his arms and made up his mind that this was the end. They would pack up and move out a soon as humanly possible."

"They left to stay with Mrs Cardew's mother that night. The house was put on the market and they moved into their new property in Docklands soon after."

"Two months later Cardew returned home one evening. He was late because he had been attending a conference and he was very hungry. The lights downstairs shone brightly but upstairs all was in darkness. Cardew called out to his wife and, without switching on the lights, he ran upstairs to use the toilet. He reached the darkness at the top of the stairs and as he did so something hard struck him on the head before swinging away. He ducked and ran to the landing light switch.

"The light revealed a horrific sight. Before him, swinging from a cord attached to the ceiling pendant light, was the body of Melissa Cardew. Her head was pulled to one side at a frightening angle; her tongue was black and lolled from between partly open, bloodless lips. The scene was exactly as in his dream.

"I asked him if she had left a note and he said that there had been one line left on a piece of paper in the kitchen. It said...

Sorry, darling, but this is the only way.

"Later the coroner bought in the verdict of suicide.

"Cardew broke down and I made him some coffee. After that we parted. The Eaves is haunted, Mr Collins. I am convinced of it. I have done nothing about it until now because, well, who would have believed me?

"I'd better go," said the inspector. "Other matters await my attention."

The Inspector looked worried. What he had heard did not make life any easier. It threw him into a state of total confusion and he needed to get back to a more rational atmosphere.

Collins took his leave of the party: "I'll get back to you on the séance and the installation of the surveillance equipment, Theynard."

The front door closed behind the Inspector. Theynard allowed himself a smile, a rare event recently, he turned to John Roylance: "I will keep you updated and thank you for your help."

Roylance replied: "If this stops whatever is going on in that house; it has been worthwhile."

Theynard then turned to face the remainder of the group: "When I hear from Collins I will contact all of you."

All the visitors then said their goodbyes and left the house apart from Letitia, she had just crossed the threshold when she felt a hand gently hold her back.

"I am tired of waiting for permission," whispered Denholme Theynard to her. "Let's collect the equipment together and I will call you when we have a clear run."

Letitia smiled excitedly, nodded, turned and left.

*****

Abel Collins entered his office, but which he would always associate with David Kayne. Dr Bond was just leaving the room as Collins arrived.

"Aah! There you are. Just brought you my final report on the body in the garden at Vale Road. It is Annie Linde. Your men discovered a discarded dental appointment card in a drawer at The Eaves. Her dentist provided me with x-rays that clearly confirmed her identity. I also have the results of the DNA profile using tissue taken from the heart in the trunk. It too belonged to Annie Linde. How about that for a turn-up for the books?

"One more thing; the organs in the loft were contaminated with a quantity of soil particles. The chemistry of that soil exactly matches the soil in the garden where the body was found and it is quite different from the soil in the garden at Rill Place. The organs had therefore been removed after the body had been initially interred. The corpse must have then been reburied."

Abel Collins slumped into his office chair and ran his fingers through his hair.

"That's great, Tom. Another piece of the puzzle. The trouble is we seem to have dozens of pieces and each from a different jigsaw. I gather that we still have no idea of the whereabouts of Julia Davenport's missing body parts."

"No, not as far as I know. I must be on my way, Abel. I will catch you later." Bond turned to go and then hesitated. "The bloody fingerprints on the outside of the room from which Kayne fell; they are not on record. The blood belonged to Julia Davenport."

"I don't understand how that can be. Are they Mr Kayne's prints?"

"I am afraid not and we can't find the owner on the database." Bond disappeared leaving Collins pondering the ever-deepening mysteries of this case. He frowned and then caught sight of his computer as it indicated an incoming email. It was from Dumairt.

I am back in my office if you want to talk to me.

"What the hell is he doing back at work?" breathed Collins to himself.

His mind turned back to the murders, the full significance of the last statement of Tom Bond striking him like a thunderbolt. Not David Kayne's prints! And how did Julia's blood get there?

Collins thoughts then turned to what he had heard that night. Logic dictated that this was merely a series of straightforward murders. The events in the house could surely be rationalised as a series of coincidental happenings. The number was the disquieting element and gave him a queasy feeling in the pit of his stomach. He decided that he would review all the evidence acquired from The Eaves. To do this he laid out all the exhibits in the form of photographs. His eyes travelled over them; the watch fob with the initials 'MJD' cut into it; the candelabra dropped by Linde by the bed in the Davenport case; the contents of the trunk in the loft; '1888' written on a sheet of paper by Kayne just before he died. The blood stains on the outside of the door of the room from which Kayne had fallen. All disparate items, seemingly unrelated and yet something nagged at the back of his mind.

He examined the articles found in the trunk. He stared long and hard at the photograph of the man seated with a book and then at the deeds of 9 Eliot Place. He sighed as he transferred his gaze to the ceiling. It was as if a veil was draped in front of the shadowed thing he was trying to see. Every now and then the edge of the veil was twitched back to reveal a glimpse of the solution. Not a big enough glimpse, however, to make out what it was. First thing in the morning he would find out where Eliot Place was in Blackheath.

He suddenly felt very cold and wondered if money was being saved by not heating the building at night. That would be typical of the authorities; saving funds when policing was a 24 hour job.

His thoughts were interrupted by a shadow falling across his desk and he looked up to see the figure of Superintendent Dumairt standing over him.

Chapter 31

A Significant Name Change

"Mr Collins, my invitation email was not voluntary," he thundered as his eyes bored their way, gimlet-like, through him.

"Surprised to see you back after such a wound, sir."

"I understand that you have not located the fugitive," winced Dumairt, leaning heavily against the desk. "That is not good enough and I have decided to take personal charge of the search. Have you any news?"

Dumairt's head was heavily bandaged and he was obviously not fit enough to be back at work. Collins rose and stretched across to aid the wounded detective but the latter shrugged him away.

"Have you found out how he got hold of the gun?"

"The prison authorities are carrying out a thorough investigation," explained Collins. "The Governor will report on progress in the morning. As for Linde, he turned up at Reverend Theynard's vicarage seeking help. We arrived at the front door as he was talking to Jim Flagg at the back. Flagg, his wife, Dr Brock and two or three others were holding a meeting and Linde knocked at the window."

"How did he know they were there?" asked Dumairt.

"Apparently he went to the Flagg house first and their cleaner told him where they had gone."

"When he heard us he legged it over the gardens at the back of the house and we lost him."

"You lost him. Your conduct during this investigation leaves much to be desired and I intend to make changes. Anything else to report?"

"Sir, there is something strange going on at The Eaves...Linde's house. There have been a number of things happening there over many years. Nobody has lived there for longer than a few months for 30 years, perhaps much longer. All the occupiers seemed to have moved because they were frightened."

"Are you telling me that we are dealing with 'The Amityville Horror', Sergeant?"

"It's 'Inspector', sir...and all I am saying is that the Reverend Theynard would like to set up some detection kit in order to monitor any paranormal activity at the house, that is all. After all, what have we got to lose?" Dumairt pulled his brows down over his eyes. Every syllable which followed was enunciated slowly and was spat from those slightly cyanotic lips. His pupils glowed like coals as he hissed: "Only the loss of our credibility before the public and our superiors. Tell me how it will lead us to an early arrest in the Kayne case, Sergeant? I think you should get used to being addressed as Sergeant again because it will not be long before you reclaim that rank. You come in here with this nonsense in the middle of a murder enquiry. Which I might add, is a total debacle and in no small measure due to your personal incompetence. Now get on with finding Linde, a murderer, and forget that last stupid notion. There is no way that I will sanction the installation of apparatus from mumbo-jumboland."

Collins realised that this was no time for rebellion. He turned on his heel and left the office.

* * * * *

Letitia Preece carried the third of six large boxes into the house she shared with Miriam Brock. She was keen to be equipped to deal with or at least measure whatever was happening at Rill Place. It was time to take matters into their own hands.

Interestingly, her opinion of Denholme Theynard had changed. The man had done his homework. His research had been thorough and, in her view, he had justified the need for further investigation. Miriam Brock agreed with her and they both thought that Denholme Theynard and Lucinda Randolph were a formidable team.

The prospect of practical research was exciting and made the checking of her detection equipment of primary importance. She would be ready when the call came.

* * * * *

It was the morning following the altercation between Collins and Dumairt. The latter had organised a meeting, with Collins present, of officers involved in the hunt for Linde. The search was widened which had involved the input from forces outside the local area. Additional officers from those forces were present for briefing and a new reporting system was organised.

It was not until late morning that Collins made his way into Lewisham Library. There resided the Lewisham Local Studies and Archives, which included archival material concerning the Blackheath area. On entering the building he sought out an archivist who directed him to the section housing the historical street maps of the Blackheath area.

The documents were stored in the form of fiches and Collins was quickly able to access street maps of Blackheath across a wide spectrum of time viewed through the projection equipment. He searched for over half-an-hour before the light from the 1861 map projected a mottled glow across his face. At first, he was confused, until he found his bearings and one street name moved into view as he wound the fiche through the viewer. A smile gently played on his lips as he raised his face and stared sightlessly at the dark wooden panelled library walls before him.

Rill Place did not exist in 1861. There was a road there, just as now, but it was called Eliot Place in those days. No 9 Eliot Place was clearly the same house as The Eaves according to these maps. The archivist, not used to seeing someone finding humour in old maps, strolled over. His appearance jerked Collins out of his triumphant thoughts.

"Have you an archive of newspapers from the 1860s through to the 1890s?" said Collins, composing himself.

"Yes, sir. Come this way."

The Archivist led him to the next floor up where the newspaper records were stored. They were bound in book form and Collins began leafing through the back numbers of the Lewisham and Greenwich Mercury from dating back to that era and beyond, to try to find some reference to Eliot Place and its environs. He had reached January 1865 when his mobile rang. It was Dumairt asking how things were going and what he was doing. Collins lied as to his where-abouts, rang off and continued thumbing through the papers.

In May 1875 a small fire had occurred in Eliot Place. No specific address was mentioned in the report but the same thing had happened in June 1876 and this time 9 Eliot Place was mentioned as the house involved. A woman called Eliza Nessling, a well-known local eccentric, had knocked over a candle and set her bed alight. She had thrown herself from an upper window, her clothes ablaze. She was killed by the impact with the flagstones below. After a neighbour had extinguished the flames engulfing her clothes and before she died, she gasped that a figure had appeared to her on the landing; a man hanging from a hook in the ceiling. This vision had caused her to let the candle drop.

The report had ended by saying that the woman was well-known for her strange behaviour and that madness had probably led to her demise.

The afternoon wore on and the light was beginning to fade as Collins reached the mid 1880s and found a reference which caused his eyes to light up and his face to assume a puzzled look. There was a name mentioned that caught his eye. It was in relation to the Blackheath Cricket, Gottball and Lawn Tennis Company. A new treasurer and honorary secretary had been elected.

The address was 9 Eliot Place. There was some-thing about the name of the man, which seemed familiar but, though he wracked his brains, he could shed no light on why it was significant to him. Eventually Collins gave up the struggle to remember, stood up and stretched himself. It was dark now and he closed the books after making a note of where he had got to in the records. He thanked the archivist, pulled on his coat and left the building.

Chapter 32

The Ghost Hunt Begins

Hundreds of emails and calls awaited his attention but late that evening Collins was intent on re-examining the Eliot Place deeds found in the loft space. He collected the plastic envelope containing the documents from the evidence store. He signed the docket offered by the officer in charge of the repository and made his way through the, now quiet, corridors back to his office.

He removed the deeds from the envelope care-fully and gently unfolded the rather delicate documents. As he did so, a yellowed, foxed, dog–eared envelope dropped from between the pages and on to the floor. Collins gently laid the deeds on his desk and bent to retrieve the envelope. He noted the tuppenny blue Victorian stamp in the corner and the address, in a bold hand, on the front. Carefully he opened it and withdrew a yellowing sheet of paper.

It was addressed to a firm of estate agents, Hartle and Block, in Lewisham. A corner of the sheet crumbled away at his touch. He managed to unfold the paper and began to read:

January 25th 1890
Re; 9 Eliot Place, Blackheath.

Dear Sirs,

I cannot understand the delay in selling this property. I hold you responsible in selling us this residence in the first instance. You misled us as to the history of the premises and I expect you to remit your fee in the circumstances. Please ensure that any further expenditure is kept to a minimum – I shall expect nothing less.

I explained the circumstances and I understand that, because of the activities of the monster, who resided here before us, the street name is to change. He has gone in body but his evil presence is still domiciled here. My wife has seen both him and the woman and has been so frightened that she now refuses to visit the first floor. She sleeps in the living room.

I have seen the old woman twice; once in the garden and in the master bedroom. I was overcome by melancholy and cold despite...

Here the fragment of letter ended but it told enough to confirm the stories he had heard earlier. There was something in that house and there might be other evidence, such as more papers in the loft, as yet unearthed, where the trunk had been found.

He stood up and pulled on his overcoat. He was hungry and he decided to head for home. He approached his car but hesitated for a moment, his hands resting on the roof. He had pocketed the key to The Eaves before leaving the office in anticipation of a visit to the house tomorrow. He was tempted to go now. There was a step-ladder in the house, which would allow him up to the loft, and he had a torch in the boot of his car.

*****

Reverend Denholme Theynard and Letitia Preece sat in camping chairs in the back garden of The Eaves. The night was cold and there was a hint of rain in the air. Lucinda Randolph had not accompanied them because she said that she had a previous engagement.

Letitia had just completed the setting up of cameras and sound equipment. One camera was directed at the house from just inside the perimeter wall and a second had a line of sight at right angles to the first, parallel to the back wall of the building. The equipment was battery-operated and built to withstand the rigours of weather. The camera pointed at the house was a time-lapse camera. This allowed an eight–hour recording to be viewed in a more man-ageable two hours via a standard DVD player.

The second camera was triggered by using a series of infrared beams. If the movement of a solid object broke any beam, the camera was immediately acti-vated. Letitia was concerned about the weather because rain would also trigger the camera.

These two people made a strange couple but they had been thrown together by circumstance, frustra-tion and the need for action.

The police had removed any cordons around The Eaves and it had been easy to enter the garden as the side gate had been left unlatched. Together they had manhandled the equipment from Letty's car before parking it further down the road outside so as to avoid attracting too much attention. They bent to their task with grim determination.

Having installed, checked and double-checked the workings of the cameras and the detection systems

Theynard poured them coffees from a Thermos flask and the two companions settled down to await developments.

A full moon sailed above them and Theynard mused on a poetic description by Percy Bysshe Shelley...

And, like a dying lady lean and pale,
Who totters forth, wrapp'd in a gauzy veil,
Out of her chamber, led by the insane
And feeble wanderings of her faded brain,
The moon arose up in the murky east
A white and shapeless mass.

What insanity would she see tonight in her feeble wanderings? They had certainly encountered some mad happenings over the last month. Letitia too, thought as she sipped her coffee, of the nightmarish events recently – several people dead, an apparently haunted house with an emerging history of death and evil. The last man who had bought this house had turned out to be guilty of multiple murders...or was he? She was pondering this question when the silence was broken by the hooting of a tawny owl.

She remembered the strange story told by that self–effacing little man, John Roylance. He had left the meeting in a cheerful mood and asked to be kept informed of progress. He was happy, at last, that something was being done about this terrible place.

This house tormented the people who came in contact with it – it changed them, tortured them and sometimes disposed of them.

The night wore on and the traffic noise subsided to an occasional distant murmur. Letitia's eyelids became heavy, her head began to droop and her chin rested on her chest. Around two hours later she was awakened by the camera whirring into life. Staring into the darkness, she saw the shape of an urban fox making his way across the lawn and she reset the system.

By now, the two of them were feeling very cold and they pulled their coats tighter round them. They poured themselves more coffee and Denholme Theynard whispered that at least the rain had kept off. They lapsed into silence and Letitia once more began to doze. Theynard too was beginning to fall into unconsciousness when something stirred him back to wakefulness. He stared across the lawn but could see nothing at first. Then he saw it. He grabbed Letitia's arm and shook her.

She followed the line of sight from his pointing finger. The window from which David Kayne had fallen had been boarded over but through gaps they perceived a feint beam of light. As they watched, a shadow passed slowly before the light and then disappeared once more into the darkness. The light then moved across the room and faded into darkness, as though it had moved to the back of the room and was then extinguished.

Letitia watched and shivered, this time with more than just the cold. She shook with fear. The window was now completely in darkness. A sudden sound came from the front of the house, causing them both to start. Theynard leapt to his feet and turning to Letitia said: "You stay here. I'll go round the front to investigate."

Before Letitia Preece could react, he had moved off round the side of the house, taking care not to step in front of any of the lasers. Just as the side gate closed after Theynard, the camera whirred into life again. One of the laser beams had been interrupted by something, and it had not been the priest.

Chapter 33

A Candle Flame Dies Again

Collins had just emerged from The Eaves when Theynard rounded the corner of the house, almost colliding with him.

"Oh, it's you, Inspector Collins," said Theynard. "We wondered who it was."

Collins spun round to face the priest and for a moment, a look of fear flickered across his face. It passed as he recognised the owner of the voice.

"Theynard, what are you doing here? Who is this 'we'?"

Theynard explained about Miss Preece and her equipment installed in the back garden. Collins frowned and said that he had not given them permission to start the work.

"Come now, Inspector. We both know that you would never gain the blessing of your superiors to do this research or to hold a séance here."

"I was thinking perhaps it could be done under my sole auspices, discreetly. I would obviously need to choose the time, however. You realise that your activities this evening could be construed as perverting the course of justice and, as well, you are trespassers."

As he spoke, the Inspector made to move into the back garden. Theynard reached out and grabbed his arm: "Mister Collins, have you just come from upstairs, the room from which Mr Kayne fell?"

Collins turned back to face the churchman, a puzzled expression on his face. His voice when he found it was husky: "I have only just arrived and had opened the door when I realised that I had forgotten my torch. I turned to retrieve it from my car and there you were."

"Did you hear anything as you entered the hall?" asked Theynard.

"Why do you say that?"

Theynard described the shadowy figure they had seen in the bedroom followed by a sound coming from the front of the house.

"It was the noise out here that prompted me to come and...well...you know the rest."

The two men faced each other, for a moment neither speaking. The Inspector collected his thoughts first and turned back to the front door. As he did so he said: "No, I heard nothing."

Collins pushed the front door open and both men entered the building. Theynard turned on the lights in the hall and landing and Collins led the way upstairs. The door of the bedroom stood ajar. It looked like a long black rectangle between it and the doorjamb. Collins pushed open the door, stepped inside the room and switched on the light.

The room stood innocently empty and both men ceased holding their breath. Theynard's eye was drawn to an object in the centre of the floor. Collins had already stepped forward to pick it up. It was a brass candelabrum, the wick of the candle was not alight but it had been and a thin wisp of smoke rose from it.

Abel Collins turned the brass holder round in his

hands as he examined the rather ordinary, presumably, Victorian object. Theynard, meanwhile, went up over to the boarded window and stared down into the garden through the gaps between the boards. As he looked, the moon sailed out from behind a cloud and illuminated the scene. His eyes fell on the shiny surfaces of the cameras they had installed.

Theynard's gaze moved on across the garden to where the camping chairs stood. Letitia Preece still sat in her chair. He was just thinking how brave she was to remain there on her own. He had expected her to follow him, especially as he had not returned for some time. It was then that he noticed that she was staring up at him. He spoke to Collins, his back still towards him. "I think we ought to go to Miss Preece, she will be worried..."

His voice tailed off as he stared down at his female conspirator. She was staring fixedly at him, a wide grin on her face. That grin frightened him. It held no warmth.

"Inspector, there is something wrong...please come."

Theynard turned and ran downstairs and out into the garden, closely followed by Collins. They both stopped when they reached the open side gate. There was no sound now; the streets had lapsed into a heavy, threatening silence. Cloud had smothered the light from the moon. The stillness carried the forbidding charge of an approaching storm. It was a few moments before their eyes became accustomed to the darkness.

The chairs were side-on to where the two men stood. Instantly Collins realised that Letitia Preece's head was lolling at an unnatural angle. He moved forward and as he did so, the moon re-emerged from cloud and cast an eerie light on the scene before him. More of her face and body came into view. As he moved round to face her his eyes widened.

The moon illuminated Letitia's terrible wounds. Her abdomen had been ripped open exposing her intestine. Blood had welled up to the top of her oesophagus and had oozed across her face from both sides of her wide-open mouth. Theynard had seen her face at a distance, through the shuttered window and in poor light: he had been given the erroneous impression that her lips were spread in a hideous grin.

Collins felt for a pulse in the neck. There was none; Letitia Preece was quite dead. Collins turned and his eyes swept around the moonlit garden. He ran back to the front of the house through the garden gate passing the astonished figure of Denholme Theynard.

"Do not touch anything, Theynard. Stay put."

Theynard stepped forward in shocked horror as his eyes lit upon the violated body of Letitia Preece. His eyes darted back and forth across the garden and then he became aware of a whirring sound. One of them had triggered the camera system.

Collins reappeared, a torch and a mobile phone in his hand. He was calling for support from colleagues. The front garden and road outside were deserted; it seemed that the murderer had made good his escape. Theynard spoke up excitedly: "Inspector, the camera is rolling. We must have set it off."

"I guess you are right, but so what?"

"Don't you see; the murderer would have triggered the camera too. We may have his image recorded in the act of killing poor Letitia. That camera is also sensitive to infra-red; the darkness would have presented no problems."

Collins looked quizzical at first because he realised that it was possible for Theynard to have killed the woman prior to their meeting at the front of the house. Theynard could have also killed Kayne, he certainly had the opportunity. The motive might even be to perpetuate the evil legend of The Eaves. Collins' instincts told him something different, however. He knew that whatever was at work here no police officer could solve without expert help. He turned to Theynard. "Ok, I will get it checked out."

Theynard stepped forward to disconnect the surveillance equipment but Collins stopped him. "Wait for my colleagues to arrive, please."

Chapter 34

Witness for the Prosecution

Once again the police circus reconvened at The Eaves. Dumairt arrived and immediately took Collins aside: "What has happened here?"

"Letitia Preece and Theynard had set up surveillance equipment in order to record whatever haunts this house; human or otherwise. I happened to be here taking another look around. I had no idea they were on the premises until I ran into Theynard as I was going to my car. While we were at the front of the house; Miss Preece was attacked and killed in the back garden."

"You fucking idiot you will be back on the beat by tomorrow and you won't have David Kayne to cover for you. You were here and what looks like a murder took place under your nose. Do you know what the press are going to do to us?

"Go home, and tomorrow morning report to my office at 9am sharp."

All the fight left Collins. He was tired, hungry and, worse still, he felt totally out of his depth. He was about to defend himself but turned away instead, leaving Dumairt to seek out Theynard, now the number one suspect.

Collins crunched along the gravel drive to his

car, his shoulders hunched. He ran his hand across his face and attempted to massage the fatigue out of his eyes. He wearily opened the car door and slumped into his seat. As he did so, a second person opened one of the rear doors and slipped into the back of the car. Breathlessly a woman's voice broke the silence. "I saw the murder. I saw the murderer, not clearly, but I saw him."

Collins turned and perceived the ample figure of Lucinda Randolph, red-faced and very flustered. Collins regained some of his composure and asked her what she was doing there. "Denholme told me what he was going to do this afternoon and I decided to keep an independent eye on things," she explained. "I know nothing of electronic surveillance but I do know about the paranormal and therefore I came here just in case."

"In case of what?"

He realised, bearing in mind subsequent events, that the question was rhetorical.

"I was worried, rightly as it turned out, that they would disturb whatever lives within these walls."

Her eyes wandered towards the house, dark and forbidding, silhouetted against the bright glow of the police arc lamps in the back garden. Collins followed her gaze; it was easy to believe in the evil now.

Lucinda Randolph continued: "I managed to hide away behind the Leylandii cypress in the passageway leading to the side gate. Theynard passed me, in my hiding place, having heard you at the front door. While you two were engaged inside the house I slipped in through the gate having heard a sound. It was a stifled cry followed by a tearing sound. I watched as the poor girl was murdered. I stood and watched. God help me. I could not move...I could not move."

Her voice died away into a series of sobs as she recalled the terrible event. Collins climbed into the back of the car and extended a comforting arm round her shaking shoulders. She nestled her head into his shoulder and gradually her sobs subsided. He held her and pondered on the events of the evening. He saw in his mind's eye a dark figure drifting across the lawn towards Letitia. He saw the expression on her startled face change to a look of sheer terror. A blade flashed as the figure wielded the mortal strokes that bled the life out of the poor woman.

"Who is it, Lucinda? Who is the killer? Did you see his face?"

She stared ahead of her, pale and distraught and at first made no answer. The tears flowed again down her reddened face and the words came slowly and quietly at first but then louder: "I could have stopped it if I could have moved but my fear of what that creature represents prevented me. I did not see his face but something about the way he moved was familiar. He is still here. He has not left the house. I can feel his presence now; it is like a cold, dead feeling in the pit of my stomach. He is not alone and yet he is isolated. There is anger, despair, fear and torment in the house but he is not the source of all those feelings, there are others. He is not the only source of evil and I can sense something else...there is madness."

Collins stared into the darkness and then back at the house. He thought about the current owner. How did he fit into this awful puzzle? He was approaching the end of his rope and knew that he needed help.

"Lucinda, I know that you're probably not in any fit state to answer this question but I will ask it anyway. I know that you, Theynard and the group would like to perform a séance but how will that help us?"

"A séance will enable us to ascertain what exactly haunts The Eaves. I believe that there are a number of entities, some of which are in conflict. Having established what we are up against, then Theynard and I have been preparing for the next stage."

"Which is?"

"We will perform an appropriate exorcism in the house. It will need to be, however, a very carefully constructed exorcism because the evil we will be facing is not going to leave without a fight. A fight which will put everyone present with us in the house at the time in mortal danger. The peril we will be facing threatens our very souls."

"You mean you could die as a result of this?"

"Oh no. Normal death would be a blessing and possibly a lucky escape. I mean that our immortal souls are in danger"

"That is way beyond me."

"Mr Collins, the evil in this house goes back to before the bricks of the building were laid. I also think that something entered this house in the 19th century, which fed on the evil that went before. This entity has grown but at first I did not understand how that could be possible. I have studied and thought about the nature of what has happened in the period since David Linde bought this house. I believe that the presence here must have grown from the evil he brought with him, but that is still not enough. David Linde is a murderer, I believe, but his crimes are as of nothing compared with those of the thing that lives within those walls. That entity has fed on something else because it is a spirit so powerful that it can physically kill. I think that it killed Mr Kayne, for example. There is only one way I can think of which will explain the acquisition of that power but that explanation only raises more questions."

Abel Collins had forgotten his tiredness now. He was transfixed by what Lucinda had to say. She was moving too fast for him now and he needed to slow her down to his pace. "I have my thoughts on the matter but at this stage I would prefer to keep my own counsel."

"Lucinda, what is the explanation?"

"I believe that something happened which has remained a legend either in this immediate area or nationally. Whatever it was, it has become so notorious that no one has forgotten it or has been allowed to forget it. This notoriety or fear, call it what you will, has remained undiminished since the time of the original event and the cause of it lives in that house and has fed on that hysterical fear ever since. It grows stronger all the time because it causes people within its reach to commit murder and that evil provides further nourishment for it. It is an ever–widening circle and it must be stopped."

"Why was Kayne killed?"

"I think that Mr Kayne was a very shrewd man and I believe that he had to be killed because he had begun to understand what was happening and he was perceived as a threat. I can think of no other explanation. Mr Kayne must have had knowledge and could do damage to it. That is where you come in, Mr Collins."

"What do you mean?"

"You need to understand all that Kayne uncovered during the investigation. Go through his notes and try to think as he did. Talk to his family."

"He had no family, only his wife; she was killed immediately before he died."

Lucinda frowned before she muttered: "Was she now? Well, that is interesting?"

Chapter 35

The Scream in the Darkness

"Lucinda, how do you hope to defeat this monster if you are rendered as helpless as you were tonight?"

"That is because I was defenceless. That will not happen again. I cannot afford to make such mistakes and I won't. I had earlier decided to take wafers with me to The Eaves but as I was not intending to enter the house I thought it would be alright to leave them behind."

Collins suddenly felt weary again.

"Ok, Lucinda, let's get you home. That is enough for one night, I think."

"Thank you but no, Mr Collins, I will walk home. I want to think."

"Are you sure? It is very late and I would be concerned about your safety."

"I don't live far away and I need to turn this situation over in my mind and plan the next move. You probably need to contemplate your position also."

Collins put out a hand to stop her but she was in no mood for any opposition. They both got out of the car and Collins said: "I have to see Dumairt in

209

the morning and then I will do the research you suggest. I have already examined most of Mr Kayne's information but I need to read it again and thoroughly digest it. I will ring you to plan the séance. That will not be until early in the New Year probably, bearing in mind Christmas and the fact that the house is once again a crime scene."

Collins climbed into his car behind the wheel. Lucinda nodded to him as she crossed in front of the headlights of the car and headed towards the front gate. Collins watched her walk away in her capacious dun-coloured maxi-coat. Moving out of his headlights he accelerated the car forward and passed her. She watched as the car turned at the gate. It was as her eyes became accustomed to the dark that she suddenly became aware of the cold in the air, a bitter clinging cold. She stopped in her tracks and turned towards the front door. Despite the darkness of the house façade, emphasised by the arc lights behind it, a dark shape moved out of the shadowed doorway. Before she had time to adjust her focus on the shape, her ears were gripped by a sudden loud scream.

It was like no other scream she had ever heard. Dante must have heard that sound as he travelled through hell. The images created in the drawings of Botticelli showing Dante and Virgil in purgatory flashed across her mind. The scream was made by a writhing tortured soul or souls. Her ears were not the only part of her sensing that awful noise. Her whole body was wracked by its sheer intensity. Lucinda clapped her hands over her ears, closed her eyes and bent double under the weight of the pain of it. The sound continued for what seemed like minutes and at last subsided into a wail of despair. The noise attenuated gradually but for a while the walls of the garden and the house seemed to echo the anguish of the cacophony.

Gingerly she dragged her hands from her eyes and raised her head. Her whole body was frozen now and she knew, it was not over yet. She began to intone the Lords Prayer. Her eyes remained tight shut.

She tried to force them open, knowing that some horror stood before her. The silence now was as deafening as the scream. The muscles in her eyelids would not work...dare not work. A tiny movement of the gravel in front of her broke the silence but confirmed her fears.

Finally, she opened her eyes and before her was...nothing...or so it first appeared. Then she realised that the house and the drive up to the house had disappeared. All was invisible behind a dense blackness. The scream must have emanated from the blackness. She stared into that stygian fog and saw, clearly, faces emerging. They were white and stark, full of pain and fear. They emerged and then faded into the blackness before again appearing as though they struggled against some hidden force. She realised that the scream came from these tortured souls trapped together in some hell, not of this world. Lucinda had only time to utter the words, "the Lord God protect me." There was a crash like thunder and she was thrown back on to the gravel and rendered senseless.

*****

With no sign of the black fog, the next thing that Lucinda saw was the face of Abel Collins staring down at her as she lay on the gravel drive at The Eaves. She remembered the poor creatures and felt again the emotions she had experienced seeing those faces.

Collins helped her into a sitting position. "What happened Lucinda?"

She did not answer but realised immediately that before she had been felled a feeling had engulfed her, which was not the fear of evil. It was an overwhelming awareness of deep fathomless despair and it emanated from the creatures before her. She had also experienced a similar feeling of despair in that scream.

"What made you come back?" asked Lucinda.

"I drove to the end of the road and realised that there was no way I could leave you to walk home," said Collins. "I was right, wasn't I?"

Lucinda did not reply but began to struggle to her feet.

"Would you like a drink of water?" asked Collins.

"No, just get me home. I think I need to be in safer surroundings. I will tell you what happened later."

Collins helped Lucinda to the car and they drove away in silence at first. Collins needed directions to her house and therefore some words were eventually exchanged. They pulled up in front of a Victorian, three-storey house, still in Blackheath.

Collins followed Lucinda up to the front door: "Do you want me to stay until you feel better?"

"I'm quite alright now, thank you."

"Look, let me come in and make tea for you? I insist, by the way."

Lucinda had lost the strength to resist.

They sat in the parlour, which was rather chintzy and cluttered, in keeping with the 19th century origins of the building. Collins noted the marble fireplace was complete with a brass companion set, a feature not seen much nowadays. His eyes wandered to the bookshelves and he noted volumes on many subjects including philosophy and the arts. His eyes lit up when he saw a large section of books covering spiritualism and religion. "What caused you to collapse?" said Collins, turning to Lucinda. "I don't see you as the Victorian lady suffering the vapours."

She told him about the faces, the scream and the feeling of despair she had experienced. His reaction at first was to blame it on autosuggestion, but deep down he knew he was just regurgitating the standard explanation of the sceptic. He had no doubts that she had seen these creatures.

"It is the same scream that John Roylance heard in his dreams," said Lucinda, standing up to pour more tea.

"When did you first find out that you were able to see things?"

"You do not want to hear all that, surely?" asked Lucinda, uncomfortably.

"Yes, indeed I do, Lucinda. What happened to make you realise that you were...were different."

"It first happened when I was 16," began Lucinda. "My father and mother took me to Haworth in North Yorkshire. I was studying the Brontes for GCSE English Literature and had become very interested in the family."

"We stayed in rooms over a teashop opposite The Black Bull where Branwell Bronte had drank and taken laudanum. My mother and father had planned for me to visit the parsonage and wander the moors as Emily Bronte had done 130 years before. Our rooms were off an old oak–panelled corridor, which, on the other side of the passage, had windows overlooking the cobbled hill leading past the parsonage. We had journeyed up from Suffolk, where we lived, and we were therefore quite tired when we arrived in Haworth. We went to bed early.

"I was soon asleep but was awakened some time later by noises in the corridor. There were footsteps running up and down and raised voices and, at one point, a scream. Sounds of children could be heard and I told myself that they would soon go to bed. The noises continued. I became annoyed and decided to say something to them. I was somewhat surprised that my father had not protested before now, as my parents were only one room away from my own.

"I climbed out of bed and approached the door. I was about to turn the handle when I heard an adult voice saying...

Come children, this way quickly. There are people out there.

"I hesitated. I decided that the adult would soon quieten things down and so it transpired. I went to bed and later woke up to a glorious Yorkshire morning. I washed and dressed in a leisurely manner and made my way down to the tearoom where breakfast was being served and my parents were already drinking coffee.

"The owner of the establishment arrived to take our order and my father said that they were ready, now that his errant daughter had arrived. I took umbrage at that point, protesting that the people running up and down outside my room half the night had kept me awake. No wonder I was late for breakfast.

"My parents said that they had heard nothing and it was then that the host spoke up. "There are certainly no children here and my wife and I sleep on the other side of the house," he said, a look of realisation crossing his face. "I will get your breakfast," he added. "Afterwards I will tell you a little story."

"After we had eaten our 'full English' and were enjoying a second cup of coffee, the owner returned, sat down at our table and told us the following story..."

'About a century and half before the Brontes, the tea–shop had been the site of an apothecary (the old equivalent of a modern pharmacy). One night a fire broke out on the upper floor of the building where a family had rooms.

'The timber structure was very susceptible to the flames and before long the building was a blazing inferno. The family on the upper floor were trapped because the fire was fiercest in the stairwell, which was the only escape route.

'People in the street below are said to have watched the terrified children running from window to window desperately searching for a way out. They failed and the entire family perished in the flames. The house was rebuilt in its current form later on.'

"I listened to this story with the hairs on the

back of my neck rising and my mouth open," continued Lucinda. "To this day I still wonder what I would have seen had I opened the door. I realised right there and then that I had heard my first ghosts."

Chapter 36

Lucinda Randolph Tells a Tale

"It must be remarkable to have this awareness?"

Lucinda hesitated for some moments before answering Abel Collins. She considered her response very carefully.

"Mr Collins, you have no idea. One does not become aware of these entities at a convenient time. I have become conscious of a spirit when I was about to attend an urgent appointment or enter a deep sleep. The entity may be friendly or malevolent. They have one thing in common; they are lost in a twilight no-man's-land between the world of the living and the afterlife. They carry with them two possible auras in their immediate vicinity. These are either a feeling of deep unhappiness or the terrifying evil. Physical energy is required in order to generate a manifestation. A sharp drop in temperature is therefore the first indication of a presence. This cold is bitter if the thing entering this world is malevolent. 'Remarkable' would not be my chosen word to describe it."

Collins said nothing as Lucinda continued: "I have experienced these happenings since puberty and it was probably my hormonal changes which triggered this awareness. When I was young, the phantoms have caused me to pass out in a dead faint. Some people call it a gift but it is more accurately described as a curse. This curse has blighted my entire adult life because I cannot hide from it and I cannot run away from it. People like me, historically, have died of fright, been committed to asylums or been burned at the stake. I have learned to live with my 'gift' by helping others who suffer because of these hauntings. It is the only way I know how to survive."

Collins leaned forward in his chair: "Is that how you met Denholme Theynard...exorcising some evil spirit?"

"Denholme Theynard was my lover. Do not look so surprised. Denholme and I were both young once and I was not always this shape. Denholme was not always the dried up husk you see. Inside he was, and still is, a brave and intelligent man. He is a disappointed individual because he has always craved my power to pierce the veil, so to speak. I still see the fire of his youth sometimes burning in his eyes and, once more, I remember our adventures when we were young. I met Theynard when I was 18. He was the new curate at my local church in Woodbridge in Suffolk. I had been troubled by a poltergeist, a not uncommon phenomenon in a girl of that age. My mother had sought out Denholme in the hope that he might save me from whatever had possessed my soul...or that was how she saw it.

"Denholme sat me down and listened to me, really listened. It was the first time that that had ever happened. Just talking to him helped and provided me with some catharsis. He had been a student of the occult since he was a teenager and he did not pour scorn on me as everyone else had done. He told me that he would help me and he set about doing that. In the process, we fell in love, much to my mother's chagrin. Denholme was forced to leave the parish and he took me with him.

"We moved to London and set up house together. Denholme managed to find a curacy at a church in Mile End Road in the East End. We had little money but when you are young and in love that is of no importance. For a while it seemed that my powers had waned and no more spirits made their presence known to me.

"One day I was in the West End walking down Oxford Street. I had acquired a job in a library in the area near our house and had settled in well. I had received my first pay packet and had decided to window shop and spend a little. I was staring into a window when I saw a familiar figure reflected in the glass before me. It was my mother standing on the other side of the road staring at me. I turned and she walked across the road towards me. I smiled happily and ran towards her, wanting to share my newfound happiness. She reached an island in the middle of the road and as she stood, she mouthed the words...

I love you, darling.

"A bus passing between us suddenly obliterated my view. I waited in the middle of the carriageway, with a growing excitement with the anticipation of telling her everything. When the traffic cleared I rushed forward but she was nowhere to be seen. I scanned the road and pavements to no avail. I began to panic. I ran searching for her familiar face but she had gone.

"The attack of panic faded, only to be replaced by a new concern; had what I had seen been a warning that something had happened to her? I searched for a phone box in order to ring my father and eventually located one near Trafalgar Square. I hastily dialled the number and waited impatiently for an answer, dancing from one foot to the other. His voice came on the line. Immediately I knew there was something wrong. He said that he had been waiting for my mother to come home from shopping. She was late and they had tickets booked for a show at the Riverside Theatre in Woodbridge. I told him that I merely wanted a chat and asked him to ring me when she finally arrived home. I then hurried home in the knowledge that my fears were about to be realised. My father rang later that evening: my mother had been crossing the road, while in town, and was hit by a motorcyclist travelling far too fast. She had been killed instantly, as had the motorcyclist.

"When we went to the funeral in Woodbridge; my father and Denholme put the past behind them and became firm friends and remained so until my father's death a few years ago. A massive tragedy like that can put old arguments into perspective. It is a pity that the price for such a coming together is so high.

"The day of the funeral came and we were standing by the graveside as the service of interment took place. My eyes wandered over the faces of my aunts and all who stood on the other side of the grave. My eyes lit upon an unfamiliar man standing behind the main group. He was a young, dark-haired man with a brooding expression on his face. He reminded me of the young James Mason in *Odd Man Out*. I determined to find out how he knew my mother when the service had finished.

"After we left the graveside I sought out the stranger but could see no sign of him anywhere. I asked Denholme if he had seen the dark boy but he had not. There was a cold wind blowing as we made our way back to the waiting cars in order to return to my father's house. My thoughts returned to my mother and I relived the last look she gave me across that busy city street. I climbed into the car and the funeral cortège moved slowly and silently away.

"I stared back to take a last look at that stark hole in the ground where the woman who bore me lay dead. A tall dark figure stood at the graveside staring down into that sad pit and I realised it was the young man I had seen earlier. I noticed that he was clad in the black leathers of a motorcyclist. I tried desperately to stop the car and eventually Denholme persuaded the driver to pull over to one side of the road. Denholme and I dashed back to the graveside but the lonely figure was gone. I explained to Denholme what I had seen and we both knew who that dark, brooding figure was.

"I shall never forget standing in that fading autumnal light, dead leaves rolling over the grass. The wind howling through the nearby yew trees and in that coldness I felt the agony of the boy, trapped here because of a moment of youthful stupidity. I clung to Denholme. He held me, and all he said was that we would try to help the boy.

"We spoke to my father about the affair and at first he was angry. Denholme told him the reasons for the spirit coming to the graveside. Eventually we persuaded him that we might all find some peace if we could make contact with the spirit of the boy. I told my father that we would need his help and after some days, turning the matter over in his mind, he agreed.

"Before we left Woodbridge we made contact with the boy's father, a widower and a broken man. We met him in his house in Framlingham and it was there that I performed my first séance. There is no great need for learning to perform such a ritual but there are a number of basic rules to know and follow.

"We four; Denholme, the boy's father, my poor father and myself sat and held hands round a table set up in the bedroom of the boy. I called upon him to come to me. It was some time before anything happened but in the end, after half-an-hour, I felt myself slipping into a trance. The boy spoke through me and said that because of what he had done he could not move on without forgiveness. When he learned of my father's presence he grew silent and I felt the terrible weight of guilt which lay on those shoulders. I cajoled him into speaking and, in the end; he broke down and begged my father for forgiveness. I shall never forget the words of my father..."

You were young and who does not make mistakes at your age? There but for the grace of God, go I. You were not deliberately setting out to do harm and therefore I willingly forgive you.

"When my father had said these words; silence reigned," added Lucinda. "It was a peaceful silence as though storm clouds had cleared and the oppressiveness of the atmosphere that had gone before was now replaced by clear air. The boy was seen no more and the two older men were able to start their healing process."

Chapter 37

The Borley Rectory Incident

Thomas Dumairt sat in his office with a furrowed brow. He had completed his progress report to Townshend and it was getting late. He stood up, walked over to the window and stared across the rooftops, shining wet with rain. There was circumstantial evidence linking Theynard to the deaths of Kayne and Letitia Preece but nothing at all to suggest that he was implicated in the murders of Annie Linde or Julia Davenport. The last two lay at the door of David Linde, together with the murder of Prison Officer Partridge and the solicitor Coldwell. He therefore had to let Theynard go.

Dumairt remembered the DVD disks, which he had personally removed from the cameras in the garden at The Eaves. He took them from his briefcase and went into the office next door where he knew there was a DVD player and television.

*****

Lucinda Randolph brought in a further supply of tea, sat down and resumed her story. "I began to gain a reputation after this last event. Helped by Denholme, more investigative work came my way culminating in an event at Borley near Sudbury on the Essex/Suffolk border," she explained. "Denholme and I had been on holiday at Flatford in Suffolk, exploring 'Constable Country', when a woman at the bed and breakfast establishment where we were staying mentioned a new outbreak of disturbances. Are you familiar with the story of Borley Rectory?"

"The name rings a bell," said Collins.

"It was once labelled as the most haunted house in Britain, mainly because of the book of that title written by the paranormal investigator Harry Price in 1946," continued Lucinda. "The house itself was gutted by a mysterious fire in 1939 and the ruin finally demolished in 1944. The ghost of a nun was frequently seen in and around the house and is still seen especially in the local churchyard. Price had seen all sorts of phenomena including poltergeist activity in the house itself in the late thirties. Harry Price has since been labelled by various people as a charlatan and much of the activity he recorded as bogus.

"Denholme and I decided to spend a day over at the site of the rectory, meet with the local vicar and perhaps shed some light on the matter. On arrival in the village we made our way towards the church. It is a lovely old building of unknown dedication although the nave is undoubtedly Norman in origin. The churchyard is graced with the most beautifully manicured yew trees and massive spreading chestnut trees. We made our way round to the lych-gate, but as we strode along the path towards the church frontage I glimpsed a man walking in our general direction across the churchyard. When I turned my head to look at him more carefully he had disappeared amongst the yew trees. I was aware only of an individual with a broad forehead, thick eyebrows, thinning hair and extenuated features. We reached the church door and as we did so I looked along the path at right angles to the one we had just taken. I expected to see 'bushy eyebrows' but of him, there was no sign. I turned to see if he had changed direction and was behind us, but there was no one.

"My attention was diverted by the opening of the door in front of us. A dog collar proclaimed the vicar we had come to see. We explained who we were and he took us into the church. The interior was relatively plain; witness to the removal of any decoration by the Puritans. The Victorians had re–introduced the gothic element with beautiful stained glass windows, while carved pews replaced uncomfortable box pews. The whitewashed walls looked down on a peaceful scene. It was difficult to believe that any unquiet souls could roam this tranquil setting.

"The vicar, the Reverend Foyster, was an old man with a shock of pure white hair. He had a quiet, fruity voice with a slight lisp. He would not have been a man to overdramatise a situation. He said that he had heard of us and that he had, that day, put a letter in the post to us outlining the problem. Divine intervention seemed to have already managed a shortcut."

'A ghost has been frequently seen in the church-yard for some forty years now. There was nothing new in that but the visitations have become more frequent in the last few years culminating in a quite frightening manifestation. It happened at a service held here on Sunday 29th March 1978.'

"At this point Denholme interrupted the vicar and asked the nature of the previous churchyard visitations," continued Lucinda. "Mister Foyster replied that there had been two distinct phantoms seen; one took the form of a nun and had been seen many times in the church and indeed Borley Rectory, before and after its destruction. The other figure seen was that of a man. Foyster described him as being of medium height with a broad forehead, prominent eyebrows and had quite heavy features. 'I have seen him this very afternoon in the churchyard,' I said, sitting forward in my chair.

"My outburst caused Denholme to turn to me in some consternation because I had not mentioned the man to him. I replied that I had thought nothing of it at the time. Reverend Foyster excused himself for a few moments and left the room. He returned carrying a small photograph. He handed it to me and I nodded as I recognised the penetrating stare of the man I had seen. "Who is he?" I asked.

"Foyster replied that I was looking at the face of Harry Price."

'His appearances had been restricted to the churchyard but, of late, he had been seen inside the church. On the morning of the 29th I had commenced the morning service when suddenly every moveable object in the church toppled over: the offertory box; communion chalice; bread plate and wine pitcher all fell to the floor. This was accompanied by a great rush of wind through the church culminating in the appearance of the figure of Harry Price before the altar behind me.

'Women screamed and children cried, it was absolute chaos and this happened again on the next Sunday. People began to stay away from the church and to be honest I am currently at my wits end as to what to do about it all.

'There was a link between Harry Price and the date of this first visitation: Harry Price died on the 29th March 1948.'

"Silence fell as Foyster imparted this last little nugget," explained Lucinda. "I was the first to speak and said: 'I can only conclude from this that he is very unhappy and wants some wrong righted. There is only one way to find out and maybe resolve this issue and that is to conduct a séance in the church.'

"Foyster initially baulked at the idea. Eventually he agreed that it was the only way forward and that the diocese did not need to know about the matter, as this would be seen in the same light as a sugges- tion to reintroduce the ducking stool.

"Three evenings later we met at the church and I set up a table at the west end...the far end of the nave from the altar. Denholme, Reverend Foyster and I sat round a single oil lamp burning at the centre of the table. I sat with my back to the altar, Denholme sat on my right and Foyster to my left. The semi–darkness and the soft light from the lamp would encourage any spirit to manifest itself. We joined hands and waited. I closed my eyes and concentrated, emptying my mind.

"The night was a stormy one and the wind howled round the building. Occasionally the creaking sound of timbers could be heard as the old structure adjusted to the tempest. I entered a trance-like state and I rely upon the testimony of Denholme for much of the next part of the story.

"After about an hour the wind began to subside. As the church became quieter; Foyster became nervous and began staring into the darkened areas of the church expecting some horror to emerge. A slight sound near the altar caused both the men to turn in that direction. Foyster spoke first in a frightened whisper...

'Did you hear that?'

"Before Denholme was able to answer, the sound came again. This time louder than before and was immediately followed by other noises. The men realised that footsteps were slowly making their way along the aisle of the nave from the altar towards us."

Chapter 38

A Warning

"The sound of the footsteps was harsh and distinct as though the walker wore a pair of hard–soled shoes," continued Lucinda. "Denholme and Foyster turned to face whoever was approaching but could see no one. For a few moments silence reigned. The end post of the rearmost pew creaked. It was as though someone had leaned on it wearily. Silence fell once more in the darkness of that old country church.

"In my trance I felt a presence standing behind me. Denholme quietly reminded Foyster not to make any sound. To which I added: 'Are you here, Mr Price? Please make your presence known.'

"Silence once again fell but then a steady voice came out of the darkness. Denholme afterwards swore that he saw a movement in the shadows. The silhouette of a large head was moving against the faint light coming from the lancet window behind the altar.

"Then a voice asked: '*What do you want? I am in agony and you disturb me and cause me more pain.*'

"I then asked Mr Price why he was in so much pain.

"No sound followed so I suggested it was because reporters and academics had ridiculed his work at Borley.

"The silence confirmed what Denholme and I had discussed prior to the séance. This was a man whose reputation had been destroyed after his death by many in the field of psychical research.

"I continued and told Mr Price that I had faith in his powers. I was a clairvoyant and I need the help of a spirit guide in order to aid those who need me. If he helped me it would also be a way for him to continue the great work he started while he was alive.

"No answer emerged from the darkness but Denholme noticed that there had been a great change in the atmosphere of the old church. The darkness in the corners was not so dark and forbidding and the storm outside had abated completely. My companions later said that they felt less fearful. I, meanwhile, raised my face to the vaulted ceiling and thanked Harry Price, reassuring him the work he had started we would continue.

"I slumped down into my chair and, with the help of Denholme, began to emerge from my trance. Since then Borley church has been troubled by this particular phantom no more."

Collins had listened intently to the story and now he leaned forward. "Do you maintain that in the spiritual work you do, you have been, and still are, helped by the spirit of Harry Price?"

"Yes, from that day Harry Price has faithfully been my spirit guide," confirmed Lucinda. "His presence has been an inspiration and my reputation as a clairvoyant has grown as a result. Unfortunately, soon after the Borley incident my relationship with Denholme began to deteriorate. He became much more involved with his work in the diocese and six months later we split up as a couple. I think I will always love him and we will always be there for each other both professionally and personally but we have not been an item for over 15 years.

"Neither of us is to blame for the break. My work had sometimes isolated me from him. I joined the Society for Psychical Research and became a committee member, and that took up a lot of my time. It was there that I made contact with Julia Davenport, a very talented girl. I knew when I was told about her reaction to the The Eaves and the circumstances of her death that the entity in that house was a significant evil presence."

Lucinda was quiet for a moment and then she said: "Have you ever thought that, maybe, David Linde did not kill Julia but that something in that house may have been responsible?"

Collins rubbed his eyes with the backs of his hands and then replied with a question; "Why do you say that?"

"Something inhabits the house and seems to orchestrate everything that happens there. It must also have been a considerable presence in life. The research Denholme and I have done indicates that the history of the house abounds with evil happenings but nothing to explain the magnitude of the malignancy I detect there. We must be missing something."

Lucinda walked over to one of the sash windows in the room and drew back the thick velvet curtains. The grey light of dawn stole into the room and fell across the thoughtful features of Abel Collins causing him to, momentarily, squint his eyes. He and Lucinda had talked all night. He stood up and pulled his head back, stretching his arms to the side at the same time.

"Aaaagh...it is time I went and cleaned myself up and faced the music. I will probably be suspended, I think. That will give me time to do some more research. I don't think there is any chance that we will be able to perform the séance until the New Year now but that's not very long away. It's December 21st now, after all."

Lucinda nodded and asked: "What do you think of your new chief?"

"I presume you mean Dumairt?"

Lucinda nodded once more.

"I can't really comment on that, can I? I have not known him very long."

Lucinda changed the subject. "I have been thinking long and hard about the séance. I do not think it would be a good idea to include the Flaggs and Miriam Brock. This is dangerous territory and the séance is going to be very tricky. I will need to protect all of us against whatever appears. I would not want the responsibility for any more people than is strictly necessary. I only anticipate you, Denholme and myself...is that ok?"

"I agree with you," said Collins. "I must go now."

Lucinda caught his arm as he turned to go: "I will let you know when I have everything I need for the séance...and one other thing?"

Collins turned and eyed her expectantly.

"Can you find out what was recorded on the disks from the cameras in the garden?"

*****

Collins was ten minutes late for his meeting with Dumairt. Traffic from his home had been very slow moving and he had been further held up by a container lorry trying to reverse into a narrow lane in front of him. He was not in the best of moods when he entered Dumairt's office.

He found himself confronted not just by Dumairt but also by Chief Superintendent Townshend, who had taken charge of the situation and had seated himself behind the desk. Dumairt stood behind Townshend, half turned towards the window, an amused expression on his face. He retained the bandage round his head. Townshend did not stand on ceremony but launched into an attack: "You're bloody late, Collins, as well as being indolent and insolent. You have not been concentrating on the job in hand. Your efforts in tracing Linde have been abysmal. You seem to be hell bent on pursuing other totally fruitless lines of enquiry in this case, against the orders of Mr Dumairt here."

Dumairt still stared through the window across the nearby rooftops. Townshend continued: "We have tried to make allowances, appreciating how affected you have been by the death of Mr Kayne but you chose to continue working. The job has to be done. Currently the case is proving to be a total embarrassment to this force. What have you got to say for yourself?"

Collins stared across the desk and said: "There is more to this business than meets the eye. I had to follow every lead. It has got to the stage where even a bizarre lead may help us."

Dumairt pushed his body away from the window frame by tensing his shoulder muscles and turned to Collins. "Does that include getting involved with that pair of crackpot ghosthunters, Randolph and Theynard?" he snapped.

Collins restrained himself from saying anything. If he put his thoughts into words, no-one would believe him anyway. A month ago, or less, if he had known what was currently running through his head, he would probably have checked himself into a hospital.

"Well?"

Collins finally spoke: "Linde *is* a murderer and must be caught. I felt, however, that as our division and other police forces were on the hunt for him that I would spend my time more profitably pursuing other lines of enquiry. I also think Linde is not the only murderer involved in this affair."

Dumairt's neck began to redden. "He is the only person we know is a murderer. He killed Davenport, his wife and the personnel in the car in Vale Road. I reckon he possibly killed Letitia Preece, unless you know anything different?"

Collins retorted: "There are things in this case that go way beyond anything I have ever encountered and to ignore them would be a dereliction of duty."

Dumairt moved to the desk, leaned towards Collins and spoke, quietly and controlled, but with frightening menace: "You have been consorting for too long with total cranks. Also talking to previous residents of The Eaves, who have nothing to do with this case. You have been burrowing in old newspapers and archive files associated with the house going back to the year dot. How can any of that benefit the investigation?"

Collins wondered how Dumairt could possibly know. Before he could answer, Townshend took up the cudgels: "I am sorry, Collins, but none of this is good enough. You are suspended until further notice. I will need to consider what the next step will be. In the meantime, leave your warrant card on the desk."

"Before I go, can you tell me what was on the disks in the cameras set up by Miss Preece and Mr Theynard?"

Dumairt curled his lip but answered Collin's question: "Nothing at all. The disks were blank. This is, of course, no surprise...since Preece and Theynard were obviously incompetent as well as cranks."

Townshend stood up with an air of finality and while tamping his papers on the desk said: "Enough of this. Go home, Collins. We will contact you later."

"Do not go near the The Eaves," hissed Dumairt, as Collins turned to go. "To do so will be seen as tampering with evidence and you are in enough trouble as it is."

Collins was unlocking his car in the under-ground car park when Dumairt appeared at his shoulder: "Do not dabble in matters which you do not understand and do not concern you. I warn you that the sack will be a minor problem compared with what else might happen."

Collins watched Dumairt's back disappear through the double doors into the office and as he did so he wondered: "What the hell do you mean by that, Mr Dumairt?"

Chapter 39

Collins Unburdens Himself

Christmas came and went...and by the end of December Lucinda had acquired all she needed for the séance. She rang Abel Collins who seemed strangely subdued.

She asked if she could help. There followed several seconds of silence, then finally he spoke: "Can you and Denholme come round to see me? I am worried about something and I need to unburden myself to someone."

*****

Miriam Brock stared down at the glass in her right hand. In her left hand lay 20 or 30 small white tablets. A tear rolled down her cheek as she sat at her dining room table. She looked round the room and her eyes fell upon a small figurine on the sideboard before her. It was the figure of a small boy, a Hummel piece called 'Boots'. He was wearing a blue apron, carried a pair of boots under his right arm and a pair of ladies shoes in his left hand. A happy boy, his lips pursed as he whistled while he worked. It was not a particularly expensive ornament but looking at it broke Miriam's heart, for it belonged to her beloved friend Letitia.

A white sheet of paper lay on the table before her. Her gaze travelled down to it. She read it once more and transferred the tablets to her mouth. She swallowed water from the glass and then, after placing the glass on a coaster on the table, she moved over to the stereo system on a small table next to the sideboard and pressed 'play' on the CD player. At once, the strains of Mozart's *Requiem* began to play.

Miriam lay down on the settee, closed her eyes and waited for blessed oblivion. The heartrending strains of the *Lachrymosa* had hardly begun when her hand slipped to the floor and the tightness around her mouth relaxed.

I have never known such happiness as I have had with Letitia. All I had before meeting her was my career. I realise now that it was as of nothing compared with her love.

Now I therefore have nothing and my only hope is that in death we can be together again.

God forgive me.

*****

David Winslade worked as a maintenance engineer on the Thames Barrier. At lunchtime on December 31st he was walking his motorcycle home, as it had broken down. He was not in the best of moods as he had some way to go and the motorcycle was heavy. He was approaching an area of the Thames, which in his great-grandfather's day had been Thorneycrofts Wharf. He had been waterman and had found a dead body in this part of the Thames a 130 years or so before.

Winslade rested the bike against a wall on the towpath. He leaned against the wall and sighed. He delved into his pocket for a cigarette. It was as he lit up that he saw the bundle of clothes floating at the water's edge. He drew in his first breath of smoke and felt the dizzying effect of the first dose of nicotine of the day. Through the haze of his dizziness it seemed to him that there was something lighter in colour attached to the bundle. The haze cleared and he saw a carnival mask coloured yellow and purple.

"It must be a Guy left over from a bonfire," he muttered to himself.

His whispered words ceased in a sharp intake of breath. The cigarette dropped from his lips. His eyes widened as he realised that the bundle was not just a ball of clothes. There was no mask: he was staring at the bloated face of a dead man.

*****

Denholme Theynard was surprised at the appearance of Abel Collins. Collins looked tired, unshaven and pale and his eyes had dark circles round them. There was no smile of greeting as he gestured him and Lucinda to enter his house. They followed the round—shouldered detective into his dining room. There were papers everywhere. Photographs were liberally distributed around the chairs and floor. Collins hurriedly made space for the pair to sit down, collecting the papers together and laid them down on the coffee table in the centre of the room.

Lucinda stared around the room. It was tastefully furnished but quite sparse. There were shelves of books from floor to ceiling on both sides of the fireplace. The titles indicated a surprisingly thoughtful man – for a policeman – she reasoned. Joseph Conrad, Graham Greene and Evelyn Waugh were well represented in his collection. This room, however, had never had the advantage of a woman's touch and most items present were functional rather than decorative.

Collins voice was hoarse. "Drink anyone?"

The two visitors refused and Collins slumped into an armchair and reached for a whisky glass on the coffee table. He took a pull on the spirit. He rubbed his stubbly chin as he prepared to begin. Before he did, Lucinda spoke; in part to break the tension created by Collins' nervousness but also to assure him that both Denholme and she were on his side.

"I have explained to Denholme that you know about our history and he is happy for the three of us to work together," she said. "Please go ahead, you are among friends."

"I have had some time to think in the last few days," began Collins. "I am currently under suspension, as I expected. It has allowed me to go through the case papers which I copied before I left the office. I have also been reading Mr Kayne's notebook and documents found in a trunk in the loft of The Eaves. Altogether, they seemed to strike a chord but, for the life of me, I could not think what it all meant. You, Lucinda, said something when we last spoke that really set me on the road to realising what is going on. You remarked that we were missing something that would explain the magnitude of the malignancy in that house."

Lucinda nodded in assent and leaned forward in anticipation.

"Kayne and I discovered a diary in the trunk I mentioned earlier and I think that it was written by this man."

At this point Collins held up a photograph, which he had retrieved, from the heap of documents on the table. The image was of the young moustached man at a table reading a book

"We found this photo in the trunk also," he explained. "On the back of it were written the letters 'MJD'. I think they are the initials of the man."

"The diary talked about a woman called Annie who was pregnant. Annie gave birth then died from childbed fever and the baby was taken from The Eaves by a man called Gull. I wondered who this Gull might be and I keyed the name into a search engine on the internet with no useful result. I thought more about it and then wondered if he might be a doctor. After all, he had taken the child and was probably present during the girl's confinement. Both of these increased the likelihood of him being a physician. I keyed 'Dr Gull' into the computer, and in the list of results was a reference to a Sir William Withey Gull, Baronet, 1816–1890, doctor to Her Majesty, Queen Victoria."

Denholme Theynard smiled. "Dr Gull was implicated in the most savage murder of the 19th century, Mr Collins."

Collins continued "Yes, but he was not the murderer. The killer was the writer of the diary and he is the monster in The Eaves. Look at this entry in the diary..."

January 17th
Mother calls upon me to avenge my "sister". She says she will help me but it is I who must do the deed. The women who must pay are known to her. I must obey her for she is my mother and I love her. I can do it – I know how and the revenge must be bloody.

"He was, and I suppose is, Jack the Ripper," said Collins.

Chapter 40

MJD

"There are things you do not know which fit the Ripper's *modus operandi*," continued Collins. "Body parts being removed – in the case of Julia, her heart and sexual organs were taken. This fact had me doing further research on the internet and I discovered the pathologists report covering the Mary Kelly murder. She represented the last of the Jack the Ripper murders and took place on November 9th, 1888 in Miller's Court in White–chapel. The report is an exact replica of that produced by our pathologist.

"The replication of detail is remarkable. Every cut, every wound and even the physical attitude of the victims were the same. Julia's demise is either a copycat murder by David Linde...or else something more mysterious has happened."

"We do know that David Linde is a murderer because Annie Linde was undoubtedly murdered by him. The self-same organs had also been removed from Annie Linde's body, which is another link with the Julia Davenport murder."

Lucinda Randolph spoke up. "Have either of these sets of organs been found?"

"Yes," confirmed Collins. "One set was found in the trunk in the loft of The Eaves. They belonged to Annie Linde whose body we dug up in the garden of Linde's previous address in Vale Road. The body parts were wrapped in an oilcloth pouch and were contained in a leather satchel. What is more the parts of both murder victims had been cut out in the same way – the cuts matched exactly according to the pathologist."

"This all points, fairly conclusively, to Linde. At least that is what one would think if one did not know what we know," interrupted Denholme Theynard. "Did you find Julia's heart and sexual parts at The Eaves?"

"No, but I still think, as you both do, that there is more to this than just Linde carrying out copycat murders," reasoned Collins. "I know that I am supposed to be a hardnosed police officer and a logical thinker. However, the other events at The Eaves, its history, your experiences, both of you, the death of Mr Kayne and your feelings anyway, Lucinda, convince me that something else is at work here. I mention the death of David Kayne specifically because Linde could not have killed him. We were holding him in custody at the time and all the evidence points to Kayne having been murdered. The only alternative is suicide, but I know that, despite the recent death of his wife, he was not capable of such a thing. Anyway, suicides do not throw themselves backwards out of windows. I do not believe Linde murdered Letitia Preece either. The last place he would go back to would be The Eaves. He knew he was a hunted man and that there was a considerable police presence at the house."

Denholme Theynard spoke quietly. "Were there any other items found at the murder scenes or in your loft trunk that might give us a clue to Lucinda's monster?"

"There were certainly some strange findings up in the loft. Firstly, when we started to open the trunk we had some difficulty because the hinges had rusted solid and yet it must have been opened recently for the relatively fresh organs to have been placed in there. Dr Bond told me that when he examined the organs there were particles of soil contaminating them. The soil was peculiar to that found at Linde's old address. Someone had disinterred the body at a later stage before mutilating it further. It still could have been David Linde but I have my doubts. I think that there is someone or some*thing* else involved…and there is another point."

Abel Collins thought for some moments and then began thumbing through the copies of the case documents on the coffee table. Eventually he found what he was looking for. "This other photograph was also found in the trunk. I believe it to show the mother of the man you have already seen, and the girl Annie referenced in the diary. The satchel containing the body parts was also monogrammed. 'MJD' was embossed in gold lettering on the flap. You will note that 'MJD' was also written on the back of the photograph of the man."

"A small silver medallion, possibly originally attached to a watch chain and embossed with the letters 'MJD,' was found clasped in Julia Davenport's dead hand. 'MJD' seems to be a recurring theme…"

Collins stopped in midflow and stared, deep in

thought, sightlessly in front of him. Eventually he spoke. "Well, I'm blowed!"

"Are you alright, Mr Collins?" asked Lucinda, putting her hand on Collins' arm.

Collins sat bolt upright, becoming very animated. He shuffled through the papers on the table but could not find what he sought. He stood up and ran out of the room, returning a few moments later with a small black covered notebook. He consulted it for a few moments, thumbing through the pages, before he spoke.

"Rill Place has not always been the name of the road in which The Eaves stands. In 1890, or thereabouts, it was changed. This fact was mentioned in a letter from the period inserted in some deeds also found in the trunk. The name was changed because a 'monster,' as it was described in the letter, had lived in the house. An angry letter was written by the resident to his solicitor.

"The writer maintained that he had been sold the property without being told of the existence of the 'monster' residing there beforehand. This 'monster' was said to have left in body but remained in the form of an evil spirit. While I was searching the local newspapers for the 1880s, I found a reference to someone who lived in The Eaves not long before the writer of the letter. The Eaves simply had the address '9 Eliot Place' at that time. This person had been elected as treasurer and honorary secretary of the Blackheath Cricket, Football and Lawn Tennis Company. His name was..."

Abel Collins' research findings were suddenly interrupted by Denholme Theynard, who interpolated the name..."Montague Druitt...and I would be astounded if his middle initial was not 'J'. There is your 'MJD'."

"Yes, Theynard. That realisation was what came to me a few moments ago."

The three were quiet for a moment until Lucinda broke the silence. "How did you know that name, Denholme?"

Denholme smiled and turned to her. "Druitt was a young man who I knew lived in Blackheath in the 1880s. I had quite forgotten him but now I remember that he was one of the chief suspects in the Jack the Ripper case. I believe he committed suicide by drowning himself in the Thames at the end of the year of the Ripper murders. Rumours apparently circulated around Blackheath about him but no one before has ever connected Druitt with events in the house after the Ripper murders. The rumours obviously became fact because it must have been decided that the name of the road should be changed because of its association. In the same way that shortly after the grisly murders perpetrated by Christie at 10 Rillington Place, in west London, the entire street was destroyed and in its place today stands Bartle Road. In Gloucester, 25 Cromwell Street was demolished and the bricks from which it was made were ground to dust because of their association with Fred West and his heinous crimes. Everyone, not just the clairvoyants, can sense and cannot live with the residual evil in a house linked with terrible murders."

"Why was this Eliot Place/Rill Place name change not published in the national newspapers, do you think?" asked Collins.

"If no one had worked it out then the local authority were not going to tell anyone. In fact, nobody in Blackheath said anything because it would have been bad for business. Houses in the area would not have sold and why publicise it? The police were not interested. Better to hush up the whole thing, change the name and pretend the whole business did not happen. After all, the local council may have known about the other horrors... even more reason to keep quiet."

Theynard paused for a moment before saying: "As for the missing body parts, maybe only Mr Montague Druitt knows the whereabouts of those items."

Collins cleared his throat and spoke: "Mr Kayne, I think, had worked out that part of the puzzle. In the bedroom, from which he fell, the SOCOs found a note on the floor. Kayne had written one thing on that paper, '1888'."

Chapter 41

Jigsaw

Abel Collins poured the coffee he had just made. Their current discussion had served to change the atmosphere and the detective had regained some of his old enthusiasm.

"Sugar, Denholme? I am glad that you came round today, particularly on New Year's Eve," he said, appreciatively. "I had all the pieces of the puzzle at my disposal but could not see how to put it all together. Talking to you two has helped me to do that, or at least to make a start."

Collins continued: "I had not made some of the connections in the case. I certainly had not seen the link between 'MJD' and Druitt. Strange that…I had accessed the website which comprehensively explores the Ripper murders but I had concentrated on the death of Mary Kelly and had missed the references there to Druitt. Reviewing the case with you allowed the penny to drop. I can only thank you."

At that moment the phone in the hallway rang and Collins went out to answer it.

Sergeant Dove sounded harassed and he spoke quickly. "In a bit of a hurry, sir. Thought you would like to know about a new development. Linde has been found drowned in the Thames."

Collins jaw dropped and he put his head round the door of the dining room and relayed the news to the other two. He then turned his attention back to Dove. "How long had he been dead and where was the body found?"

"Dr Bond estimates that the corpse had been in the water approximately ten days. There is no evidence of any injuries pointing to murder. The body was about a mile down river from the Thames Barrier. An engineer who works at the Barrier discovered it, name of Windslade. I must go now. We have had an urgent call to check on Dr Brock. She failed to turn up at an important meeting at the hospital. She cannot be raised by telephone or by neighbours knocking on her door."

Collins thanked Dove, replaced the receiver and returned to the others. They were in deep conversation about Linde's death.

Denholme was saying: "There are two possible reasons for his death: one is his utter despair leading to his suicide; the other may be a more sinister one – maybe he was removed."

Collins entered the conversation. "He must have died not long after the police hunt for him began. He knew the game was up and that he was going to go down for multiple murders. There was, however, something strange about the killings leading to his escape. Those were out of character and we never did establish how he got hold of a gun while he was on remand. None of that made sense to me at the time."

They all sat quietly for a while.

The churchman rubbed his temple thoughtfully. "You have internet access, I believe, Mr Collins?"

Collins nodded and Theynard continued, "Let us

explore your Ripper website and see if further research will yield any more helpful clues to this affair."

They all rose and Lucinda moved towards the door saying: "While you boys are playing your computer games I have final preparations to make for the séance. Can you ascertain if we will be able to move into the house, Mr Collins? We will need several hours to prepare the house and ourselves. I intend to take no risks...to do so would compromise our lives and worse. The devil is quite literally in the detail."

Collins agreed and the three went about their tasks, each feeling the first coil of fear and apprehension in their stomachs. Lucinda left the house, agreeing to return that evening at seven.

*****

Lucinda spent the afternoon making a wax prepared from Holy Wafers. Having completed the task she laid out all the impedimenta needed for the exorcism. She had discussed the intricacies of the whole process with Denholme Theynard who, as an ordained priest of the Roman Catholic faith, would be taking the service.

She ticked off the items on a list they had prepared, at the same time imagining each step of the ritual to ensure that she forgot nothing. They were a strange array of items: Garlic flowers; pieces of chalk; Holy Water; hyssop twigs; a censer; candelabra; a Bible and a number of crucifixes. Finally, she grabbed a small paraffin burner, a gas stove and a metal dish from a cupboard in the hall and placed them in a bag. The bag joined the other items on the table.

Lucinda stared down at them, worried about possible omissions but she had forgotten nothing. Still she stood staring at them and began to mouth some words: "Our Father, who art in heaven..."

*****

Lucinda knocked on the door of Collins' house, just as the clock in his kitchen chimed seven. The door opened. He looked flushed but at the same time more refreshed than when she had seen him last. He had shaved, showered and looked like he had caught up with some sleep.

He invited her in and led her to the dining room. Papers were still scattered across the floor but the previous atmosphere of gloom no longer pervaded the place. Theynard was seated in an armchair sipping tea. He stood up as she entered and placed the cup on a small nearby table. He kissed her on both cheeks.

"You both look a good deal happier than when I saw you last," smiled Lucinda.

Collins offered her tea or coffee. She refused. Then Collins began to apprise her of latest developments in their research.

"We found a photograph of Druitt which is a precise match of the one found in the loft. Druitt is pictured seated at a table, his head resting on his right hand reading a book. We also know his full name...Montague John Druitt. This tallies with the initials 'MJD', engraved on the watch chain medallion found in Julia's dead hand.

At this point Theynard interrupted. "We have not only confirmed the identity of the mysterious 'MJD', we also think that he *was* probably Jack the

Ripper. It is not a positive identification and would not stand up in any court of law but it is close enough for me."

"Druitt writes in the diary, well, we think that he wrote it, that he used 'his metal' on a girl he later discovered was Annie Millwood," explained Collins. "On the 'Casebook' website, which is the most comprehensive 'Ripper' site on the 'net', she is described as having been attacked on February 25th,1888. She was not killed but it was a knife attack and the diary entry is recorded on the same day. It is six months before the accepted Ripper murders but it has many similarities to a murder that took place later – that of Martha Tabram. Many regard her as the first of the true 'Jack the Ripper' killings. It seems logical that when Druitt encountered Millwood he had not killed before and was not experienced enough or sure of himself to carry it through.

"Annie Millwood was a prostitute, Martha Tabram was a prostitute," continued Collins. "They were of a similar age: Millwood was 38 and Tabram was 39. They were attacked only a few minutes walk apart. Both were attacked with knives. Both women were also subjected to repeated stab wounds to the lower abdomen.

"In the loft diary the names of the sisters of the diarist were mentioned: Ethel, Edith and Georgiana. A census record from 1881 is included on the 'Casebook' website for the Druitt family when they lived in Wimbourne, Dorset. Druitt had three sisters called Ethel, Edith and Georgiana. This I think is the final confirmation of the identity of 'MJD' as Montague John Druitt.

"One other fact that also points to Druitt being

involved are the embossed initials on the trunk in the loft: "AH". Druitt's mother's maiden name was Ann Harvey. The trunk may have therefore belonged to his mother. Not a key fact but an indication we are on the right track."

Theynard and Collins fell silent to await Lucinda's reaction. She was amazed at the ground they had covered in such a short time and said so. Further discussion was cut short, however, by the ringing of the telephone. Collins picked up the receiver and his companions watched as the deep furrows of a frown crossed his face.

"It isn't murder then, Dove...you are sure? How long had she been dead?"

Collins nodded to himself and pursed his lips before finally asking. "Has everyone pulled out of Rill Place now?"

Theynard and Lucinda Randolph stared expectantly as Collins replaced the receiver and addressed his companions. "Miriam Brock has been found dead at her house. She apparently took an overdose of barbiturates."

"Not another murder, surely?" interrupted a shocked Lucinda.

"No, she left a suicide note saying that the loss of Miss Preece was too much to bear."

"It may not be directly attributable to Druitt but he did it as surely as if he poured the water for her to swallow the tablets," fumed Lucinda, unable to keep the bitterness from her voice.

She added: "He represents a powerful evil, which has prospered for a long time. Who knows when he may come to call on each one of us?"

She had only just voiced this fear when the doorbell began to ring. They all jumped. A dark figure was outlined by the light of the street lamps on the frosted glass window of the front door as Abel Collins made his way, with some trepidation, down the hall.

Chapter 42

An Unexpected Arrival

Collins was in normal circumstances a very pragmatic individual – not given to flights of imagination – but he swore that when he opened the door he beheld the moustached figure of Druitt waiting for him. In fact, the light from the hall fell on the frightened face of Jim Flagg, unshaven and somewhat dishevelled. For an instant, the apparent sight of Druitt wakened in Collins a disturbing realisation, a recognition that, as soon as it entered his brain, disappeared. No matter how he tried, it would not come back to him.

"Hello, Mr Collins. Sorry to disturb you but I had to talk to you. I went to see Miriam Brock, after I heard about Letitia Preece, to commiserate with her and found the place surrounded by police. A Sergeant Dove told me about you and, rightly or wrongly, gave me your address. He also said you were no longer on the case but he then questioned me about the state of mind of Dr Brock. It transpires that Miriam Brock has taken her own life."

"Go home, Mr Flagg. You are correct in that I am no longer officially on the case, as explained by Dove. You will need to talk to Mr Dumairt, who is now in charge of the operation."

"I can't go home because I am afraid. It is as simple as that. My wife has had a nervous breakdown and is in a private clinic. One of my best friends is a mass murderer on the run. Julia Davenport, Miriam Brock and Letitia Preece are all dead. The detective initially in charge of the case has died and to cap it all, Mr Collins, my agent rang me this evening to say that Sam Plaid was killed in a road accident in the States today. He was a client of mine and was at that first dinner party at our house after Linde moved into The Eaves. I am either going mad...or I am next." At this point, Flagg sank to his knees and broke down in tears.

Collins stepped forward and raised the wretched man to his feet. He helped him inside and called to Theynard for help. Together, they led Flagg into the dining room and Lucinda fetched a glass of water from the kitchen. After a few minutes, and some kind words he began to collect himself. It was obvious that he had had a terrible time with his wife Jane since they had learned of Annie Linde's murder. Jane had been unable to accept it and further developments had only added to her instability and contributed to his current state.

After some coaxing and further water to drink, Jim Flagg began to pull himself together. He remained quite pale and he looked very tired. There was however some fire in his eyes and he insisted on hearing the new developments. At first the trio were unwilling to upset him further but, Collins thought, he had to know sometime: "I have some further bad news. Before I explain, you should know that we intend to confront the thing that lurks in The Eaves head on. We now think we know the nature of the manifestation."

"What the hell is the bad news?" asked Flagg, his hands gripping the water glass more tightly with nervous anticipation.

Lucinda took the empty glass and Collins spoke quietly. "David Linde is dead. He was found drowned in the Thames. It is believed that he may have committed suicide."

Lucinda laid the glass aside and took Flagg's two hands in hers. "You know many of the stories surrounding The Eaves. You heard what Denholme and I have discovered. You listened to some of the tales told by people who have lived in that house. I know you have always been a diehard sceptic but I think even you are coming round to the fact that the evil in that building spreads its influence way beyond the boundaries of Rill Place. We are going to do our best to put an end to it. The risks are huge and we may not survive – our research tells us that the original source of the evil was born in the Middle Ages. It has gained strength over the centuries by drawing to it and using people who are themselves reprehensible. In the 19th century, the evil increased a hundredfold. By confronting this powerful entity we may look directly, quite literally, into the mouth of hell."

Flagg stared into her eyes and nodded. His tear–stained face was a window into a beaten man. "I...I know you are right. I have known the truth since the meeting in Denholme's house when Mr Roylance told us his story. My cynicism may have cost me my wife. Maybe I could have done something about this from the beginning, if only I had not been so blind. Now I have lost virtually everything, my friends are dead and my wife is so ill there may not be a way back. I *can* do something now. What do you intend to do to fight this thing? Whatever it is, I will help you."

Lucinda let go of his hands and began to explain the plan. "I was going, as a first stage, to hold a séance in the house in order to establish the precise nature of the evil. That, I have decided, is far too dangerous particularly if some of those present are not knowledgeable enough. They would be used against Denholme and myself. I now intend to perform, with Denholme, the act of exorcism in The Eaves. To do so will require us to clean the house thoroughly and to seal all openings before we perform the act. I do not think you should be there because it is far too dangerous."

Flagg had begun to protest when the front doorbell rang. They all fell silent as the sound of the bell once more rang through the house. Without warning, a line of Macbeth ran through Collins' head as he stood up and headed towards the door.

Hear it not, Duncan, for it is a knell that summons thee to heaven or to hell.

The shadow across the frosted glass of the door revealed nothing to the detective except perhaps a sense of foreboding. He opened the door and there before him was his boss, Superintendent Dumairt, seeming as elegant and supercilious as ever. He had almost a contrite air as he shuffled from one foot to the other.

"Collins, I am worried and I need to talk to you. I may have been somewhat hasty in my condemnation of your methods. There seems to be something going on that I do not understand. I am, to be honest, out of my depth. I think you may be on the right lines in that something beyond our understanding is operating. May I come in to talk through the matter with you?"

This was a new Dumairt who entered the house and as Collins gazed at his back, he wondered how the former would react when he found the trio sitting in the dining room. Collins hesitated because the same feeling descended on him that had occurred when Flagg had stood at the door. He looked out into the night and saw the first whirling flakes of snow falling in the darkness and a cold wind blew against his cheek. He turned and moved forward quickly to block the path of Dumairt into the back room where the others sat quietly awaiting developments.

"Come into the front room."

Collins took Dumairt's coat to hang on a hat–stand in the hall. The front room was furnished quite differently from the other ground floor room. The floor consisted of varnished wood. A large oak table stood in the centre of the room, around which were distributed four oak chairs and two carvers, made from the same wood. The two men sat down. Dumairt spoke first. "You are convinced that there is a supernatural evil and you and your friends intend to destroy it...is that not so?"

Chapter 43

Mr Dumairt Insists

Collins was dumbstruck for a few moments but Dumairt continued talking. He collected his thoughts: "I have had time to think about our last meeting and I realise I was being unfair. It was the incident with the disks which changed my attitude," said Dumairt.

Collins looked mystified "What disks?"

"The disks from the cameras set up by Miss Preece and the Reverend Denholme Theynard in the garden. I could not understand why they were blank. I had all the equipment including the disks checked by our people and they said that there should have been no problem with any of them. We should have had a recording. That caused me to check other things such as the detail surrounding the deaths of Superintendent Kayne and Julia Davenport. Several things do not add up and are not explained except by some paranormal phenomenon."

Dumairt paused to run his hand across his brow: "I don't mind telling you, I am at my wits end. That is why I decided to come to talk to you and to apologise. I was very harsh on you before and I hope that I am man enough to eat the necessary humble pie. I know that you are planning something at The Eaves, and probably with Lucinda Randolph and Denholme Theynard. I read between the lines of phone calls you have had with Sergeant Dove. I gather that you are also up to speed with the latest developments."

Collins spoke warily. "I know that Dr Brock and David Linde are both dead. I learned recently that Sam Plaid, an American who had attended the initial meetings at or around the time of the death of Julia Davenport, has met with an accident and is also dead."

Dumairt spoke and the bombshell came: "You think that much of what is happening is traceable to a suspect in the Jack the Ripper murders 130 years ago...is that not so?"

Collins was dumbfounded and he could not reply for a few moments. Dumairt did not wait for him. "Come now, Collins, I merely followed the same trail as you did...the diary, the *modus operandi* involved in the killing of Julia Davenport compared with that of Mary Jane Kelly in 1888. All of it points in the same direction. It all culminates in the fact that M J Druitt lived in Blackheath and was found in the Thames on the December 31st, 1888 on exactly the same day of the year as Mr Linde was found. All these coincidences began to make me think...those and the fact that every time I walked into that bloody house the hairs on the back of my neck stood on end. There is something in that house and you and your friends intend to confront it – is that not so?"

Collins voice came as a croak. "The same day as Druitt...Druitt died in the Thames?"

"Druitt died in the Thames and at the same place

as Linde. Linde was also found, coincidentally, by a direct descendant of the man who found Druitt."

This last point caused Collins to make a conscious decision. "I think it is time you met the others in the back room. Before we go in, do I get my warrant card back?"

"I think you misunderstand the position here. I am going out on a limb for you and that separates us from the Establishment. Chief Superintendent Townshend has your warrant card and I am certainly not going to ask him to return it...yet. This is all part of a piece of private enterprise on our part and nothing to do with the police. If I mentioned this in official circles we would both be consigned to a secure unit somewhere, I assure you. No, you must stay as *persona non grata*. I do believe that you and your associates are correct in your conclusions about the house and I would like to help you. If we can resolve this case then I can promise you a way out of your problems with Townshend."

Collins said nothing but turned away and led Dumairt into the room where the other three were waiting. As they entered, it was evident that Lucinda was unwell as she held her head and leaned heavily against the coffee table before her. As she did so, a cup and saucer standing on the edge of the table fell to the ground. Theynard immediately stood up, took her arm and led her to a nearby armchair before she fell.

Once again, a glass of water was poured and this time administered to Lucinda by Collins. Although pale, she seemed to recover herself. "Sorry, everyone, I think it must be the stress. You must understand that despite being an experienced medium I have never encountered a situation like this. There have been many people hurt and so much unhappiness."

Superintendent Dumairt sat down before Lucinda and spoke: "I am glad you are feeling better now, Miss Randolph. I hope it was not my arrival that upset you. I have explained to Collins here that I have only come here in the hope of helping.

"The more I study the situation at The Eaves, the more I realise that there is indeed something paranormal at work there. I have no wish to interfere with any investigations you decide, as a group, to initiate. I would like to lend a hand and maintain an open–minded approach to the problem while doing so."

At first silence reigned and Theynard placed his arm around his old friend, Lucinda, in order to reassure her with his presence. This at least had the effect of diverting attention from the obvious fact that no-one wanted Dumairt there. The latter continued: "I understand the fact that you are all wary of my motives. I assure you that I am sincere in my wish to help. I have examined all aspects of this case and there is but one inevitable conclusion. It is unpalatable to me, I have to confess, but the blank disks clinched it for me."

He went on to speak about the testing of the disks from the recording equipment set up by Letitia Preece, and the fact that Linde had drowned in the Thames on the same day of the year as Druitt.

Collins spoke first: "Theynard, Miss Randolph and I have made our plans. There would be too many people if you and Mr Flagg came. It will be dangerous enough for us three and we may not survive."

Lucinda Randolph stood up. She went towards the mantelpiece, deep in thought, then turned and spoke. "Mr Collins is correct in what he says because I am responsible for the safety of you all. I know that you will say that you are adults and as such are masters of your own fate but that is not the point. I am the expert and your presence could cause me additional worries which might make me vulnerable. It might be enough to allow the thing in that house to gain the upper hand. I need all my powers to be directed at this entity. Nothing must divert me and your presence could cause me additional worries which might make me vulnerable and lower my guard."

Dumairt listened to what she had to say and his features hardened. His voice came as almost a whisper and the menace in it was palpable. "I think you have all misunderstood my position here. My offer of help is not negotiable. The Eaves is still under police jurisdiction. I say who goes in and out of the place."

Chapter 44

Decision at Sundown

Collins spoke first. "Mr Dumairt is correct – we have to include him in our group. He will be in a position to clear the way for us and I am sure that he will be no hindrance to us."

Miss Randolph was beside herself and Theynard was purple with rage but managed to find words: "Good grief man, we might as well sell tickets. This is no way to conduct the operation we are planning."

Collins raised his hand to calm the situation.

He noted, out of the corner of his eye, that Dumairt was staring impassively at the floor as the initial reaction to his ultimatum died down. Lucinda Randolph spoke with some emotion: "This is blackmail and, apart from the reasons I have already stated, we must enter that house as one. Any antipathy within the group will be a weakness to be exploited by the powers present there. It will act as a hole in our defences and this weakness will kill us all. That is why I was initially worried about Mr Flagg's inclusion: his cynicism in the past could have led to our downfall."

"My cynicism is long gone; it has been beaten

out of me by events," said a tired Flagg, brushing the hair from his eyes.

Dumairt was about to speak again but Collins interjected: "Look, Lucinda, we have no choice. Dumairt has all four aces. I suggest that we set up a plan to enter the place with all of us present. You, Lucinda, said before Dumairt appeared that you have much work to do...how long do you think you will need to complete your preparations. You said something about another 24 hours?"

Collins' face betrayed no change of expression as he spoke. Only his eyes, flicking sideways towards Dumairt, showed any trace of his intentions. Lucinda saw the glance and took her lead from it.

"Very well. I can see that we have Hobson's choice," she added. "I will need another day and probably an additional eight hours or so for preparations. We must start at daybreak in order to complete preparations and carry out the exorcism before nightfall. When the night comes I cannot be sure of containing what may come at us. If we are still there after midnight then God help us."

Lucinda glanced at Denholme Theynard and he knew that look so well. It told him, silently, that further protestations were unnecessary so he kept his own counsel. Flagg seemed slightly bemused.

Dumairt's expression softened as he started to speak. "I must say that I think you are taking the most sensible route. I do not intend to cause antipathy within the group. I am head of the investigating unit and, although this operation is all highly unorthodox, I need to be present at the denouement. If nothing else, it will get you off the hook with the chief, Collins. I will take the flak. When and where do we meet?"

Collins stood up with an air of finality. "To allow Lucinda plenty of time I would suggest that we meet here at 6am the day after tomorrow, January 2nd."

Lucinda also rose and smiled. "You mean tomorrow, Abel. It is just after midnight...Happy New Year."

As she spoke, sounds of ringing church bells and the crackle of fireworks came from outside the house. All the parties shook hands. After some discussion about how dreadful the year had been, they hoped that the next one would be better. Dumairt said he would see them later. He then left the house.

Collins waited for Dumairt's car to gun into life and for the sound of it to recede into the distance. He turned, closed the door and gestured to the remaining three to return into the room they had recently vacated. He knew that as he re-entered the room they would besiege him with protestations about Dumairt's inclusion, which they did, all with the exception of Lucinda.

Theynard was particularly vexed. "We don't need another day, Lucinda is ready now. Why did you ignore her reaction to your suggestion that we restrict numbers and particularly the inclusion of him, Dumairt?"

Lucinda's calm voice broke in. "You saw my look, Denholme. I do not think we are waiting a day are we, Mr Collins?"

Abel Collins smiled enigmatically. "No, Lucinda, you are quite correct. We enter the house early in the morning, without Mr Dumairt. I know that the house is now free of any police presence because Dove told me as much when he phoned earlier. I will go to the house in a few moments to reconnoitre the ground. I would suggest that the rest of you get a couple of hours' sleep. You can bed down here while I am away."

"Can I come with you, Abel?" asked Lucinda. "We can go on to my place to collect my equipment. We must then have time to prepare ourselves. No one must eat anything from now on and drink water only. This is part of the cleansing process and is most important."

Collins then turned to Jim Flagg who had remained silent during all the discussion. "I think, on reflection, that you have paid a considerable personal price. You have earned the right to be with us on this expedition and I know that you are no longer a sceptic. What do you think, Lucinda?"

"If Mr Flagg wants to be part of our group, he will be welcome," said Lucinda, turning to Denholme, who nodded his agreement.

Flagg made a sad smile, thanked them all and asked if he could take a bath before he slept. Lucinda said that they should all do the same as part of the cleansing process.

Collins went off to the kitchen to collect a torch while Lucinda put on her coat and scarf.

She glanced out of the dining room window and noted the whirling flakes of snow, which at times were whipped horizontally by a howling gale. The snow already lay an inch thick on the lawn and was beginning to settle on the trees outside. She shivered but not from cold or the sight of the snow. Lucinda knew that only Theynard and she realised the dangers they were facing in the house. Each time a death linked to the house had occurred the evil within would grow. God only knew what would be unleashed if they failed in their quest.

"We will be helped by Harry Price, you know," said Lucinda, turning her head as Theynard placed his hand on her shoulder.

"Don't take any risks," he said. "Remember that you will be unprotected tonight. Please don't go inside the house? I want you to promise me."

"Don't worry, Denholme. I have retained my senses," stressed Lucinda, kissing him on the cheek. "We are only checking that all the police have gone. I need Abel to help me with my gear anyway."

"Ok, Lucinda, let's go," said Collins, standing in the doorway, well wrapped up in a tartan scarf and heavy coat. His face was set in a determined expression.

Collins spoke to Flagg and Theynard. "Lucinda has already emphasised the need to start early, so we will be back in time to leave for The Eaves at 5am. See you later."

Sleep for Flagg and Theynard would not come easily.

Chapter 45

The Eaves in the Snow

They drove in silence. The road conditions required Collin's full concentration. Snow whirled before him and the lights gave the impression that the car was travelling through a long black tunnel with snow as a layer of mobile polka dots on the inner surface. Each junction had to be negotiated with care.

Eventually they turned into Rill Place and drew slowly past The Eaves. It looked completely deserted and if windows reveal the soul of a building, these stared back lifelessly. Snow covered the two lions on the entrance pillars. There was no sign of any police presence and no cordon was in place. Collins slowed to a halt 20 yards further down the road and switched off the engine. He turned to Lucinda. "I will just go and give the place the 'once over.' I won't be long."

"Have you still got a key?" she asked. "Or are we going to have to break in when we return?"

"Thought of that," said Collins. "I kept the spare door keys which I found in a cupboard when we searched the house after Kayne's death."

He drew a ring holding a Yale and Squire keys from his pocket as he spoke. Lucinda reminded him:

"I promised Denholme that I would not enter the house until after daybreak."

"Don't worry. I only want to look round the garden, that's all. I think everybody has gone but after Dumairt's statement tonight I don't want to risk any possibility of there being any police presence when we do this."

Before Lucinda could speak, Collins had shut his door, left the car and headed down the road with Lucinda's voice trailing unheard behind him.

"I think I would like to come with…"

She exited the car and closed its door in time to see Collins turn into The Eaves drive. She looked straight ahead. She walked and listened to the rusty hinge sound of her feet in the thickening layer of fallen snow. She arrived at the two pillars and their covered lions atop them. She turned to face the dark shape of the house. The tiny amount of light reflected pallidly from the front windows, which stared blankly back at her.

She was not fooled by their pretended innocence. Her last visit had removed any scales from her eyes. The silence was palpable; snow always imparts a unique brand of eerie silence to any landscape, even an innocent one. The small hours are always quiet, but this was different. Something waited in that silence…that white–blanketed brooding silence.

Lucinda moved forward and noted, as she did so, that before her showing up dimly in the nocturnal gloom were the rapidly disappearing prints of Collins' feet. She followed in his wake in the direction of the side gate, which was slightly ajar. It tapped gently against its latch. Ahead she glimpsed the flash of torchlight as Collins made his inspection.

Snow was still fitfully whirling about her as she made her way down the side of the house. She did not know why she had wanted to go with Collins in the car or follow him now. All she knew was that any action was better than sitting alone in that car. She would not have been able to sleep had she gone straight home.

She stopped and turned to look through the pane. She was sure that out of the corner of her eye she had perceived a group of shadowy figures pressed close against the window, lit by a dim light from below them. When she turned to stare directly at them the shapes had dissolved as though they had not been there.

This time she thought she recognised the shape and attitude of one of them. The temptation to look directly at them was too strong and her full gaze revealed only a dark empty room again. She caught her breath as she uttered a single word under her breath, "Denholme."

His form was unmistakeable and yet she knew it was not possible. One of the other dimly seen figures was also familiar but her memory, as yet, would not allow her to recognise it. Just then, the sound of a snowy footfall came to her ears. She jumped as a dark silhouette moved against the dark greyness of the background sky. This was no phantom however and the familiar face of Abel Collins loomed out of the snowy darkness.

He snapped on the beam of his torch and it temporarily blinded her.

"Sorry to have startled you. I didn't think you would wait in the car, somehow. There's no-one here. I have checked the garden and all round the house and all is quiet. Are you ok, Lucinda, you look as if you have seen a ghost?"

She assumed a rueful expression. "Let's go round to my place now."

"I have something else to do before I rest. Can I drop you off and collect you later. Your car is parked outside my house, I believe?"

"Yes it is. But you must get some sleep, you know. We will need to be sharp for what is ahead of us."

Collins grunted an enigmatic response. "What I need to do may help us in this struggle."

They approached the gates and Lucinda turned and looked back at the house expecting to see figures staring back from the windows. Only a quiet black façade stared back at her through the whirling flakes and she turned to follow Collins back to the car.

Collins drove to Lucinda Randolph's house in silence. She was still thinking about those figures in the window. She had decided to ring Denholme Theynard when she got home to check that all was well. It was as she decided on this action that the identity of that second shadowy form occurred to her...it was Jim Flagg. She was now desperate to ring Theynard and, luckily, Collins was pulling into the curb at her house.

"OK, I will be back at about 4.30 to pick you up. See you later."

Lucinda opened her door and was about to climb out of the car when Collins placed his hand on her arm. "It is ironic that maybe Jack the Ripper will face me as a part of the group that proves to be his nemesis."

"Why is that?"

"My mother's maiden name was Abberline. Do

you recognise it?"

"No, should I?"

"Maybe not, but I mention it because my great, great, grandfather was Inspector Frederick Abberline. He was the detective who led the hunt for the Ripper in Whitechapel in 1888."

*****

Lucinda pushed open the door of her house. Before she entered, she stared after the taillights of Collins' car as it disappeared down the road. Collins was a man who revealed relevant knowledge he had a little at a time. She pondered over his last statement. Did he now see the imminent confrontation as a final reckoning between two old adversaries, Abberline and the Ripper? The emotional and genetic link could be dangerous because it might affect Collins' judgement at a critical moment.

Now she thought that she had better ring Theynard; the sight of those figures pressed against that window in the house had unnerved her. She was afraid that something might have happened to him and Flagg.

The sleepy voice from the other end of the line indicated that all was well, apart from having been unceremoniously woken. Lucinda made the excuse that she had felt vulnerable on her own and wanted to hear a friendly voice. Having rung off she set about ensuring that she had forgotten nothing in the way of defences for the mornings work but all was well. She had checked it all before she had left home earlier in the day. Nevertheless, one could not take any chances.

Eventually, after a hot bath, she settled down in her fireside armchair and dozed. Outside the wind continued to howl, more snow fell and the hours became less small. In her fitful dozing she wondered what Collins was doing which "would help us", as he had said.

Chapter 46

Strange Conflict

Collins had completed what he needed to do and was driving through the snow to pick up Lucinda. During the journey, his thoughts had turned to the number of coincidences and links with the Ripper case. One or two he had only recently realised, but others had emerged earlier; how Julia Davenport had been murdered by a method mirroring that of Mary Kelly; the removal of organs resembling the Mary Kelly killing; David Linde dying in a similar way to Druitt, at the same location, on the same day and month of the year. A man called Winslade finding Linde's body in the same way as an ancestor of Winslade found Druitt in 1888. Last, but by no means least he, Collins, was a descendant of Abberline; the Ripper hunter. It all seemed to be part of some diabolical pattern. It was as if Jack the Ripper was trying to relive the events in Whitechapel of late 1888.

His car drew up outside Lucinda Randolph's house and he saw the curtains in a front window twitch, indicating that Lucinda was awake and ready to go to work. Her front door opened and she emerged carrying a suitcase and several parcels.

Collins opened the boot for her and asked if there was any more to be collected.

Lucinda replied breathlessly: "I'm afraid so", having deposited the first load, she returned to the house for the remainder. Eventually they were ready to leave. Lucinda wondered whether she would ever see her house again and she stared back longingly at it as they drove off.

Denholme Theynard and Jim Flagg were waiting for them. Theynard was carrying a small attaché case and both men strode out to climb into the car.

Lucinda calmly asked them: "Before we go can you wait while I have a few words with Denholme about the Service of Exorcism." Flagg and Collins waited and after a few minutes of consultation they drove in silence. Each one of them was lost in their own private thoughts.

On arrival at The Eaves Lucinda addressed the group as they left the car: "I will enter first on my own in order to assess the atmosphere. Make no mistake; we must be careful at every step. What lies in there will defend itself at all costs...at all costs.

"Denholme and I will assign each of you jobs to do as the first stage of the exorcism. You must follow our instructions to the letter – do I make myself clear?" There were nods and murmurs of agreement.

Collins parked the car in the drive of the house. A hint of gunmetal greyness was beginning to adorn the eastern sky heralding the beginning of the day.

The snow had ceased falling as they made their way down the drive towards the front door. Flagg looked up at the dark house towering above him and thought that he had never been so frightened in his life.

Collins handed Lucinda the keys and they waited

as she pushed open the door. She shivered in the cold air as she walked forward down the hall after leaving the front door slightly ajar. Her three companions waited outside moving from foot to foot in the bitterly cold morning air. They wore heavy winter coats but this did not seem to be any defence against the bitterness in the air.

Theynard turned to them: "We may as well unload the car. We can bring the bags and cases as far as the front door. It may warm us up a bit." They were all only too glad to begin some physical activity.

After some minutes, all the impedimenta they would need lay on a plastic sheet by the front door. Theynard blew on his cold hands and spoke: "We must give her as much time as she needs. Perhaps, Abel, you should move the car down the road away from here."

Theynard and Flagg stood back and watched the car disappear, leaving a cloud of water vapour hanging in the frosty air.

A crash rent the air; it came from inside the house. Theynard pushed open the door.

The sight that met their eyes caused them to step back. At the far end of the hall, the mirror that had graced the wall facing the door now lay face down on the floor. Shards of glass could be seen spread across the floor. Scrawled on the wall in red were the following words.

The Juwes are the men that will not be blamed for nothing.

The sentence had been written recently because

they could see the shiny wetness of the liquid used and a dribble of it was running down the wall from the letter 's' in 'Juwes'. Beneath the words and in front of the broken mirror lay the prone figure of Lucinda Randolph.

Theynard dashed forward but was beaten to her side by Collins. He checked her pulse. She groaned and raised her head. She held it in a cupped hand.

"I'm OK, I think."

Theynard held her hands: "What happened, Lucy?"

Collins said: "Let's get her to a chair." Flagg brought one into the hall from the dining room. Gently, they lifted her to her feet and guided her to the chair.

Collins asked: "Did you see anybody while you were in here?"

"No, I took a look round the house and was about to come back outside to you when I was struck on the back of the head and fell forward. The mirror must have hit me. I did feel an intense cold just before it happened and I did feel a presence but I was not surprised, bearing in mind where we are."

Theynard asked: "Is your head OK?"

Lucinda looked up: "I feel a bit better now. I think I have been more mentally shaken up than physically harmed."

Collins stood up and his attention strayed to the writing on the wall. Jim Flagg strolled over and stood with Collins.

"What do you make of this?" asked Flagg.

Collins hesitated for a moment before turning to face the assembled group. "I know where these words come from. The Ripper killed Catherine Eddowes on Sunday, September 30th 1888 in Mitre

Square. Before he went on his way he tore off a piece of her apron in order to wipe his hands. It was later found in a doorway in Goulston Street, about a third of a mile from Mitre Square. On the wall of a passageway leading from that doorway to a staircase this message was scrawled on the wall in bloodstained chalk."

He pointed to the writing on the wall in the hallway.

Lucinda said: "Jack is making his presence felt. This is his way of saying that we are now on his patch and that he is the leader of the pack. He knows we are here and he will protect himself against us. His power is such that he can even operate during daylight hours."

After making this statement, Lucinda stood up and moved over to where the shattered glass lay on the floor and knelt beside it. Jim Flagg strode towards her. "How can we possibly fight this? No matter what we do this thing will win," he said.

Denholme Theynard moved between them. "He *is* powerful but daylight will limit his strength. We must set to work now while we can. I think he is attempting to wrong-foot us, waste time and weaken our resolve. I suggest that we start our preparations and remember…we must not expect to have everything our own way. He has a lot to lose and he has been here a long time in one form or another. We must work with a will. Think positively and not fall at the first hurdle, which after all is not a particularly high one."

"You are right, Denholme. He is using our fear of his reputation to unsettle us. Let me outline to you all that we must do and then let us set to work."

Lucinda led them first outside to bring all the

impedimenta she had assembled inside the house. She then told them what needed to be done and within a few minutes they had begun their work.

The furniture was removed from the bedroom where Julia Davenport was murdered and the back bedroom where Mr Kayne had met his fate. These rooms were to be spotlessly clean. Next, the carpets were rolled up, taken downstairs and dumped in the garden.

While the men were manhandling the carpets Lucinda began cleaning the floors and walls with hot water heated in a kettle in the kitchen on a small gas stove she had brought with her. On her own in the larger bedroom, she pondered as she worked. When she had knelt by the shattered mirror in the hall earlier, she had looked into a shard of glass. Jim Flagg had stood directly behind her but all she could see in the mirror piece was the front door. Flagg had cast no reflection!

Chapter 47

Preparations for a
Strange Ritual Begin

The house echoed to the sounds of sweeping and washing. The two rooms were soon spick and span and after four to five hours' work a break was called for 'refreshments'. This consisted of water. Collins volunteered to fetch and fill a jug in the kitchen downstairs. He turned on the tap and allowed it to run for a while before filling the vessel. Collins' gaze wandered to the draining board by the sink. A mug stood on the board and Collins noted a dribble of dried coffee running down the outside of it.

He at first thought that it had been left by the police during their investigations at the house. Absentmindedly he reached out to examine it all round. A transfer print of Saint Paul's Cathedral came into view. He revolved it further in order to look at the coffee stain, which was the same shape as the one he had seen on the mug in David Kayne's office when he had returned there after the death of the detective...he remembered it clearly. In fact, he remembered everything clearly on that terrible day. What is more, the mug in the office also had a picture of Saint Paul's Cathedral on it." What was David Kayne's coffee mug doing here?

He became aware of a movement at the periphery of his vision. Collins turned, but only the anonymous doors of a cupboard stood before him. A shadowy figure had passed him and moved out of the room...he was sure of it. He ran out into the hall but there was no one and no sound of movement. He could just hear the murmur of the others upstairs. He looked in each of the downstairs rooms and rationalised the phantom as being the product of an overactive imagination. The house was affecting him and he needed to get a grip. He walked back into the kitchen and found four glasses in one of the cupboards. He placed the jug under the still running tap. It was then he noticed the ring of wetness on the draining board where the mug had previously stood.

Collins became aware of a figure in the kitchen doorway and jumped back, his face turning deathly pale.

"How long are you going to be with the water...? Are you ok, Abel, you look as if you have seen a ghost?" Lucinda Randolph moved into the room, went over to the sink and moved the now full jug from under the tap.

"Either my mind is playing tricks on me or David Kayne is in this house." He explained what he had just seen and she listened without comment. When he had finished she did not laugh, as he expected, but stared at the wet ring left by the mug.

"I am not surprised. I think what you saw was real," said Lucinda. "This house is a portal for all the spirits associated with it. Some associations are so powerful they sometimes leave behind palpable items. This may be what has happened in this case. The wetness left by the mug is real enough. I do not think that you are losing your grip on reality. I do, however, think that we should get on as soon as possible because daylight is limited at this time of year."

They found a tray for the glasses and water to take upstairs. On the way, Lucinda suggested that it would probably be best not to mention the mug to the others, particularly in front of Flagg. He was nervous enough.

Collins wondered if Kayne had made his presence felt in order to reassure him that there was more here than just the powers of darkness. Little did he know that Lucinda Randolph had drawn the same conclusion and would use it, if it became necessary.

The quartet drank the water. Lucinda began the preparations. She explained and issued instructions to them. She then set to work sealing all the windows, front and back doors with the wax she had prepared from the holy wafers. She made the sign of the cross in holy water over each seal before moving on to the next door or window.

Flagg and Collins took pieces of chalk and marked each of the internal doors with a cross. She had told them that the crosses must be in the shape of a crucifix and the transverse stroke must be near the top of the cross. An inverted cross anywhere would surely destroy all of them during this ritual because it would be an open invitation to any beings from the Pit.

Denholme Theynard, meanwhile, built a large fire in the grate of the fireplace of the room where Julia had died. He lined the grate with newspaper and then added wood kindling brought along in a bag by Lucinda. Soon a reassuring glow lit the room, which had become so gloomy in the after-noon winter greyness. By this time Lucinda had begun the construction of a chalk pentacle on the floor of the room. She enlisted the help of Flagg and Theynard to help her.

She explained: "The Pentacle of Solomon is a fortress against any dark spirits. To be effective it must be drawn accurately."

To this end, she had brought string and a meas-uring tape. She first constructed two chalk circles, one inside the other, some six feet in diameter at the maximum. She left a small gap in the circum-ference of both circles approximately one foot wide. A five pointed star was then drawn, after much calculation and measuring, in the space be-tween the two circles. As the group worked, their shadows danced on the walls in the orange glow from the fire.

Collins, meanwhile, had set to work making garlands of asafoetida and garlic flowers for each of them.

Flagg joked: "This is like being in a Hammer horror film from the sixties; I would not be sur-prised if Peter Cushing and Christopher Lee turned up."

Theynard brought a serious note to the proceed-ings: "Look gentlemen, what we are doing could save our lives...perhaps even our souls."

Denholme Theynard commenced chalking in the space between the two circles...

IN NOMINA PATRIS + ALPHA + OMEGA + ELELOHYM + SOTHER + AGIA + TETRA-GRAMERTON + AGIOS + OTHEOS + ISCHIROS

A cross was drawn between each word and after

chalking each cross Theynard made the sign of the cross with his hand over the symbol and said the words of the Benediction. Lucinda then poured holy water into five small silver chalices and she placed each of these in the valleys of the pentacle. Theynard blessed each of the cups in turn. Then he lit five long tapering candles, placing each above the five points of the star.

By now, night had fallen and they could hear the wind howling outside as once more winter made its presence felt. It was much later than Lucinda had hoped they would begin the service but it could not now be helped. More drinking water was brought from the kitchen. Each one of the group was lost in their thoughts as they drank and listened to the gale outside. Collins stared into the glow of the fire and wondered what ordeal lay before them.

Lucinda switched the lights on all round the house and took from a velvet bag white robes and a cassock.

Chapter 48

To the Brink of the Abyss

Lucinda wore the white robes and Theynard the cassock, as all four of them placed the wreaths made by Collins on their heads. Lucinda spoke to Flagg and Collins. "We will now perform the Ritual of Exorcism. Please step inside the pentacle through the gap I have made in the circles. I will then close the pentacle. Whatever happens from now on, you must not move out of the circles."

Theynard placed a hand on each of Flagg and Collins' arms before they moved. He had sensed some scepticism on the part of the two younger men and decided to address this issue.

"The pentacle is an ancient symbol. The Celts believed it was the sign of the Goddess of the Underground, who they called Morgan. Some Christians believe that the five points of the star represent the five wounds of Christ and has also been described by them as the Star of Bethlehem or the Three Kings' star. The latter having led three Zoastrian astrologers to the baby Jesus in Bethlehem. The English warrior Sir Gawain, a nephew of King Arthur, adopted the pentagram as his personal symbol and painted it on his shield. The religion of

Wicca is based, in part, on ancient Celtic deities, symbols, days of celebration, etc. The pentacle and pentagram are their main symbols.

"It is tradition and strongly held beliefs that make any symbol so potent. The pentacle is a fortress, which, because of the mind-set of millions of good people from the past, has the power to repel any evil that may try to enter it. It is one of many symbols made supremely strong by the power of many minds. If you walk out from within its protective barrier, it will be the same as opening a gate to any evil entity, which may be conjured by what we are about to do. Make no mistake, the dangers we face now are the most serious that Lucinda and I have ever encountered because they too have been nurtured by hundreds of years of tradition. The difference between them and the symbols of light is that they have been sustained by a succession of evil-doers. They therefore have acquired a similar potency to the symbols we are using as a defence but in a totally negative sense. If you ignore our warnings, you do so at your peril. We will have no power to save you or your immortal soul. Believe me, death is not the only threat ahead of us."

Prompted by Theynard's speech, Lucinda gave a gasp as she remembered an important omission and once again rummaged in the bag. She stepped forward with four objects made of silver on silver chains. She encircled each of the men's necks and her own with the chains and stepped back. Collins lifted the crucifix on the chain in his hand to look at it. The plain silver cross shone brightly in the reflected firelight. Theynard said: "I will bless each of these; the most ancient and potent symbols of the

Christian church."

After the blessing Flagg and Collins stepped into the pentacle through the gap in the chalk and stood awkwardly in the centre of the circles. Lucinda carefully completed the circles with chalk and as she did so Theynard recited the Lord's Prayer and finally the Blessing. He told them that if they felt threatened or frightened during the proceedings the best defence was to recite the Lord's Prayer and make the sign of the cross in the air.

Theynard then made up the fire with further wood and sprinkled frankincense on the fire. Dense white smoke was generated, filling the air with a strong aroma. Lucinda retrieved a censer, a sprig of hyssop, a bottle of holy water, a metal bowl, a tripod and a spoon.

She moved over to the fire and tentatively removed some of the burning twigs from it using the spoon. She deposited them in the metal bowl, which Theynard had placed on the tripod on the floor near the window. Further frankincense was sprinkled on the ignited wood, clouds of white smoke again rose in the air. She transferred a portion of the burning incense into the censer. Theynard, meanwhile, inserted the hyssop twig into the bottle of holy water in order to ensure that the twig was thoroughly wetted by the liquid.

Lucinda and Theynard were now ready and they rose to their feet, Lucinda carrying the censer and Theynard the bottle of holy water in one hand and the hyssop twig in the other. Theynard took the lead and started to walk back and forth across the room, scattering water from the hyssop as he went. Lucinda followed him, moving the censer gently back and forth across her body, allowing the perfume from the incense to permeate all corners of the room. "I exorcise thee, O unclean spirits, in the name of the Father and of the Son and of the Holy Ghost," intoned Theynard, in a low gentle voice.

The two robed figures then made their way out on to the landing out of sight of the men waiting tensely within the pentacle. They could still hear Theynard intoning the exorcism prayer as he and Lucinda moved across the landing to the computer room.

A burning log fell in the grate of the fire and Flagg and Collins turned to stare into the orange glow of the flames, which crackled with the movement. The sound died away and it was then that the two men noticed the silence. They could no longer hear Theynard's voice or indeed any sound from the landing and beyond.

Flagg stared into the fire and then round the room. Collins called softly to Theynard and Lucinda but there was no answer. Only the echoes of Collins' voice dying away through the house broke that cloying silence.

It was then that Flagg noticed that the light from the fire seemed to be stronger. He looked across at their shadows dancing on the walls and they seemed darker. "The lights are dimming!" he said, grabbing Collins' arm.

Chapter 49

Forces Divided

Theynard and Lucinda continued the service across the landing and into the rear computer room. They circled the room and were about to return to the bedroom occupied by the others. Theynard continued to intone the Prayer for Exorcism when the door slammed shut. They had noticed nothing untoward before this moment and Theynard assumed that a draught had caused the problem. Lucinda however immediately ran to the door and desperately tried the handle, with no result. They were locked in the room.

"Denholme, it begins...our forces have been split," said Lucinda, despairingly. "I was stupid not to foresee this. Can't you feel the intense cold? There is something happening out there. Pray, Denholme, for God's sake, pray."

*****

Collins stared around the room, the shadows in the corners were definitely deepening. By now, there was no light from the electrical bulbs in the room and the firelight had faded so that only the glow from red-hot coals was visible. All the flames had disappeared. The room had also become icy cold. Collins watched as tendrils of mist formed from his breath. A deep sinking feeling of fear had wormed its way like a snake into his stomach. Beside him, he heard Flagg sniff the air and he too became aware of a smell filling his nostrils. It was a sweet sickly odour and it seemed familiar to him. Flagg coughed and held his hand to his face and uttered an oath.

At first quietly and then more loudly Collins began to intone the opening lines of the Lord's Prayer. Flagg recovered himself and, on hearing Collins, he too joined him in prayer.

Collins remembered where he had experienced that foul odour before – it was the smell of the charnel house, the odour of rotting corpses. The two men were so cold now that they were shivering and wrapping their arms around themselves in order to keep warm. Their prayers faltered as their teeth began to chatter. Flagg was turning this way and that, desperately staring with fearful wide eyes. "Remember what Lucinda and Denholme said," whispered Collins hoarsely to him. "Do not be tempted to move out of the pentacle. Pray as hard as you can and try to imagine the figure of Christ."

Collins took Flagg by a clammy hand and held it to him. Flagg knew that something was about to happen. He too stared round the room in panic.

A dark shadow had begun to form in the doorway to the room and rose from the floor. It looked like black smoke, but as it rose it began to thicken and solidify into a form. At first they could not make out what it was and their minds were working overtime. They imagined all manner of devils appearing before them before the shape resolved itself into a flat surface, which moved forward into the room. Four legs formed below the flat shape and the men realised that a table had materialised before them immediately outside the pentacle.

The table had formed itself into a solid object and something had appeared in the middle of its top surface. The object was dark coloured in the faded light and was approximately the size of a fist. It began to pulse rhythmically before their eyes and a thumping sound echoed round the room. The thumping noise rose in volume and was accompanied by a swishing sound.

Very soon the thumping was echoing round the walls of the entire house. Thump, boomp, swish, thump, boomp, swish...louder and louder it became. Collins and Flagg could stand it no longer. They bent down beneath the weight of the sound and held their hands up over their ears. Collins felt as if his brain would burst. He took one hand down to hold Flagg back before he could step out of the pentacle and run from this horror. The pain must stop soon.

Collins realised that the thing on the table creating this ear-splitting sound was a beating heart. He looked up at the pulsing heart on the table and saw a dark figure was now seated behind the table. The figure appeared to be wearing the habit of a monk and the cowl was pulled up over its brow. He could make out no features within the dark cavern of that cowl. As he watched the figure it leant forward and picked up the beating heart in its left hand. It held the heart before it. The sound of the heart subsided until it was just audible. The hand was the colour of bleached bone. The fingers were long, smooth, tapering and ended in long nails.

The creature spoke in a whispered voice. "You are right to be afraid. I have your lives in my hand as surely as I have this heart. You were foolish to listen to the shaman and his stupid woman. I have defeated them even before the battle has begun. Do you know with whom you are crossing swords? "

Each syllable was measured, as though much thought had been put into each of them before they were uttered. The coldness of the tone chilled their bones. The whisper held no emotion and was spoken as if, at any second, the two men could be swatted and killed like hapless houseflies slapped by a descending newspaper. Collins was absolutely certain that his end had come and with that certainty came clarity of mind. He had nothing to lose and he might as well go on the attack.

He watched that left hand holding the heart and listened to that measured terrible tone and a piece of the jigsaw fell into place. Collins had remembered his initial meeting with a left-handed measured thinker and all at once he knew the identity of this evil creature before him. His late suspicions and the subsequent research had borne fruit.

"Julia Davenport's heart, I presume?" said Collins.

"I have assumed all along that you would be a worthy opponent," said the figure. "You will never know the lengths to which I have gone in order to make sure that you did not come too close to me. I knew you were a danger for two reasons; firstly, you were a loner until you met the priest and his harlot. A lone wolf is always a difficult proposition; two, you were very close to only one person and that was the astute but very dead Superintendent Kayne. You would harbour a revenge motive, therefore, which could be a problem or an advantage to me. It can lead to uncontrollable anger and that lack of moderation could be your downfall. I think that before I discuss anything further with you, Mr Collins, Flagg should leave."

"Stay where you are, Jim," said Collins, turning to Flagg. He was horrified at what he saw. Flagg's eyes were widened in abject terror. He held the knuckles of his right hand to his mouth and shook to his very core. Collins could only watch as Flagg's hand dropped and a terrified rasping voice came to his lips. "Oh my God, Collins, it's my wife. I can see her poor mad eyes in the darkness of that cowl and she wants me to come to her."

Chapter 50

A New Danger

"No, Flagg, it's not your wife. It's an illusion," barked Collins. "Don't, for God's sake, leave the pentacle."

Before Collins could move Flagg stepped forward and was across the chalk circles, lurching forward to save what he saw as his poor insane wife. Collins made a grab for him, missed and fell to the floor close to the inner circle. He stared round for anything that might help and his eyes alighted on one of the small chalices of holy water, which Lucinda had placed in the valleys of the pentacle. He grabbed for one of them and turned to face the monk. Flagg had approached the table in a rush. The left hand of the monk, with a frightening calmness, reached out and grabbed him by the throat with one hand at the same time the chain of the crucifix about his neck was torn apart by the other. Flagg was spun round to face Collins, just as the latter hurled the chalice and its contents at the blackness of the interior of the monk's cowl.

The vessel, however, struck the hapless Flagg on the chin and the holy water spewed down the front of his jacket. In one movement, the monk reached from behind Flagg, encircling his face. There was a flash of metal and a gaping, grotesquely grinning slit appeared across Flagg's exposed throat. Blood spurted from the wound and Collins' face was spattered in the fountain of blood. The monk threw the shaking, convulsing body of Flagg sideways towards the window. His body rolled over, twitched, uttered a terrible gurgling sound and finally lay still. At that moment, two figures appeared in the doorway and the attention of the monk was diverted towards them. Collins, without a moment's thought, sprang into action. He reached down and grabbed up a second chalice and hurled the vessel and its contents in the direction of the monk. There was no noise from the monk but he seemed to dissolve into shadows and the chalice crashed to the floor behind where the evil cleric had been. The vessel then rolled against a skirting board with a resounding clunk.

Collins, meanwhile, turned to the two figures in the doorway. Expecting more horrors, instead before him stood the welcome, but terrified forms of Lucinda and Theynard. Collins wiped his sleeve across his blood-spattered face. He stared in horror at the awful tableau before him, all eerily lit by the flickering glow of the fire. They all stood for a moment, transfixed by the charnel house scene before them. There was no sign of the monk, the table or the beating heart. An ominous silence hung like a pall over the house.

"Wh...what happened to you two?" stammered Abel Collins.

"We went into the back bedroom and when we tried to get out of the room the door seemed to be locked," said Denholme Theynard, looking totally stunned as he spoke. "We could not shift it. I tried everything until, for no apparent reason, I turned the door handle and it opened quite easily. How did this terrible thing happen?"

Collins related the frightening experiences of the last few minutes. He almost broke down when he reached the point at which Jim Flagg died. "I told him not to leave the pentacle but he seemed to see his wife inside that monk's cowl. I tried to stop him but he went to her and the monk cut his..."

Lucinda went forward to comfort Collins. "It is my fault," she said. "We should never have split our forces as we did. That evil thing trapped Denholme and I in that room in order to attack you and Jim. I also think that when Flagg ran to it and you threw the holy water, it was enough to cause it to momentarily release its hold on us and allowed us two to escape that computer room. It may be that the Service of Exorcism, although not completed, did enough to reduce some of its power."

"Do you really think so, Lucinda?" The voice that uttered these words seemed to come from everywhere and nowhere. It was that same measured tone of the monk but, although the trio turned in every direction, they could see no sign of the creature in that room. "You have come here to destroy me but you do not understand what you are up against."

Lucinda whispered urgently to the other two men: "Get into the pentacle as quickly as possible and do not leave it on any pretext."

They all stared round warily, no light had returned to the light bulbs in the room and hence only the firelight caused their tortured shadows to squirm on the walls. It was as Abel Collins stared at the shadows of the trio that he noticed that additional dark shapes were moving back and forth on the wall. They were not as sharp as their human shadows and exhibited a larger penumbra.

A glow from downstairs flickered into view on the wall of the stairwell. It began to move remorselessly upwards and Lucinda saw it. She pointed and whispered as loudly as she dared: "Something is coming."

The hapless trio could now hear the tread of more than one person steadily climbing the stairs.

"Hold hands and pray," said Lucinda.

She had no sooner whispered this when two figures emerged from the gloom on the landing and entered the room. In the lead, carrying a candle before him, was the figure of a dark haired, pale complexioned young man of approximately 30 years of age. His hair was parted in the middle. The candle illuminated heavy-lidded cold eyes and a cleft chin. A dark moustache grew above a mouth, which had quite generous lips. The overall impression Lucinda took from that candle-lit face was that this was a heartless but weak character. The figure was dressed in what appeared to be a tweed jacket unfastened, but with buttons up to a high point on the chest, a waistcoat and trousers. A generously knotted tie hung from a neck bearing a very pronounced 'Adam's apple'. He looked the very epitome of a late Victorian or Edwardian gentleman.

The figure behind him was that of a woman who was but a silhouette in the shadow of the man. She seemed to be wearing a long dress and her hair was pulled back from her forehead. It was impossible to make out the features of the dark, rather ominous figure entering the room behind her male companion. He stood just inside the door and the woman stood on the threshold.

The man's features became clearer when illuminated in the light from the fire but his companion remained very much in the shadows. The man spoke: "You know who I am, Mr Collins."

His voice was deep and measured. This statement was not said with the rising inflection of a question but merely stated a fact.

Chapter 51

Evil Personified

"Who am I, Mr Collins?"

The speaker bent and placed the candlestick on the floor before him then stood up and folded his arms. He bent his head forward so that he fixed Abel Collins with a stare that was the more pene-trating for having much of the whites of his eyes visible; the heavy silence did the rest.

"Come now, you know...you know." Once more he fixed Collins with that gimlet–like stare.

"Do you need a little help?"

Collins felt the wetness of his palms as he stood and thought that no matter how one tried to hide one's feelings sweat glands always gave one away. He knew who this man was but the dryness in his mouth prevented him from speaking.

The wetness in his right hand increased beyond the capability of any sweat glands and he felt the sudden presence of a solid or semi-solid substance growing in his palm. He looked down and raised his hand, revealing the pulsating human heart once more.

Collins looked up, his face a mask of horror and saw the features of the creature before him break into an evil grin. "You would have liked Julia when she was alive. Now you have won her heart." The humourless grin exploded into a cacophony of mirthless laughter. Collins threw the pulsating organ across the room at the creature but the heart dissolved into a cloud of smoke before it ever reached it. Collins gagged and desperately wiped his hands on the front of his clothes.

"Why such pathetic conjuring tricks?" said Lucinda, stepping forward in front of Collins in a defiant gesture.

"That heart is a symbol, a symbol of life and one of my identities," said the man. "The vaginas I took because that organ represents the source of woman's evil in the world. The heart you held also, I might add, indicates that your safe haven is no longer...erm...safe, having crossed your pathetic defensive wall."

Collins' face was filled with rage. "You think that pathetic demonstrations of your powers place you next to the devil himself. Power; that is what this is all about and that is what you lost when you died."

Collins paused before he spoke again. "You are Montague Druitt, the real Jack the Ripper, killer of pathetic, helpless women and you are dead. Life is the one source of power we have which causes you to envy us. You resent the living deeply which is why in death you continue as a plague on mankind."

Druitt's features remained motionless, betraying nothing. His voice came with a low and threatening tone. "On the contrary, death has deprived me of nothing, least of all the ability to kill. Jack the Ripper was but a stepping-stone on a road I have travelled now for centuries. One of my guises or entities, you might say, you saw earlier – Brother

Jacob. In the form of Brother Jacob, I have been here since the eleventh century. Long before this house was built and this road that runs by was but a lane in open countryside."

"The monk who killed three of the brothers in his monastery and then himself?" asked Lucinda.

"I used a knife. The same weapon of choice eight centuries later in Whitechapel. I killed the brothers because I discovered that the three of them had lain together. They professed to be men of God, prayed to Him and yet they succumbed to the pleasures of the flesh like harlots. They were an abomination and they had to die. I did not throw myself from the roof of the monastery. The Prior had me hurled to my death in order to cover up the foul acts of the three brothers. He knew I could never remain silent if I was left alive. I avenged myself by driving him to suicide two years later. It was my presence that caused the monastery to be abandoned because, as the monks wrote, 'God had forsaken this place.'"

Denholme Theynard moved forward to join his two friends. "What is the point of perpetuating all this killing and evil? What do you hope to gain from it all?"

"Gain and loss. These are but mortal concepts. In your pathetic terms I gain power. This is probably the only common ground shared by you and I. I also fulfil much in biblical prophecy, which has documented the failure of women from Eve onwards. I am the instrument to administer punish-ment to them because they are weak. Even in Shakespearian literature the evil and weakness of women is underlined. 'Frailty thy name is woman' was said by Hamlet of Gertrude, his mother."

"Were you responsible for the killing of Elizabeth Rayner by the highwayman Thomas Rowden? If so why did you rape, steal and take the life of a totally innocent woman?" said Lucinda.

"Hah...totally innocent? What contemporary accounts do not tell is that Rayner was a whore and a blackmailer. The money taken was booty she had extorted from married men, whom she had earlier seduced. She demanded money in order to buy her silence. If they did not pay then she would tell their wives. This is another example of the scheming female using her body to destroy men. I draw your attention to what is written in the Revelation of Saint John the Divine in the New Testament. 'I will show unto thee the judgement of the great whore: with whom the kings of the earth have been made drunk by the wine of her fornication.'"

"John was talking about Babylon as the whore, not a woman," scoffed Theynard.

"The source of the evil in Babylon and later in London in 1888 *was* the female of the species. You should look deeper into the scriptures than just under the superficial surface layer, preacher.

"Whitechapel in the 1880s was a den of iniquity with huge numbers of prostitutes walking the streets," continued Druitt. "I did London a great favour and that is something that everyone overlooks. Donald McCormick in his book 'The Identity of the Ripper' said: "The significant fact is that the Ripper murders not only focused attention on the social evils of the East End, but marked the beginning of a positive attempt to control them. The author got that right even if he identified the wrong man as the killer.""

Collins decided that it was time to bring the subject of the contents of the chest found in the loft into the mix. "I read Druitt's diary entries and they spoke of a pregnant girl, Annie Crook. Who was she? If you call yourself Druitt, that is."

"A name is but a label, 'a rose by any other name would smell as sweet'. I am an amalgam of personalities but as Druitt I did write that diary," he confirmed. "Annie Crook was a wretched victim of the whores of Whitechapel. Mary Kelly led her into prostitution and I saw to it that she, Kelly, paid the price for that. Annie was a pretty girl and she came to the attention of a royal personage who managed to impregnate her. My mother knew Sir William Gull through my father who was a doctor, a Fellow of the Royal College of Surgeons. Gull was the personal physician to Queen Victoria and he persuaded my mother to take Annie in for the period of her pregnancy and confinement. Unfortunately, we watched Annie grow weaker by the day and eventually she died. It was then that we felt that her death must be avenged on those women of the street who had caused Annie to take up the filthy life of a prostitute.

"It has given me much amusement to hear all the royal conspiracy theories, particularly the idea that Prince Eddie was the killer. Everyone held the two pieces of the jigsaw for over 100 years, the royal connection and us, but no-one put the two together."

"Who are the 'we' and 'us' you speak of?" asked Theynard.

Chapter 52

All Is Revealed

"You have joined in again, have you, priest? Call yourself a man of God, and yet you do not see that I was doing His work through the ages.You are a fool. The retribution I will wreak on you will act as a lesson to your friends here. It will also aid them in their understanding of my powers and will make even more pathetic your group's attempts to destroy me."

During Druitt's last speech the shadowy figure behind him had become even more indistinct and had formed into a dark cloudlike shape. When Druitt finished his words, the cloud moved past him, and crossed the space that lay between Druitt and Theynard. It formed a dark halo about the churchman's head in a moment and, before he could utter a cry, it encircled his throat lifted him bodily from the ground as if it were a length of rope and moved him forward across the room towards the door. He made desperate choking sounds and tried to struggle but to no avail.

Collins tried desperately to move forward to help Theynard but it was as if his limbs were constructed from lead. Lucinda tried to work her mouth in order to appeal to Druitt but she too could neither speak nor move.

Druitt raised the candle and the two hapless companions could only watch in horror as Theynard's body was lifted into the air above the landing. The dark snaking cloud extended into a long tendril, which encircled the flex of the pendant electric light in the ceiling. Theynard's body rotated so that his face became visible to Collins and Lucinda. It was very red, rapidly turning purple. His eyes bulged and he continued to choke until he extended his almost black tongue and his body shook spasmodically. At last his eyes rolled up into their sockets and with one last twitch he expired.

For a moment he swung from the cloud and pendant, his body limp. Collins watched fascinated and horrified, as the flex was pulled taut by the dark vapour and the corpse hanging from it. Theynard's dead heels struck the banister with a thump. The flex broke free from the ceiling rose under the weight of the dead man. The body was released and fell, disappearing from view behind the banister on the landing. Lucinda and Collins winced as they heard the crash of the body striking the stairs and bouncing down, to land in the hall with a sickening thud.

The silence, which followed, was almost a solid entity. The dark vaporous cloud had withdrawn into the shadowy shape in its previous position behind Druitt.

Lucinda cried out and, now able to move, fell to her knees. She realised the significance of why she could not see Flagg and Theynard's reflections in the glass shards earlier in the hall. She also remembered seeing them in the ghostly throng through the kitchen window on the previous night at The

Eaves...the two men were effectively marked for death. She sobbed uncontrollably and buried her head in her hands. Collins went over to her, raised her up and put his arms around her to comfort her. When she had regained some control over her emotions, Collins raised his face angrily to Druitt.

The latter placed the candlestick once more at his feet. His face was illuminated from a new angle as he did so and Collins caught his breath. The face of Druitt, in this light, resembled someone he expected to appear eventually. The manner and the preferred use of the left hand was a confirmation.

"Presumably, you think that all these killings will stop me?" fumed Collins. "Well, that shows how little you know me...Mr Dumairt! I knew there was something suspicious about you from the moment I met you. Dumairt and Druitt are one and the same creature.

Lucinda raised her tearstained face and in an instant she saw Druitt's face transform into that of Dumairt. Collins continued. "It was you who killed Coldwell, Linde's solicitor, and Partridge, the prison officer, in the car in Vale Road. You released Linde from the handcuffs and he ran from the scene, terrified. It was a clever ruse to wound yourself, by the way. It was you who also drowned Linde after pinning the murders on him...presumably some kind of poetic justice as you chose the same calendar date as your own, or should I say Druitt's, death in 1888."

"Go on, Collins!" goaded Dumairt. "As I said before, you are a worthy adversary. I also chose a descendant of the man who found my body all those years ago to discover Linde's corpse."

"I did some checking on Superintendent Dumairt,

and he seems to have appeared out of nowhere," continued Collins. "I therefore contacted a friend of mine in the Human Resources Records Office at the Yard. There is no record of you before 1998 and you seemed to have apparently moved into a very senior position and left no trace. People would have re-membered you along the way with a name like Du-mairt but we could find no one who knew you. I checked you out because I was suspicious of you. I thought that at first it was my prejudice and loyalty to my old boss. But you had said things to me that did not make sense."

"When I left the meeting with Townshend at which I was suspended, you caught up with me in the car park afterwards, remember, and warned me off.

"You told me not to dabble in matters, which I did not understand and which do not concern me. You warned me that the sack will be a minor prob-lem compared with what else might happen. That was a direct threat and it made no sense to me then but now I realise that...

"Now you realise these are the consequences of your actions I warned you against," interrupted Dumairt. "Mr Kayne got too close and he was taken care of accordingly. You should have realised that you were treading a dangerous path a long time ago."

Lucinda now entered the fray. "Where does Linde fit into all this...did you kill his wife and bury her in Vale Road?"

"Linde was merely an instrument...a very blunt one. He had killed his wife and buried her. Fortu-itously, he found this house to move into. I did remove his wife's heart and vagina later as a means of implicating him further in the killing of Julia Davenport. The overall purpose of all this was to increase our powers. Death makes us stronger and more able to complete our work. A murderer, such as Linde, coming to live here meant that our power was magnified enormously, especially as his murdered wife was an adulterer. When Linde brought Davenport back to this house I sensed that because of her extraordinary psychic powers she represented a further threat to me. I frightened her off by showing her that Linde was going to die but I knew it would not be enough. We sensed the sexual magnetism between Linde and Davenport and this, we thought, would lead her into probing deeper into our affairs. A message was sent to her computer, ostensibly from Linde, inviting her to meet him here. It seemed right that she should end her days in the same way as Mary Kelly, who had introduced poor Annie Crook to the evils of prostitution. Davenport had slept with a senior manager at the BBC in order to get on television, you know? Yet another promiscuous bitch."

Collins spoke again: "You have not had things all your own way. I have been on to you for some time. Julia Davenport was killed by a left-handed individual and in her struggle for life she had torn a monogrammed medallion from your watch. The monogram read 'MJD' – Montague John Druitt. The trinket was clutched in her hand when we examined the body. It was another link between Druitt and the killing. It was also another link between Dumairt and Druitt because you, as Dumairt, are left-handed. Tenuous, I grant you, but a link nonetheless and from little acorns grow mighty oaks. Linde gave us another clue when we interviewed him after the murder. He described a phone call he had received from Julia, from this house immediately prior to her death and she was cut off as she mentioned a name. It sounded something like 'Drew'. I think we all know what she meant, don't you Druitt, or would you prefer Dumairt?"

Dumairt remained externally, it appeared, very calm. "I have been 'Druitt' for so much longer - but no-one outside this house will ever believe what you say anyway because your story is just too fantastical."

Collins continued: "I do have evidence which I finally obtained today, although difficult to believe. It is one of two clinching facts. You left some bloody finger prints on the outside of the doorframe when you killed Kayne. I took a pen from your – Dumairt's – desk at the station and lifted the prints from it. I then checked those prints against the doorframe dabs. Guess what? They matched. There were in excess of 25 points of agreement between the two sets of prints…a perfect match, indisputable in any court in the land…enough to convince Townshend anyway.

"One other thing, you egotistical creep. Your name – T. I. Dumairt. Switch the letters around and out pops, 'I am Druitt.' Your inflated ego couldn't resist that. I was always destined to be part of your downfall because I am a direct descendant of the man who hunted you in Whitechapel, Inspector Frederick Abberline. Now I can help him to rest more easily."

Chapter 53

The Worm Turns

Dumairt's face contorted in anger for the first time. He was about to speak when the dark shadow moved forward from behind him. As it did so, its shadowy structure began to take on a more tangible, solid form. An icily pallid face materialised out of the gloom and seemed to glow in the light from the candle. The sound of a sharp intake of breath issued from Lucinda as there before them stood the solid form of a dark, forbidding and formidable woman. Her hair was scraped back severely from her forehead into a bun at the back of her head. She was tall and wore a long black dress, which reached her ankles. The dress was in a late Victorian style and it glittered in the candlelight. Collins could make out small black beads covering the dress, which caught the light. The dress finished high at the neck and seemed too tight. The wrinkled neck of a woman in late middle age emerged from this tight collar. They realised with horror that the face had no features, appearing at first as a flattened visage of stretched skin and was all the more horrific for that. The surface of that frightening face began to change as they watched, frozen to the spot. Black pits appeared and from their depths; two cold eyes glittered into life. Within a few seconds cheekbones and a nose emerged, followed by the frightening slit of a mouth. The face, now fully formed, had once been handsome with high cheekbones but was now disfigured by age and the severity of its expression. The eyes glittered like two chips of black marble in the candlelight and they narrowed, turning the face into a mask of hatred. Her thin lips drew back revealing yellowing teeth and she spat at the two hapless people before her. "Enough...I have heard enough from you two. I must take this sorry situation in hand. There is only one thing to be done... you must be removed finally from our presence. You must die as those foul prostitutes did and your stupid allies have done tonight."

Collins stared into that face of hatred and madness and recognised it – the face of the elder female of the two women in the photograph found in the chest...the chest he and Kayne had brought down from the loft. She was wearing the same beaded dress that was found. Collins realised that she was the driving force behind the evil in this house.

She was the previously unseen monster behind the Ripper killings in Whitechapel a century and a quarter ago. It all made sense now. The girl, Annie Crook, had been a prostitute impregnated by a client. The presence of the royal surgeon, William Gull, confirmed that client as Eddie, Duke of Clarence. All this evidence could be inferred from the entries in the diary in the trunk found in the loft. This woman was the mother of Druitt and she decided, in her madness, that the women of the streets of Whitechapel had led Crook into the pain and the eventual death she had suffered. They had had to pay for their evil and her son had been the instrument of that revenge. A deranged woman, who had herself known the pain of bearing children and now saw this poor girl Crook as a daughter led astray.

It also explained the royal cover up but not because Eddie was the murderer, as postulated by many Ripper authorities. The cover up was to hide Eddie's involvement in what would have been a scandal; the scandal of a child born of a Whitechapel prostitute. The smokescreen had protected not only Eddie but also these two fiends born of the evil already present in this house. The Eaves was already built upon past foul madness and death and was ripe to drive any inhabitants to commit the foul excesses seen in the Whitechapel murders of 1888. This was especially so if those inhabitants were already unstable and on the brink of insanity anyway.

Collins thoughts were interrupted by a howl from Lucinda and he became aware of the fact that the two figures before them had quickly grown in stature in a quite literal sense. The evil woman now towered over them and as she grew she leaned forward, raising her right hand, from which emerged a bladed scalpel. Her son, beside her, also towered over them, brandishing a similar weapon. At the same moment, their faces seem to grow down towards the frightened pair and they knew that their end had come. Lucinda closed her eyes and prayed for help from God and her guardian. Collins cowered, raised an arm across his face in an effort to protect himself, and as he did so the faces, it seemed to him, transformed into death-dealing screaming skulls. The hideous mouths became cavernous and the screams seemed to fill his senses. He remembered, for a moment, the story of John

Roylance when he told of his dream of waking in terror and the house echoed with the screams that he thought were only in his recent nightmare, but were now all too real. Collins closed his eyes and waited to die.

He tensed all his muscles for the first scything blow of those murderous blades. Collins realised that the screaming had ceased and had transformed into an angry hiss. He cautiously half opened an eye and saw that a huge dark figure had risen between them and the two monsters. The figure was that of an old man with thinning hair but to Collins he seemed to stand before them like a colossus. The man held the candleholder above his head, brandishing it like a weapon. The candle itself seemed to burn like a fierce torch. Druitt and the woman shrunk back, both in size and position, and appeared nonplussed by the appearance of this new gladiatorial spectre.

Collins turned to Lucinda who had collapsed to her knees. He became aware of ghostly figures beginning to appear out of the gloom away from the candlelight in the darkness behind Lucinda. They massed towards the two monsters and a sound began to grow out of the dying hiss. It was the angry clamour of the murdered throng from the dark past of this deadly house.

Collins turned back to the Druitts and saw for the first time a look of fear appear on those evil faces. The woman's visage soon turned to a mask of anger and the wizened face contorted with rage. The man with the candle moved threateningly towards them, as did the assembled ghostly throng.

Collins now began to recognise the faces of some of the group. In the forefront was a figure he knew well and he could not assuage the pang of pain accompanying that recognition. David Kayne was a heroic figure with a face full of vengeful anger. Beside him was a woman he remembered from photographs he had seen. It was Samantha Kayne and by her side was Julia Davenport. Others crowded in on the Druitts and Collins recognised Jim Flagg, Denholme Theynard, Letitia Preece and Miriam Brock. Others present wore dress from the 19th century; women who had care-worn faces and were obviously much younger than their appearance belied. He guessed that these were the poor murdered prostitutes from Whitechapel, come to settle the final accounts of the creatures who had ended their miserable lives over a century earlier.

Lucinda raised herself to her feet and took Collins' hand. She whispered to him that the figure holding the candleholder was her protector Harry Price. Even before she had uttered his name the old man pulled back his arm and threw the blazing candle into the faces of the evil Druitts. The flame from the candle seemed to grow as it flew through the air and the foul pair were at once engulfed in a sheet of flame. The throng of dead immediately began a chorus of triumph and all of them flew forward into the growing conflagration. Lucinda and Abel Collins watched as the flames spread and ran across the floor of the room. It was as if burning petrol had been thrown into the centre of the room and Collins was shaken into immediate action. He tightened his grip on Lucinda's hand and yelled over the sound of the crackling inferno. "We must get out of here *now.*"

Chapter 54

Out of the Conflagration

Abel Collins felt the searing heat on his hands as he raised them to protect his face. He quickly grabbed Lucinda's hand and pulled her through the doorway of the bedroom. She screamed with pain and fear as he dragged her along the landing. He became aware of the flames licking up from her burning clothes.

He ran into the back bedroom to tear down the curtains. Returning to her, he smothered the flames with the curtain fabric. By then her face and hands had been terribly burned but her dress was now merely smouldering. Collins held her as she fell into his arms in a dead faint. The couple were now engulfed in thick black smoke and he coughed and choked as he lifted her and attempted to try to carry her down the stairs. Her dead weight caused him to fall against the wall of the stairwell. Luckily, she recovered consciousness enough to allow Collins to drop her on to her feet and together they staggered down the stairs to the hall. Above them they could hear the screams of the tormented souls of the Druitts as they met their fate in the all consuming, cleansing fire. Collins tripped at the foot of the stairs and both of them fell headlong across something lying across the floor near the front door.

Collins lay flat, his body against the front door and he stared through the smoke filled gloom where he lay. The smoke cleared for a moment and before him was the face of a man. It was deathly white; as white as parchment. Panic rose in his stomach as the eyes stared sightlessly into his. A trickle of blood had run from the scalp into one of the eyes. Collins realised that he had tripped over the dead body of Denholme Theynard.

Collins closed his mind to this new horror, regained his feet and looked round for Lucinda Randolph. Through the thickening smoke he saw that she lay across the body of her former lover, moaning softly, obviously in terrible pain. Collins raised her and helped her to regain her feet. He staggered with her towards the front door and attempted to open it. The body of the dead churchman, however, impeded the door, and Collins could only open it two or three inches. He allowed Lucinda to drop gently to the floor and he pulled at the door with both hands. Eventually he managed to force the body back so that the door opened, allowing a gap of about 18 inches.

He turned to pick up Lucinda and saw the flames now licking along the stair rail above them. The smoke blinded him but he managed to locate her with his flailing hands. With his remaining breath, he hauled her through the gap on to the drive where helping hands took her from him. Collins lay in the snow on the drive for a while, choking on the smoke from the inferno, which was now out of control. Collins wretched and eventually vomited violently. Two strong hands lifted him into a sitting position and then draped a metal foil blanket around his shoulders.

The luminous yellow jackets told him that he was now in the care of an ambulance crew. He could hear the caterwauling of a siren and its increasing volume indicated that it was headed for The Eaves.

Collins was lifted on to a stretcher and an oxygen mask was placed over his mouth. He sucked in the life–giving gas and attempted to rise. He was immediately restrained by the medics but just before he lay back he caught a glimpse of an upper bedroom window of the house which had just shattered from the heat. He swore that he saw a figure emerge for an instant from the smoke, only to be dragged back into the flames by a second shadowy shape.

Collins lay in the relative quiet of the ambulance and immediately became aware of the pain from his hands and face. He opened his eyes and looked up into the face of Chief Superintendent Townshend.

"You lay quiet, Abel, for a bit. Everything is under control. Can you give him something for the pain?" Townshend asked of the calm paramedic nearby.

"Is Miss Randolph alright? She needs help more than me." Collins raised his shoulders from the stretcher but Townshend restrained him and said: "She is in good hands now. You lay back and we will talk later."

The paramedic sank a syringe of morphine into his upper arm and Collins closed his eyes and waited for it to take its blissful effect. The doors of the ambulance were closed and it drew away down the drive, just as the roof of The Eaves collapsed in a shower sparks and flames down on to that bedroom of death.

Collins lay and contemplated in his mind that figure which had appeared at the bedroom window. It had been the mad, evil Mrs Druitt and the figure pulling her back into the inferno, he swore, was David Kayne.

Chapter 55

Six Months Later

Six months had passed since the extraordinary affair at The Eaves. The remains of two dead bodies had been found in the gutted wreck of a house. Dental records showed that they were all that were left of James Flagg and the Reverend Denholme Theynard. Rumours had abounded that a third body had been present but, in truth, no mortal remains were ever found of Superintendent Thomas Dumairt, although he could not have escaped the inferno.

Abel Collins had been held for a time after he recovered...accused of murder. The partial recovery of Lucinda Randolph and her statement to the police exonerated the inspector. Miss Randolph corroborated Collins contention that a tragic accident had occurred. A candle had been lit because of a power cut in the house, a fact that could not be verified because of the fire damage. The candlestick had fallen as a séance was being performed and the resultant fire had caused Denholme to stumble on the stairs in his desperate attempt to flee the flames. He had fallen and broken his neck.

Jim Flagg had been buried under the roof wreckage and was so badly burned that the cause of his death could not be ascertained, at least that was what the official police press release said. Some experts questioned this statement but if the police records said anything to the contrary, it was never revealed to the public.

Collins had been reprimanded for agreeing to the séance in the house in the first place, but this was never revealed to the press. Neither was any of the other evidence, given by witnesses and former residents, that the house had been the source of terrible evil. The Sunday Sport had reported a story involving witchcraft and satanic worship in the house. The devil had been abroad and caused the deaths. Very soon the public memory of the events faded to be replaced by terrorist attacks and rows about immigration.

Collins and Townshend discussed the fact that Dumairt had no history recorded in police records. He had appeared as if from nowhere. Police service systems were immediately reviewed and improvements introduced. Systems fail, in every walk of life, because complacency causes people to relax. If a new person appears on the scene at the appropriate moment then it is human nature to believe their history as they tell it.

Townshend believed that Dumairt may have been the perpetrator of most of the murders. When pressed as to the motive, he would only say that motivation is a difficult area where insanity is involved. Dumairt, he said, may have been an accomplice to Linde in the murders of Annie Linde and Julia Davenport. Linde, he felt, had committed suicide because of pangs of remorse.

Collins kept his own counsel on all these matters because who would believe the absolute truth. It was possible to bury that truth in this instance because of the fire and the subsequent investigations and inquests chose to do so. The establishment has maintained that silence in these matters ever since.

Another mystery in this affair was the timely appearance of the emergency services at the scene of the final fire. Collins had discovered that an anonymous 999 phone call had been sent preceding the fire. Maybe a neighbour or passerby was disturbed by the noise from the house.

Chapter 56

The End of the Affair

A year passed very quickly and Collins had returned to duty after having relocated to Liverpool and Merseyside Police. He had maintained contact with the hospital where Lucinda was slowly but surely recovering from the physical injuries she had sustained. She had been transferred to the famous specialist Burns Unit at Pinderfields Hospital in Wakefield.

She had been too ill to attend the funeral of Denholme Theynard. Collins had sent a floral tribute on her behalf and attended the ceremony in her stead.

He visited her in hospital during her recovery period but they had kept the conversation to trivialities and no mention was made of their terrible experiences in Blackheath. They had both attended a memorial service for Flagg in London later in the year and the artistic glitterati of the country were present. Lucinda had sat with Collins at the back of the church seated in a wheelchair. During the service Jane Flagg was mentioned as being too ill to attend. She was the last victim of the Druitts because two months after the service; she was released from hospital and, within days of going home, had leaped to her death from Beachy Head while ostensibly on holiday in Eastbourne. She had been the last remaining member of the group who had first met in her house and discussed Linde's ghostly woman at Rill Place.

*****

It was a bright cool morning in May when Abel Collins walked up the drive of the home of Lucinda Randolph. The latter opened her door and the two friends embraced...no words were spoken, no words were necessary. They turned and walked through to the book–lined room where, on that cold December night a lifetime ago, Lucinda had told Collins of her life as a medium. It looked warm and cosy, a fire burned in the grate and it was a million light years from their last meeting there. Lucinda had been home from hospital for a couple of weeks and although several skin graft operations lay ahead, she felt much better. She prepared tea and brought a tray through to the room with chocolate biscuits.

"I am quite addicted to those, Lucinda." This confession caused them both to laugh.

Lucinda spoke in serious vein: "The doctors tell me I have to undergo three more skin graft operations. What about you?"

"My burns were superficial compared to your injuries," said Collins. "There has been some mental scarring. I suffered terrible nightmares for a while, but they are not as bad as they were, or as frequent."

"Yes, I have had similar problems. I too am healing now."

326

Collins took the first tentative step into the, so far, untouched territory: "I have been back to talk to neighbours and they say that all has been quiet since the fire. Do you think that this business is at an end now? The house itself is gone but has the evil also departed?"

"I believe so, and for three reasons," explained Lucinda. "Firstly, as you say, there have been no further events since that night. Secondly, that fire would have had a cleansing effect on the ground in and around the house. Thirdly, and more importantly, the spirits of those poor victims effectively took revenge on the Druitts that night and they have driven away any evil influences."

"There are still one or two things I do not understand," said Collins. "Why was the woman who appeared to several of the people faceless, and horrifically so?"

"I think that her spirit wanted to remain anonymous," continued Lucinda. "She was the power behind the throne, as it were. Remember, that in her day women were subservient to men in so many ways but they could wield power behind the scenes. The old saying: 'Behind every great man there is a woman' is a great truth. In this case instead of 'great' we can substitute the word 'evil'.

"There was one interesting testimony from Mr Cardew that his wife had seen the woman's face peel and melt before her during one awful visitation. I think that Melissa Cardew was seeing the final demise of Mrs Druitt's spirit in the fire. It was a scene from the future."

Collins nodded but still retained a quizzical expression: "What about the despair Linde felt and described when he saw her?"

"That was the despair she had felt for Annie Crook," reasoned Lucinda. "Which had spawned the murders in 1888 and the later activity. I'm afraid that I did underestimate Mrs Druitt's power although the clue to that lay in the fact that she could appear away from the house. There were also solid artifacts present at the hauntings such as candles, beads from her dress and the use of a computer to send messages as the Druitts had done to lure Julia Davenport to Rill Place and her death. These creatures were powerful entities."

"Why do you think the woman appeared to Linde at Julia Davenport's flat as well as at his house?" asked Collins.

"I think that there were two good reasons for those appearances. It served as an attempt to push an already unstable man over the edge and most people think that ghosts are phenomena that occur at only one given locale. By appearing at the flat it therefore also undermined his credibility in the eyes of the ghost–hunting group. He would also be a convenient scapegoat for further atrocities committed by the Druitts. His instability was confirmed because he was later unmasked as the proven killer of his wife."

Collins' face brightened and he spoke excitedly. "Kayne believed that Linde was unstable from very early on. He told me after we had visited the Flaggs, soon after Julia was murdered, and we were leaving the house. He had seen Linde standing at a bedroom window…Linde was staying at the Flagg house at the time. Linde was smiling and Kayne had shivered when he told me about it. That smile was very unsettling, not normal at all. I always listened to him on such matters because he had an instinct for these things and read people well. He had few doubts that Linde had killed Annie...even then."

"The Druitts knew this as well and had removed Annie's organs after burial to mimic the Whitechapel Ripper's methods," reasoned Lucinda.

"That makes sense; those organs were contaminated with dirt from the earth in which they had initially lain." Collins sipped more tea as the whole jigsaw puzzle began to take shape in his mind. "Julia almost named her killer during her final phone conversation with Linde, you know. She said that it was 'Drew...' but did not finish the name because she was attacked by Druitt. It was all there if we had cared to look closely. Linde even said that he had seen a ghostly figure leaving the murder room just before he entered it."

"Yes, you mentioned Julia's phone call during the encounter with Druitt," remembered Lucinda. "Don't be too hard on yourself, Abel. Even David Kayne had help in getting as far as he did on this case."

"What do you mean?"

"I always considered the death of Kayne's wife intriguing," said Lucinda. "Not that the death itself was linked to the events at The Eaves. I think, however, his recently dead wife took a hand helping Mr Kayne. It was soon after her death that Kayne went back to the house and, I think, was given the clue to the affair in the shape of the number '1888'. You remember that officers found a piece of paper which Kayne had left in the room where he died. He was killed immediately after he had written the note because he was getting too close.

"Before the note business...that old trunk found in the loft, Abel? I think Mr Kayne was again pointed in the direction of that item. Why would he check the loft again? As far as he was concerned officers had already looked up there and found nothing? I believe Samantha Kayne helped her husband in death and Druitt killed him before he uncovered the whole disagreeable truth. Druitt/Dumairt was confirmed as the killer of Kayne by the finding of his bloody fingerprints on the door frame of the computer room. Following up on that clue was an excellent piece of work on your part, Mr Collins."

"Letitia Preece was killed because her instruments in the garden could have recorded something significant. In fact, I bet they did. But Druitt, in his Dumairt disguise, destroyed the disks."

Collin's realised that one of the last pieces of the puzzle had dropped into place: "Your body may have been damaged by the fire but it did not affect your mind."

Lucinda continued: "We had help, you know. Harry Price and the other poor dead souls saved our lives. Among that group there was a woman's spirit keeping close to that of David Kayne. I think Samantha Kayne was there too."

"Yes – I saw her too."

The two friends sat and stared into the fire for a minute or two as their minds replayed the events of that night. Lucinda spoke first. "The Druitts had the cunning born of an evil centuries old. When I went to The Eaves on the very first occasion with Denholme, I saw the full horror of them. I entered the hall and there was a mirror facing me, the one which broke on that last day. I saw the face of a monster staring back at me. It was standing behind me. I spun round and there in front of me was

Thomas Dumairt. At first I was in shock but later I realised the connection...stupid of me."

Lucinda paused once more before asking "Why has there been no mention by the authorities about the paranormal aspects of this case?"

Collins shrugged his shoulders before replying: "They think that the truth, although it is staring them in the face, cannot be reported to the general public because they would not accept it and the police would be held up to ridicule. All of the wrongdoers in this case are dead and there will be no trial; hence why not just close the file. There will be bit of filleting before closure but no good would come from revealing the truth."

Lucinda nodded in understanding but then frowned.

"Don't let it get to you, Lucinda. We know the truth of what really happened. Anyway, the evil in Rill Place has gone."

Collins stood up, realizing that Lucinda Randolph looked tired. He thanked her for the tea and the two friends parted. They promised to keep in touch...and they would.

Epilogue

Six months later Collins stood by the gate of platform nine at Liverpool Street Station. He had been to visit Lucinda and was now on his way to Suffolk. He and other members of his Merseyside team had been asked to help with a case in Ipswich. A series of murders of prostitutes had taken place. The case had been very high profile and Suffolk police badly needed a result. Police and equipment from all parts of the country had been drafted into the area.

Collins was tired and he did not relish the thought of several weeks in a hotel. He moved through the gate on the platform and idly gazed into the carriage windows as he passed. People were finding their seats and children were being told to sit quietly. In another compartment, a man was opening his laptop. It amazed Collins how some people could hardly take their seats on a train before checking their emails. Just then, a man and a woman passed the computer man and sat down opposite him at the same table.

Collins turned his head and glanced back at them through the window. He had only a glimpse as he moved forward before the reflected image of the station platform replaced any internal view of the carriage. The man stared back at him for an instant as he lowered himself into the seat; he was tall, aged about 30 and moustachioed. A half—smile played around his lips. The woman was dressed in a long black old–fashioned dress; she had her back to Collins.

Collins walked towards the next carriage door. It was open and he placed his foot on the threshold and paused. Realisation dawned on him and he felt a cold foreboding in the pit of his stomach. He moved quickly on board, stood his case in a corner and turned through the doorway linking the two carriages, back towards computer man's table. He had to wait a few moments as a stout businessman, sweating and breathing heavily, blocked his path through the doorway. Collins waited until he had passed and then raced down the centre aisle.

He arrived at the table and stared in disbelief. Two elderly ladies sat where he expected to see the man and woman. He thought at first that he had selected the wrong table, but there opposite the two ladies, was Mr Laptop, concentrating hard on his computer screen.

Collins addressed the man. "Excuse me, did you see a man and woman seated here before?"

"No, the ladies have been here for some little time now."

Collins moved quickly forward to the door at the end of the carriage and jumped down on to the platform. He looked up and down the platform from one end of the train to the other but all he saw were a group of young backpackers about to climb on board. He ran down the platform towards the gate staring into the carriage windows as he ran. There was no sign of the couple. Just then a uniformed rail-wayman emerged from his lair and told him that he had better board the train as it was about to depart.

Collins climbed aboard, retrieved his case and

sat down in the nearest free seat. He sat for a while regaining his composure and squeezing the bridge of his nose. He began to doubt the evidence of his eyes and felt angry.

At Ipswich Station Collins waited on the platform. He watched people disembark. He climbed the steps up to the bridge over the lines and waited at the other end, pretending he had forgotten something. The empty enclosed bridge he had just traversed yawned ahead of him. He was the last one across it. There was no man or woman lagging behind him.

He shook his head and walked towards the station exit, a thoughtful expression on his face. He remembered that when he had examined the file on the Ipswich murders, two of the victims had names closely matching the name of one of the poor victims that had been so brutally despatched in Whitechapel in that long ago autumn of 1888.

Notes by the Author

Many of the characters in this book are based on real people, as are some of the facts associated with them:

Thomas Rowden, the highwayman mentioned in Chapter 28, did exist and was a sometime member of the Gregory Gang in the 1730s, as was the more infamous Dick Turpin. The tales of the rape of Elizabeth Rayner and Rowden's hanging are not true.

Arpad Vass is mentioned as being a pathologist working at the Body Farm in Tennessee. He is described as using a strange device to detect buried dead bodies. This is all true.

Harry Price (1881–1948) was the medium associated with Borley Rectory.

Montague John Druitt (1857–1888) did live at 9 Eliot Street in Blackheath and was treasurer and honorary secretary of Blackheath Cricket, Gottball and Lawn Tennis Company in 1885. He is one of the suspects in the Jack the Ripper case. He did drown near Thorneycroft's Wharf and was discovered by a waterman called Henry Winslade on Monday December 31st 1888.

His father, William Druitt, was a Fellow of the Royal College of Surgeons but I have no idea if he knew William Gull (see below) as asserted in this book.

Druitt's mother, Ann Druitt (nee Harvey) did succumb to mental illness and was committed to the Brook Asylum in Clapton. It may be noted that Druitt did leave a suicide note in which he stated: *Since Friday I felt I was going to be like mother and the best thing for me was to die.*

The description of the mutilated corpse of Julia Davenport closely mirrors the autopsy report of the time describing the state of the body of Mary Kelly. A report written by a pathologist called Dr Bond.

Dr William Withey Gull (1816–1890) was indeed physician to Queen Victoria and it has been postulated that he was associated with a royal cover–up involving a girl called Annie Crook and her baby. Prince Eddy, Duke of Clarence, was said to be the father of her child. I should add that both Eddy and Gull have been suspected of being Jack the Ripper at one time or another. The assertion that Gull was the killer was made in the 1988 Michael Caine film *Jack the Ripper* and in the 2003 Johnny Depp film *From Hell*.

Inspector Frederick Abberline (1843–1929) was the investigating officer on the ground during the Whitechapel murders and is buried, ironically, in Wimbourne churchyard. The same churchyard where lies the body of Montague Druitt.

The text of the writing on the wall in the house was the same as that found on a wall in Goulston Street in the early hours of 30th September 1888 when Elizabeth Stride and Catherine Eddowes were murdered. The writing was supposedly chalked by the Ripper (see Chapter 46).

Finally: Abel Collins is said to have come down to Ipswich at the invitation of the Suffolk police to help them solve the murders of five Ipswich prostitutes in the last months of 2006. This is mentioned in the epilogue of this book when Collins is said to have worked for the Liverpool and Merseyside police. The latter force did send representatives at that time but they did not, of–course, include an Abel Collins in their number. Ultimately Stephen Wright, a Norfolk born fork–lift truck driver, was convicted of the crimes and was sentenced to life imprisonment with a recommended whole life tariff.

Maybe there is a house in Blackheath that harbours the horrors described within these covers
...who knows?

M R Russen

About the Author

Mervyn Russen was born in 1946 in Ipswich to a stonemason and his seamstress wife. At Westbourne Secondary Boys' School he acquired a taste for chemistry (via production of homemade fireworks) and gothic literature.

After completing his A' levels Mervyn joined Fisons as a trainee chemist, remaining with the company for the next 36 years. He met his wife, Susan, there and they married in May 1971, and later had two daughters, a son and four grandchildren.

Mervyn graduated in chemistry and was elected a Fellow of the Royal Society of Chemiry and is a Chartered Chemist. He taught chemistry at evening classes at the local technical college for many years. He retired as Quality Assurance Manager with The Scotts Company (a successor to Fisons) at the end of 2001 and almost immediately began writing this novel, *Terror by Candlelight*, orginally under the working title of *Cold*.

Mervyn is a cartoonist, a steam railway fanatic, loves old films (especially the silents and the film noir of the 1940s) and the history of his town.

Acknowledgements

No book ever appears out of a vacuum and this one is no exception. It is a product of my imagination, shaped by years of reading the great tales of terror from the distant and recent past.

The authors of these include M R James, William Hope Hodgson, Edgar Allan Poe, Sir Arthur Conan Doyle, Dorothy Macardle, Dennis Wheatley, Stephen King and Susan Hill.

Information on the occult came from The Black Art, a book by Rollo Ahmed (1936).

My favourite book in the horror genre, and one is inspirational to me, is *The Haunting of Hill House*, in which American author Shirley Jackson writes one of the most frighteningly beautiful pieces of prose to end her story:

Hill House, not sane, stood by itself against its hills, holding darkness within; it had stood so for 80 years and might stand for 80 more. Within, walls continued upright, bricks met neatly, floors were firm, and doors were sensibly shut; silence lay steadily against the wood and stone of Hill House, and whatever walked there, walked alone.

To all these influential authors I owe a debt that can never be repaid.

Others to whom I am eternally grateful, are my editors and advisors namely: KT Forster, Matt Trollope, Jax Etta Elliott, Andrew Hollis and Lisa Hollis.

Mervyn Russen, Ipswich, Suffolk, 2016

65756429R00186

Made in the USA
Charleston, SC
07 January 2017